Dear Reader:

Julia Blues, a "storyteller on a mission," embarks on her publishing journey with *Parallel Pasts*, a debut novel about two young lovers, Cory and Fatima, who struggle to develop a rewarding relationship despite their haunting pasts but slowly grow closer as they discover commonalities.

It is my pleasure to introduce such a talented newcomer to the literary scene. Sit back and observe how these characters with undesirable family backgrounds learn to fill the missing void in their lives—love.

Julia is a fantastic writer who takes her experiences from traveling throughout the world and translates them into the written word. Her captivating story, "Heated Waters," appears in my anthology, *Zane's Z-Rated: Chocolate Flava 3*.

As always, thanks for supporting Julia Blues and the authors whom I publish under Strebor Books. We appreciate the love and we strive to bring you the best, most prolific authors who write outside of the traditional publishing box.

You can contact me directly at zane@eroticanoir.com and find me on Twitter @planetzane and on Facebook at www.facebook.com/AuthorZane.

Blessings,

Zane

Zane
Publisher
Strebor Books
www.simonandschuster.com

ZANE PRESENTS

Parallel Pasts

A NOVEL

JULIA BLUES

SBI

STREBOR BOOKS

NEW YORK LONDON TORONTO SYDNEY

Strebor Books
P.O. Box 6505
Largo, MD 20792
http://www.streborbooks.com

© 2013 by Julia Blues

ISBN 978-1-59309-495-9
ISBN 978-1-4767-1147-8 (ebook)
LCCN 2013933634

First Strebor Books trade paperback edition June 2013

Cover design: www.mariondesigns.com
Cover photograph: © Keith Saunders/Marion Designs

10 9 8 7 6 5 4 3 2 1

Manufactured in the United States of America

For information regarding special discounts for bulk purchases, please contact Simon & Schuster Special Sales at 1-866-506-1949 or business@simonandschuster.com

The Simon & Schuster Speakers Bureau can bring authors to your live event. For more information or to book an event, contact the Simon & Schuster Speakers Bureau at 1-866-248-3049 or visit our website at www.simonspeakers.com.

This book is dedicated to Sugar Williams,
LaShon "Butterfly" Campbell, Grandma Della Hudson,
and Kayla Marie Williams.
Your love forever remains in my heart

Grandma is sitting in her rocking chair when I walk through the door. The television is showing an old episode of *Perry Mason*. "You still up?"

She doesn't answer. The chair is rocking; her eyes are closed. Can't tell if she's watching the TV or if it's watching her.

The remote is in her lap. I try not to make too much noise as I walk through the dining room to where her chair is positioned in the living room. Grab the remote and hit the power off button.

"I was watching that."

"Looked like the opposite to me."

"What you see isn't always how it looks," she says with her eyes still closed.

I roll my eyes. *Wish I would've gone straight home.* Tonight is not the night for Grandma and her I-was-Confucius-in-my-past-life moments.

"What brings you by?"

I wonder the same thing myself. "Left a friend's house not far from here. Wanted to stop by and see how you're doing."

She pulls her glasses down from the top of her head, checks the time. Looks up at me with questioning eyes. "It's well after midnight. The only thing you're going to see at this hour is me sleeping." She yawns. "Now, tell me, what's the real reason you're here?"

I take a deep breath. Sit on the edge of the green sofa that's been here for as long as I can remember. Try not to get too comfortable.

"I'm waiting," she presses.

"It's nothing. Really."

"If it was nothing, you wouldn't be here. Especially not at this hour."

I exhale. "Guess I'm looking for answers."

"Here we go again." She straightens up in the rocking chair. "How many times do I have to tell you that I don't have the answers, Fatima?"

My adrenaline pumps. "For some reason, I don't believe you."

"You saying I'm lying?"

I look at her with raised eyebrows. "You tell me."

She gets up from her rocking chair. Stands in front of me with hands on her spreading hips. "Watch your mouth. I raised you with better manners than that. Didn't let you talk to me like that as a child and I'll be damned if I let you talk to me like you don't have any sense now."

I get up from my seat. Throw some gasoline on her growing fire. "Then quit treating me like a kid. I'm not far from thirty's door and I have yet to know where my parents are. Don't even know if they're dead or alive. Do you even care? She's your daughter, for goodness sake."

My heart is beating so hard it feels like my chest is about to explode. Breathing is tight. An asthma attack is on the horizon. I grab my purse, search its contents for my inhaler. It's not in there. It dawns on me...I don't have asthma.

"You need to just let it go, Fatima. Look what it's doing to you."

I fume. "Why are you protecting her?"

My mother's mother stares me down. Tries to understand my need to understand. "Why won't you just leave well enough alone?"

I've tried to make it without my parents. Tried to live my life without thinking of them, wondering where they are. But every day, my struggle grows harder. Each day, I feel a piece of history drifting further away from me. Too many pieces of the puzzle are missing. If only Grandma would talk, give me some kind of clue. She's stubborn as a mule; has always been that way.

"I can't. As long as I have breath in my body, I'll never leave it alone."

"Sometimes the truth can kill you."

With my keys in hand, I tell her, "Too late. I died a long time ago."

I turn on the shower as hot as I can stand it.

I watch as the steam fogs up the bathroom. Stand in front of the mirror, stare at my disheveled reflection until the fog restricts my view. Feel like I'm falling apart at the seams. My reflection tells me the same story.

David opened this can of worms. Then, going to see Grandma, I swear she opened my mouth and dropped them down my throat. This has got to stop.

I tie my locs up and put on a shower cap. Brush my teeth before getting in the shower. I grab my purple exfoliating gloves off the rack behind me. Lather up with a sea kelp and aloe body wash I made, try my best to scrub the scent of David off of me. Want to get rid of every trace of him from my skin. I knew I should not have gone over there.

Tears mixed with sweat from the steam run down my face. I taste the salt on my top lip. Pain from yesteryear consumes me. Pain from my parents' departure. Pain from my own departure.

When my parents left me, I left me as well. Figured, if my own mother and father didn't love me, how could I? What is love anyway? Nothing more than an overused four-letter word synonymous with pain.

The tears continue to fall. I quit trying to understand why I'm such an emotional wreck. Quit trying to understand the things I'm not meant to understand. I just let the tears flow. Allow them to cleanse my soul as the soap cleanses David from my pores.

❂ ❂ ❂

"Stay here with me tonight," David had said.

"I can't."

"Fatima, look at me." He turned my face to his. "I'm not asking you to move in. You're in and out of here at your convenience. I just want a little more time with you. Stay awhile. That's all I'm asking."

I brushed his hand off me. "This never should have happened."

My skirt was on the floor. I picked it up, grabbed the rest of my clothes. Needed to get out of his room, out of his space.

David didn't let my silence stop him. He followed me to the bathroom. Pushed the door open, pushed his way back into my space. "Where are you going?"

"Shouldn't ask questions when you know the answer." I moved toward the door.

He put his hand up, blocked my departure. Showed me a side of him I didn't like.

"David, please." I pushed his hand away from the door. "Is that really necessary?"

"Talk to me," he persisted.

"There's nothing to talk about. You knew where I stood before we slept together, before we crossed that line. Tonight was no different. Don't act like this is new to you."

I stood at the front door. Purse and keys in hand, ready to close that chapter of my life.

"Don't leave like this," he demanded.

"Tell me, what difference will it make if I stay?"

David took the keys and purse from my hands, put them on the couch. Held my empty hands in his. "Look, Fatima." He sighed. "I'm not going to sit up here and lie to you. I care about you. I want more than this. I want more than what you've been giving me."

I shook my head defiantly, stopped him in his tracks and released my hands from his. "Well, I'm not going to lie either. I *don't* want more with you."

His eyes let me know I'd hurt his feelings; I'd let him down. "If you don't want more, if having no balance in your life is fine with you, then by all means, don't let me keep you."

"Balance? What makes you think my life isn't balanced?"

"Do you even have to ask?" He grabbed my stuff from the couch, put the purse and keys back in my hands. His tone dripped with frustration. He was getting desperate. Needed me to see the needy side of him so I wouldn't walk out on him. "You are so afraid of being hurt that you're in and out of my bed before your legs can stop shaking. That can't be all you want, a good orgasm. You can do that on your own."

"You're right, I can. I'll do that from now on." A smirk crossed my face. Then I got serious. "Look, you and I go way back. We have a history. But just because two people share time doesn't mean they should be together. All we have is that. Nothing more, nothing less."

His voice changed. Softer, no longer attacking. "Nobody's going to hurt you, Fatima. I'm not going to hurt you. Why can't you understand that?"

I was annoyed more than anything. Somehow, someway, he always brought my past into my present. "This isn't about me getting hurt." My voice raised.

"Yes it is. You know it. You're afraid to get close to me, to anyone for that matter, because you think we'll leave you just like your parents did."

"Don't patronize me. I'm not one of your clients, David."

He ignored me. "I am not your mom or dad. I'm not going anywhere."

He moved closer to me, looked me in the face. Wanted me to know his plight went beyond his nine-to-five. He wanted me to know I was more than a j-o-b to him. He wanted me to see what he saw, but all I saw was pain. All I saw was resentment. David sensed my fury and moved back.

"How dare you go there? This has nothing to do with them and you know it." I tried to convince myself more than him.

It did hurt me when my parents left. In many ways, I hadn't recovered. My father left, then my mother disappeared three days later. Their leaving changed the way I looked at people, especially those who used the "L" word. Made that four-letter emotion null and void in my vocabulary. Made me not feel anything for anyone. If I did, they'd just end up leaving me, too. Just like my parents.

"Do you even care about me?" He pulled me out of my past, out of my angst. Brought me to the here and now.

I shook my head. "Not the way you want me to."

He reached around me, closed the door I had opened when I'd planned to walk away from everything minutes ago. I was on my way out. Was about to finish the final chapter to our book; the one I never should've begun writing.

I was weak. Tired of fighting, tired of running.

David escorted me to the couch. He gave me space, sat on the opposite side.

"You've got to feel something, Fatima," he said. "We've been sleeping with each other for months now and you're telling me you don't feel anything?"

I shook my head, sighed. "You don't listen. I didn't say I don't feel 'anything.' I just don't feel for you the way you feel for me."

"Did I do something wrong? Is it something I'm not doing?" he wanted to know.

"David, this is not about you. It's me."

"Self-blame is the easy way out. I need a better answer than that."

My head throbbed. Too much tension. I set my hair loose, hoped to relieve some of the pressure from my head. My locs fell with ease. The ends tapped me on my shoulders as a symbolic gesture that everything would be all right.

David came to where I was. Put his hands on my shoulders, brushed my hair to the side. Took my stress as his opportunity to get closer. Wanted to work out my kinks in more ways than one.

I felt my frustration mount. Questioned myself as to why I was allowing him to touch me like that, to torture me unapologetically.

I moved forward, let his hands slide off of me. "You don't know when to quit, do you?"

"Just want you to know I'm here for you, Fatima. I've always been here. I'm not going anywhere."

"Quit saying that."

"It's true. I want you to believe me."

"Well, you can want all you want, but if you keep a pot boiling long enough, it runs out of water."

A what-the-hell look crossed his face. "What is that supposed to mean?"

"You know what..." I threw my hands in the air. "Don't worry about it."

I grabbed my belongings off the couch. Told him not to call me anymore, told him to forget he ever knew me.

"It's like that?" he asked on my way out.

The door slammed shut in his face.

Yeah, it's like that.

I pick up the phone on its third ring.

"We need to talk," the voice on the other end tells me.

I move the cordless away from my ear. Look at the caller ID display, then over at the clock on my nightstand. "It's two in the morning."

She huffs. "I know what time it is. We need to talk," she says again with no regard to what I have to do before the sun cracks the sky.

I wipe the sleep out of my eyes. "We need to talk right this minute?"

"I'm on the phone, you're on the phone. What does that tell you?"

"It tells me you haven't changed."

She huffs again. Her patience runs thin. "Whatever. Look, I'm on my way over there."

"As you said before, we're both on the phone now, so talk."

"Negative. Feels too impersonal. It'd be better to talk in person."

"Look, Trish—"

"My name is Patricia. I hate it when you call me Trish," she confesses.

"Never heard you complain before."

"That's beside the point. I'll be there in ten minutes," she tells me before pressing the end button to our conversation.

She's still the same. Always wants things her way. No ifs, ands, or buts about it.

❃ ❃ ❃

"I love you," she told me the night it all ended.

"Come on, Trish. Don't ruin the moment."

She lifted her head up from my chest. Stared me in the face. "*Ruin the moment?*" she scoffed. "What is that supposed to mean?"

I let out a deep sigh.

"Ohhhhkay." She braced herself. "I'm listening."

"I'm just saying. We had a good time as usual. No need to get all emotional."

"But if it's how I feel…" She rubbed my hairless chest. "…why should I deny my feelings for you?"

I got up from the bed. Left her and her confessions of love tangled in the dank sheets.

In the kitchen, I grabbed a bottle of Johnnie Walker. The good stuff. Needed something to calm my nerves before Trish got me to the point of no return.

Not far behind me, she grabbed the bottle out of my hands and poured its contents down the sink.

I snatched it back from her before she could waste the whole bottle. "What the hell is wrong with you?" I could feel anger boiling in my veins.

"You drink too much," she told me. "I need you to be honest with me without any coaxing from a bottle."

"I don't have time for this," I said while walking back toward the bedroom. Wanted her out of sight, out of mind.

Trish grabbed my arm as I attempted to leave her presence once again. "Do not walk away from me while I'm talking."

My pace came to a standstill. I became a statue with its fists balled up, frozen in a premature battle. Waited. Took five deep breaths. In through my nose, slow exhales out of my mouth. Then turned around to face her. Allowed her to get off her chest whatever was weighing her down before I did something I'd regret.

"Three questions."

Confusion crossed my face. Made a home in my brows. "Three questions?"

"That's what I said." She demanded my full attention with her I'm-in-charge tone as she explained the rules to her game. "I'm going to ask you three questions. What I want from you is the truth, nothing but."

Trish put her hand on her bare hip. Added, "And don't try to spare my feelings either. I want your God's honest truth."

My tone dripped with sarcasm. "Anything else?"

She gave me the look of death.

I sighed again. Let her know my patience was running thin. "Just hurry up and get this over with."

"Fine. Question number one: Where is this relationship headed?"

I took my time answering. Pondered if I should be honest like she ordered or just tell her what I thought she wanted to hear. "You said you want the truth, right?"

"Nothing but," she reiterated.

I settled to give her what she had asked for. "Okay. I, umm…" I hesitated, felt all eyes on me. Even though she was the only other person in there, I felt like there was a throng of women standing in my living room watching, waiting. Women I had been with. Women I had treated with the same distance I treated the woman who stood before me. Women who had pressured me to make a commitment I didn't want to make.

She interrupted my thoughts. "You're stalling."

I got my bearings, then said, "I don't consider what we have as a relationship. Never have. We just happen to be friends who have great sex."

"Friends. That's all I am to you…your friend?" Her eyes hardened. Took on a look I had never seen in the eight months I had known her. "So basically you're telling me that this is about nothing more than just sex?" She swallowed hard, hard enough for my own throat to hurt. Let me know I'd struck a nerve.

"You asked for the truth."

"Don't, Cory."

I got us back on target. "Next question."

She stalled just as I had moments ago, blinked. Didn't know I was going to cut her Ace of Hearts. She needed to come stronger, but I wasn't sweating it. I had a hand full of trumps. If I continued to play my cards right, I'd head straight to Boston. Frustration made her face tight. Mine loosened. The game was over.

"Question two."

I looked at her. No feelings at all registered in my eyes. "Okay."

"Are you sleeping with someone else?"

Her downcast eyes told me that she already knew the answer to that question. She wanted the truth. No matter how much it would hurt her. I gave her my truth. "No."

Tears streamed down her face. "Why are you lying? It's not gonna hurt me. Just tell me the truth."

"I gave it to you." She asked for the truth and couldn't even handle it. That annoyed me. "Hurry up and ask your last question so we can get this over with," I stressed.

"What if I told you I was pregnant?"

Bam. She slapped the Big Joker in my face, played her highest card. Didn't see that one coming so early in the game.

I spread the rest of my cards on the table. She had nothing else to beat me with. Game over.

"Are you?" I wanted to know, needed to know.

Trish swiped my cards off the table. "I'm asking the questions here." Said that with no loss of control. Dangled that Big Joker in my face like a piece of mistletoe tacked to her tailbone.

I got up from the table. Went back to the kitchen to finish what was left of the Black Label. Wasn't much, but enough to help me keep things in perspective. This is just a game, I told myself. But it wasn't. It was deeper than a deck of cards.

She was behind me. I could feel her.

"Are you pregnant?" I asked again.

Her tears resurfaced as she left the kitchen and headed back to the bedroom. I watched her put on the jeans I helped her shed not over an hour ago. The pink Victoria's Secret bra I'd had no problems releasing her 36D's from. Everything we took off in the heat of passion, she put back on. Grabbed her purse and waltzed straight to the front door.

I contemplated stopping her. Decided that maybe it was best to let her go. What was the point in letting her stay? But still, I didn't want her to leave like that. Wanted her to say something. "I may not give you what you want, but I'm honest. Haven't lied to you, haven't slept around on you. You want me to be this bad guy, Trish, but I'm not. Just don't want a commitment. Told you that from the beginning. Nothing's changed."

She couldn't look at me. Couldn't look truth in the eye.

With that, Trish walked out my front door and obviously out of my life. No goodbye. No nothing. Nada.

◉ ◉ ◉

Not even ten minutes after hanging up with Trish, I hear a loud knock at my door. No way she got here this quick. I look out the peephole knowing it can't be anyone else. Sure enough, it's her.

She barely gives me a chance to open the door before her foot grazes my threshold. She pushes me out the way and trots to the bathroom. No hello. No nothing. Nada.

I close the door, walk over and sit on the loveseat, leaving her all the room in the world on the couch. Wonder what the hell is going on.

A muffled voice comes from the back of the apartment. Sounds like she's on her cell phone.

I walk up to the door. "Trish."

The bathroom door jerks open. "Patricia. My. Name. Is. Patricia."

"What can I say. Old habits are hard to break." A smirk of victory splashes across my face.

For some reason, she smiles back. Her eyes try hard to fight the flame seeing me has rekindled. She tries to blink it away, but it's too late. I saw it and she knows I saw it.

Trish turns her head, clears her throat. "I'll be out in a second."

She comes out of the bathroom a few seconds later. Her stride slow, labored. Sits on the opposite side of me on the loveseat. I want to move, but I don't.

"Aren't you going to offer your guest something to drink?" she asks.

I think about what I have to offer before getting up. Do that to force my thoughts elsewhere. Don't want my weakness to show. I'm not ready for her to know her presence has turned my anger into arousal. Waking up parts of me I thought I had laid to rest for her.

Inside the kitchen, my thoughts remain on her thighs. Think

about them wrapped around my waist as I bring her to ecstasy. Her breasts, I can feel them in my mouth.

She's never been a heavy drinker, so I settle for a Smirnoff Ice. Something nice and light. Straight scotch for me.

She takes the bottle, looks at it with a hint of disgust, puts it down on the end table. "Swear you're an alcoholic. Do you have anything virgin?"

Obviously I take too long to answer. She huffs, gets up to find her own non-alcoholic beverage. Comes back empty-handed.

I let her know her comment struck a nerve. Let her know she's treading on thin ice. "That wasn't cool what you said. I'm *not* by far qualified to attend any AA meetings."

"Whatever."

When she walked in minutes ago, thought we could've had a roll in the hay for old times' sake. Thought that's what the call was really all about. It *is* after three in the a.m. What could we really have to talk about at this hour? Doesn't matter now. Rather go to one of those Alcoholics Anonymous meetings than get between her thighs again anyway. She's always been good about ruining the moment.

It hits me for the umpteenth time why it has never been more than sex with her: her attitude. Always finds something to huff and puff about. Nothing's changed.

I stand up, ready to escort her out of my apartment. Ms. Ruin the Moment comes to me, stands face to face, eye to eye. Pushes me back down on the loveseat.

My anger rises. "What the—"

Her lips greet mine, shush my anger. She straddles me. Calms me down, makes my nature rise.

I want to stop her. Want to stop what I'm feeling. But I can't. No matter how hard I try, I can't stop the inevitable.

I kiss her back. Take her pleading tongue into my accepting mouth.

She slides off my lap, grabs my hands. Pulls me toward my bedroom, facing me the whole way. Eyes begging me to feel what she feels. Love her the way she loves me. Wants her persistence to pay off.

I ignore what I see in her eyes. Focus on my own wants and needs for the night.

Clothes hit the floor. Hers, mine. Mix with the rest of my dirty laundry on the floor. I stop us to flick the lights on. Don't want to trip over anything.

Trish pushes my hand down. "Keep the lights off."

I do as instructed. Wonder if she might renege if light is shed on our sin. Wonder if I might.

Trish straddles me again. Gives me permission to enter her gates.

Her eyes close; she bites down on her bottom lip. Takes no mercy on me tonight. Wants me to know what I've been missing out on.

All of a sudden, her movements cease.

"Don't stop," I instruct, not wanting to lose this feeling.

She tries to regain her momentum, continue pleasing me. Desire fails her. She fails me.

Consciousness sets in for both of us. We shouldn't be here, shouldn't be doing this. No point in trying to make something happen that simply isn't meant to be. We don't care for each other. If she cared for me, she never would've left. If I cared about her, I never would have let her walk out. Whatever we shared is in the past. A place it should've stayed.

Trish shifts.

I slide out of her.

"Cory." She says my name with too much emotion.

I don't respond. Nothing left to say.

No more words are spoken. Just movement. She climbs out of the bed. Walks over to the light switch. I brace myself for the light, but temporary blindness still sets in. Not from the light, though. A secret has been revealed without any words being shared. She doesn't need to say anything because my eyes let her know that I know.

"How long have you known?"

"Not long."

Trish sees her naked reflection in the mirror. Moves toward her clothes like Eve did in the Garden of Eden once she bit from the forbidden fruit.

"How long have you known?" I ask again.

"Let's not talk in here," she says, moving out into the hallway. "Put some clothes on. I'll be out here."

Before her call, she was out of my life for good. Now she might be in my life forever. This is not what I want. Not what I need.

Trish is sitting on the couch. Nervousness makes her bite at her fingernails. Nervousness makes me clench my fists.

"Sit down, Cory."

I do, but not because she told me to. I sit because I'm afraid of what I might do if I remain standing.

"I'm twenty-two weeks pregnant, a little over five months."

I look at her, realize she's not looking at me. In her hand are pictures of a life growing inside of her. A life I do not want any part of.

I have to know. "Is it mine?"

"I can't believe you just asked me that." Trish throws the ultrasound pictures on the coffee table. They slide toward me.

I match her discord. "I can't believe you're almost five months pregnant and I'm just now finding out." For the third time, I ask, "How long have you known?"

"Does it even matter? I'm pregnant and you're the father." She looks at the scattered pictures. A sign of the life to come. Scattered lives that created one.

"You knew I didn't want kids, Trish."

"Damn it, Cory. My name is Patricia. And I couldn't care less if you wanted kids or not. It's not going to change the fact that I'm pregnant."

I feel my anger mounting. Feel my father's blood running through my veins. Need to calm myself down. Can't lose control like he did.

"Cory, look. This is not what I wanted. Not like this."

"Then why continue with the pregnancy?"

She gets up, grabs the pictures. Stuffs them back in her purse. "You know what, I've been doing this on my own since I found out. Coming over here was a bad idea."

"Next time, go with your first instincts."

"Fuck you, Cory. Fuck. You."

I see the tears forming in her eyes, see the bulge growing in her belly. See her tremble as she tries to put the pieces of her life back together. See all of that, but act like I don't. I can't. If I see, I have to care. If I care, I have to act. Every cause has an effect that will affect the lives of all involved.

"Good morning, Lauren." I walk from behind the front desk, reach out my hand. "Welcome to Conscious Kneads."

Making the decision to become an entrepreneur was the best decision I've ever made. Well, that and making the transition from relaxed tresses to a beautiful head of cultured acceptance. Every time I look in the mirror at my locs, I can't help but smile. That's the same way I feel about my spa. Conscious Kneads brings me joy.

"Thank you." The petite woman hesitates before shaking my hand. "I'm a little nervous."

"What are you nervous about?"

She hesitates. Her voice becomes soft and innocent. "I've never been waxed before. Not even my eyebrows."

"Oh, Lauren. It's nothing to be nervous about. I promise."

She gives me a skeptical look as if I don't know what I'm talking about.

"I tell you what, I'll go ahead and give you your massage first. That way you can get all relaxed before the wax."

She shrugs. Hesitant, money-green eyes still displaying her timidness. "I guess."

We walk toward the back to room number three. "Have you had a massage before?"

My question catches her thoughts elsewhere. It takes her a minute to respond. "I'm sorry, Fatima. What did you say?"

I repeat my question.

"Actually, this will be my first professional massage. My husband and I have rubbed each other down, but I'm sure it's nothing like what you're about to do."

I open the door for Lauren. "When giving massages, a lot of non-professionals barely penetrate the surface because they aren't aware of our many pressure points and such. As a massage therapist, I'm able to go beyond the surface. I hit those deep tissues you don't even realize you have."

I walk over to the cabinet, open the door. Pull out three vials of fragranced oils. Hold them out one by one for her to smell. "Now, don't get me wrong. Not all massages have to be therapeutic."

She takes each scent in. Makes her selection.

Bergamot. Perfect choice. Fresh. Light. Rejuvenating. Balancing, something David says I need in my life.

I pour a couple of drops of the oil into the aromatherapy diffuser. Burn the candle underneath to release the scent. "Undress to your comfort level." I hand her a fresh robe. "The switch on the right will cut on a signal light outside the door. Flip it when you're ready."

Weariness shows in her eyes. I ask, "Are you still worried about the waxing?"

She throws her hand in the air. "I'm over that."

"Good," I say and walk out the door, leaving Lauren to her thoughts.

Adrian is walking out of room number two just as the light to my room lets me know my client is ready.

"Hey, Fatima."

"Make it quick. My client is waiting."

She leans against the wall, arms folded. "You look like you've been in a fight with death. What's going on with you?" Her eyes are squinting in on me.

I brush her off. "Do I need to go pick your son up from school so you can mind his business and stay the heck out of mine?" I walk back toward my room before giving her time to answer.

"We'll talk about it later," she tells me.

"No, we won't."

❂ ❂ ❂

Lauren is sitting on the table twisting her wedding ring back and forth. She looks up at me, unanswered questions dangling in her eyes. I act like I don't see them. Reach for the curtain in the corner. Put some space between us. "Go ahead and untie your robe." I tell her. "I'm going to start on your back, so lay face down on the table. When you're in position, simply say, 'Okay,' and I will place a sheet on you from the waist down."

"Okay."

I draw the curtain back. Lauren is on the table. I remove her arms from the robe and lay them at her side. As I lift the robe from her, I cover her with a sheet. Push play on the portable CD player on the counter. Sounds of tranquility pour through the speakers. No words, only melodic vibrations resound from the little device.

I flick the light switch to a soft blue. Walk back toward the massage table with a warmed bottle of unscented oil. I squeeze a few drops in my hand and position them on the timid woman's back. Let my fingers act as her therapist and work out whatever issues plague her.

❂ ❂ ❂

An hour later, Lauren is fully massaged. All the stress written on her face sixty minutes ago, evaporated. Balance has been renewed.

I cover her up with the sheet, hand her the robe from the chair. "We have two showers available if you'd like to wash off the oil before redressing."

She rubs her neck, arms. "I'm not that greasy. I'll be okay."

"Okay. You can redress from the waist down." I hand her an armless robe to wrap around the top part of her body. "Flick the light when you're done."

Seconds pass. The light comes on.

I pop Bilal's *1st Born Second* in the CD player. Press the shuffle button. "Sometimes, I wish I wasn't me...sometimes." I sing as if the song is my own track while applying a small amount of wax to my wrist to make sure the temperature is not too hot. "I wish I was drug free, sometimes. Wish I saw the exit sign first..."

Lauren joins in, "Sometimes, wish I knew the truth without search." Wow. I was not expecting that. I try not to let my shock from her knowing the words show on my face. We both hum the next couple of verses before our melodies fade out.

"Lay back."

Bilal's words are so true to my life right now, minus the wish for being drug free...unless you include hate as an emotional drug of choice. I wish I knew the truth without search. I wish I didn't have to search for truth. Apparently, Lauren feels the same way.

I raise her right arm. Spray some skin preparation cleanser on a cosmetic pad. Lightly moisten her underarm. Allow it to air-dry, coat it lightly with lavender oil. Remove the applicator stick from the wax, smooth on a thick layer under her arm. Her eyes are tightly closed in anticipation of this new feeling. I test a small spot to make sure the hard wax is dry before I hold her skin taut and pull in the opposite direction of her hair growth. I quickly press my gloved fingers firmly on her hairless underarm.

"Oh. My. Goodness!" she exclaims through clenched teeth. Water leaks from her closed eyes. One leg is rocking back and forth on the table.

"You okay?"

"Yeah." She closes her eyes and hums out some more "sometimes."

That's exactly why I choose to use music with words during waxing. It helps keep a client's focus off of the waxing.

I apply another layer of wax to get the remaining hairs, then spread some aloe vera gel on her reddened skin before I repeat the procedure on her left arm.

"That wasn't too bad, was it?"

"I survived," she says. A look of relief that it's over with is plastered on her face.

"Maybe next time I can talk you into getting a Brazilian wax. You'd be surprised how much of a difference it makes."

She raises her eyebrows. "Umm, I think I'll leave that one alone. My arms are my stopping point."

"Just imagine if I had used wax strips. You would've begged me to stop after the first pull. They are torturous. The strips actually pull off the top layer of skin as well as the hairs. Double ouch." I put my hand on the doorknob. "I'll let you finish getting dressed and meet you right outside the door."

A few moments later, Lauren comes out the room fully dressed. Her face full of satisfaction. "My arms are so smooth. I might have to keep this up."

"You should. Your hair will grow in much softer and thinner since it isn't being bluntly cut off. You won't have to get waxed as often, but when you do, it won't be anything like today."

"I like the sound of that."

"Make sure you don't put on any deodorant or use fragranced body wash under your arm for twenty-four hours." I hand her a pamphlet on waxing aftercare. "This should cover everything, but please, don't hesitate to call if you have any questions or concerns."

She reaches in her purse. Pulls out a silver Visa.

"We have some complimentary refreshments that you are more than welcome to."

She declines. "Thanks, but I have a few things to get to. Hey, Fatima, can I ask you something?"

"Sure."

"Well," she hesitates. "I get a good vibe from you and I was wondering if maybe you want to check out this new poetry spot on the east side of town. Or maybe get some coffee or something one day."

"Umm—"

"I don't mean to put you on the spot or anything. It's just that with kids and a husband, my friend list is pretty empty." Lauren bites down on her bottom lip. Looks away for a minute. "My mom and I aren't on speaking terms these days and I guess I just want some female company, you know."

I think about my own lack of friends. Think about the few women in my life whom I can share with. A mom is not included in my list. No choice of mine, though. "What the heck," I say. I write down my cell number on the back of my business card and hand it to her. "Call me later."

I'm numb.

Been this way since the revelation that stood before me weeks ago.

With her eyes she told me, "I'm pregnant. I need you. *We* need you."

Words I never wanted to hear. I've never wanted to be a father. Never wanted to reproduce or see someone carry a part of me, my seed. That's the main reason why I've shied away from relationships. Because the possibility of becoming a father would exist.

Feels like ten years have passed me by without any consideration of time, any consideration of me. Time doesn't consider circumstance. It has an obligation to keep ticking. Whether I want it to or not.

I'm driving.

Going to see my brother, Cole. He has a healthy habit of injecting me with doses of the bullshit reality we live in. Unfortunately, that's the main reason why I rarely visit him now. The distance is simply a given.

Heavy traffic on the interstate gives me plenty of time to rehearse my words. It's a shame that I have to watch what I say around my own flesh and blood, but Cole reminds me a lot of our father. And you had to be cautious around him or else...

It takes me over an hour to reach his home.

Cole opens the door and my reservations evaporate like the morning mist.

He reaches out, pulls me close. Gives me an it's-been-too-long hug.

"Hey, brother."

"Well, well, well. To what do I owe this honor?" my older brother asks.

"You going to let me in first?"

"I'll think about it."

He doesn't laugh. Makes me think he's not joking.

I second guess my decision on coming. Maybe this wasn't such a good idea after all.

Cole notices my apprehension. Says, "Come on in, Meathead."

I smile at his childhood nickname for me.

"You always did have a big behind head, and that afro makes it even bigger." He gives me a light slap across my cushioned head. "What brings you all the way out to my side of the world?"

"It's been a while. Wanted to see what my family was up to."

He plops down on the tan leather sofa. I sit across from him on the love seat. Feel my burdens tense up in my shoulders as I try to relax.

"If you came around or called more often, you'd know how your fam is doing."

"Spare me the guilt trip. Working a full-time job and running my own business has taken its toll on a brother. Plus, it ain't like you live around the corner." I rub some sweat from my forehead. "Who told y'all to move this far anyway?"

"Yeah, well, distance shouldn't keep family miles apart."

Feels like he's putting the responsibility on me. "It's not like you come out to my side of town to see me."

"Either way you look at it, all of us could do better."

On the coffee table, in the center of the living room, is a picture of Cole and Dawn at their wedding ceremony. They look happy. The kind of happiness that building a solid foundation gives you. I change the subject. "How's Dawn?"

"The wife is good. She's in that career change mode again."

"She's at it again, huh? I thought she was happy with culinary school. Wasn't she planning to open her own restaurant?"

"I digress." He shakes his head in frustration. "Since the kids have started grade school, Dawn's burning desire to make a difference in the educational system has taken precedence over all her other career moves."

"That's got to get old."

"It's been old, but as long as she's happy, that's all that matters. I'd hate for her to look at me or the kids with regret years down the line because we held her back in some way."

"I hear you. How are my niece and nephew anyway?"

"A mess." He sighs. "Samantha is eight going on twenty-eight. She thinks she knows everything. Wants to do things her own way, you know. Cole Jr. is starting to smell himself. And I see why…the boy refuses to take baths."

We laugh at adolescence.

"You know he'll be ten next week."

"Man, already?"

"Yep. Time flies when you're having fun."

"That's what they say."

All the talk about kids makes me think about the seed growing in Trish's stomach. A sour taste is on my tongue. A grimace covers my face.

"What's that look about?" Cole asks, concern in his voice. "Looks like you just bit into a lemon."

I lean forward on the couch. Elbows planted firmly on top of my knees, hands tucked under my chin.

"What's on your mind, brother?"

I ask, "You got anything to drink in here?"

"No, sir. Kids in this house. Told you to leave the liquor alone anyway. You're too old to be dependent on a bottle. Now speak up."

"Why does everyone think I got a drinking problem? Ain't nothing wrong with a drink here and there."

"You're right. There isn't anything wrong with sipping on a drink here and there, but we both know you do more than sip. Don't sit up in here and act like it's okay."

"I ain't got a problem with it," I declare, feeling the need to defend myself.

"Yeah, well maybe *that* is your problem. The fact that you don't have a problem with it," he reiterates. "Look at you, all that education and you're using double negatives. '*Ain't got.*'" He shakes his head in shame.

My temperature rises. Feels like my head is about to burst. I get up, pace the living room for a second. Decide it's better to find the exit before I say some things I may never be able to retract. I pull my keys out of my pocket, head toward the front door.

"Cory, sit your always-running-from-your-problems behind down."

As mad as I am, I sit as ordered.

"Now I know you didn't drive all this way to get mad and walk back out of here. Get whatever it is off your chest, man. And look at me when I'm talking to you, damn it."

He calls out my weakness. It's too hard for me to look him in the face since he reminds me so much of our dad. Always has been. Something I've been trying to overcome for years, to no avail.

I find the strength. Look at my brother who has been more of a father than my own. Say the first thing that comes to my mind. "You ever hit 'em?"

"Hit who?"

"The kids." My voice is faintly above a whisper.

He moves to the edge of his seat. "Where did that come from?"

"Just wondering."

"I discipline my kids like any father would." He looks at me sternly. "What is this about, Cory?"

Cole keeps his eyes on me. Penetrates my thoughts. I try to block his entry, but he's stronger than I am.

"Cory, listen to me, man. That was almost thirty years ago. You have got to get on with your life and stop holding on to what used to be. Can't change what has already happened."

"She's pregnant," I blurt out.

"Who? Angela?"

I shake my head. "I haven't dealt with her in over a year."

"Tasha?"

I shake my head again.

"See, there's another one of your problems. You can't keep hopping from bed to bed. Too many diseases and baby mamas out there. You don't need to be caught up in all of that."

"Not trying to be." I rub my temples. "See, you just don't understand these women today, being all married and stuff. They are nothing like what they were ten years ago. These women out here are looking for someone to jump the broom with. When they find a man, they do their damnedest to make him *The One*. They forget about everything else. They forget about life. I'm not looking for that, Cole. I'm not looking for a commitment. A good time is all I want. I'm good with that."

He's not buying it. "That's what you're telling yourself these days, huh?" Cole shakes his head for the umpteenth time. "You'll learn."

"Maybe, maybe not."

"See, that's why you are in the situation you're in now." He looks at me with scolding eyes. "So who is she?"

"Trish," I tell him.

"Damn, man." Reality sets in. "Somebody new and already about to make me an uncle."

"What should I do?"

The stress of carrying his younger brother for all these years shows on his face, makes him look older than thirty-four. "Are you sure it's yours?"

I nod.

"Then why are you asking me what to do? Because of your irresponsibility, you've got to take care of a responsibility. For life. Next time, protect yourself or this type of thing will keep happening."

"I'm no fool, man. I protect myself each and every time. You think I wanted this to happen? The condom broke."

"Next time, put it on right. Ninety-five percent of the time, condoms break because they are put on improperly."

I laugh out loud at his statistics. "I'm damn near thirty years old. I think I know how to wear a condom."

"Well, Cory, you've got all the answers. I'm sure you will make the best decision. Just remember it's not only you now."

There's nothing else to say.

I've heard enough.

Said too much.

❈ ❈ ❈

Trish agreed to meet me after her class adjourned at eight-thirty. I suggested the Starbucks half a mile down from the school.

I'm running late. I find a parking space in front of the overrated coffee shop at a quarter to nine.

Apparently, Trish is running late as well. Either that or she changed her mind about coming. There's no sign of her inside and her car is nowhere outside.

People are in and out of this place left and right. They act like this is the last hour that Starbucks' doors will be open. Surprisingly, I find an empty table not too far from the front door.

The caffeine heads keep my attention as I wait for Trish to arrive. Sometimes I swear coffee shops are nothing more than liquid crackhouses. To my left, by the front entrance, sits an average-looking guy with a bad haircut. His hair is skin close on the sides with a little patch of hair on the top. Reminds me of the buzz cut they give Marines. He wears a face with no emotion as he talks into his cell phone. He gets up, throws his coffee cup away before he jogs out the door.

At another table in front of him are two students. The only sounds coming from their direction are fingers pounding keys on portable computers. Both type as if they have a fifteen-page paper due in the morning and they're only on the first half of page one.

Commotion from a table toward the back end of the shop grabs my attention. It's two men. Looks like a little domestic altercation. Lovers. Can't see what a man gets out of being with someone who carries the same thing he does. Different strokes for different folks. That's one pool I never plan to swim in. I shake my head in disgust. My silent condemnation must be written all over my face because the softer looking dude glares at me, committing an act of homicide with his eyes. He sucks his teeth and bulges his eyes out as if delivering his own judgments on the skeletons in my closet. I turn my attention elsewhere.

If it weren't for the loc-wearing brother working behind the counter, I'd be the only one of color in the place.

Trish sashays in about a half hour later than the time we set, the bulge in her stomach more noticeable than the last time we saw each other. She pauses, silently contemplates. Decides to greet me with a hug once she reaches my table in the corner.

I reciprocate her greeting. Might as well start things off in a positive direction. "Glad you could make it."

She sits down in the chair I pull out for her. "Thanks." She pushes her new rectangle-shaped frames closer to her eyes. "Sorry, I'm running a little behind. My professor had a few extra things on his mind tonight."

"Not a problem. You want something to drink?"

From her purse, she pulls out a honey bun. She tears open the wrapping as if it's her last meal. Her eyes roll back as she inhales two hefty bites. "This is so good."

I leave her with the taste of heaven on her tongue, head to the order counter. Bring back an Iced Caramel Macchiato for me, ice water for her.

"How's school going?"

"Six more classes and I'm done until the winter. Summer session is out of the question and I'm not registering for the fall semester either," she tells me in between bites of her five-hundred calorie treat.

"Thought you wanted to hurry up and finish. It's not like you to take breaks," I say.

"Baby is due June twenty-second."

She stares at me. Waits for a reaction.

The baby. The reason we're here. I fidget in my seat. Lean forward, take a sip of chilled coffee. It doesn't go down easily.

Forms a lump in my throat before going down with one hard swallow.

"June is less than four months away, Trish."

"Patricia. And don't raise your voice at the mother of your child."

I ignore her correction, ignore the smirk on her face. "I can't believe you've been keeping this from me all of this time."

"I found out the last time we were together."

"That was three weeks ago."

She shakes her head. "The time before that, when you kicked me out. I had found out earlier that day. Was coming to tell you, but after the way you acted, I couldn't bring myself to say anything."

"Hold up. I didn't kick you out. You left, remember?"

Her eyes tell me I left her with no other choice at that time. I wanted her to leave, to disappear. Just like right now. Wish her and the half of me inside her would walk away and never come back.

"Well, whatever."

"I don't have time for games, Trish."

She rolls her eyes. "I'm going to ignore that *this* time." Her voice doesn't hold attitude, though. "Look, I know you don't believe me, but I didn't know I was pregnant. I was still having my monthly cycle and everything. I wasn't sick or having weird cravings. Life went on as usual until my eyes started going blurry. My perfect vision went downhill overnight. Thought it was from all the reading and staying up late on the computer. The doctor said blurred vision could be the result of a number of things. One thing led to another and I found myself taking a pregnancy test."

Blurred vision is the reason why I'm sitting here. Never would've thought.

I'm silent, numb again. Frozen in time.

Being a daddy is the last thing I ever wanted to be. Never wanted the responsibility. Never wanted something so fragile to depend on me for support. Never wanted to be looked up to or trusted. Never wanted to do what my daddy did to me.

"Cory."

I'm thawed by the heat from my anger. Thoughts of the man whose seed produced me always take me to a place I hate going.

"Cory?"

I still don't respond. Not ready to produce words. Just look at the woman in front of me, wishing I could rewind time. Rewind it back to before the time I lay between her thighs. Rewind it to before the time I was born, before I slid from between my mother's thighs. Maybe then I would have a better chance.

"Why you get all silent on me?"

"Nothing to say right now," I tell her.

She huffs in frustration. "Look, you're the one who wanted to meet me. Either you start talking or I'm out of here."

"I don't want you to have my baby." There I said it. I tell her I'm not going to give her the support she needs, or wants. Can't be the father she expects me to be.

"Cory, I want you to understand one thing," she starts, her tone crisp. "This is not about me. It is not about us. I am not asking you to be with me. A child is growing inside of me. Part of me and part of you. Either you take care of your responsibilities the way you did when *you* were inside of me or I will do what I need to do to make sure this child is provided for."

"So this is about money, huh? I should've known." My voice echoes with the anger growing inside of me. "Knowing you, you probably messed the condom up on purpose."

We've made a scene. The two students pack up their studies,

leave within seconds. The loc-wearing brother behind the counter looks at us, directs his eyes to the front door. Makes a non-verbal request for us to leave.

Trish gets up, throws away her trash. Comes back to the table. *Slap*.

It takes all of the strength in my body to hold me back from raising my hand toward Trish in defense. She actually hit me. Slapped me like my mama did in her times of despair.

The only other brother in the place marches to our table. Seeing the battle brewing inside my eyes, he orders us to leave.

"I'm done here," Trish says, turns and walks out the door to my life again.

"Sir, I need you to leave as well," he tells me.

Minutes go by before I make any move. I am dazed by what just transpired.

Sitting in my car, I look inside Starbucks. See the gay man in the light blue shirt staring at me, making the same accusations I made toward him during his scene-causing moment. He rubs his hand up and down his cheek, makes a sad face, laughs.

I put my car in reverse. Drive my embarrassment away.

The phone rings. Rings four times before I pick it up.

"What's going on, Cory?"

I wipe sweat off my brow. Realize I was having a nightmare. "Carl."

"I haven't talked to you in months and that's the best you can do?"

"Was sleep. You woke me up."

"It's damn near two in the afternoon. What you doing sleep?"

"I swear, sometimes you act just like Cole," I tell my younger brother. "I'm a grown man. If I want to sleep until the Rapture, that's my business."

"Bet you wouldn't tell him that."

He laughs.

I don't.

"Look, man, didn't mean to wake you up, but I got to talk to you about something."

I get off the couch, go into the kitchen, pour myself a glass of J.W. straight like I had grown up watching my mama do. "I'm listening."

His voice lowers to a whisper.

"Speak up, man. Can barely hear you."

"I can't. Tameka's here."

"Can you go in another room or something?" I sip on a little scotch. Let it marinate on my palate.

I hear ruffling on the other end of the phone. "How's that?"

"Better."

"Man, I'm thinking about asking Tameka to marry me." He lets the idea sit for a minute. "I mean, I'm not going anywhere, she's not going anywhere. It just makes sense."

"Sounds like you got it all planned out. What do you need my opinion for?"

"I didn't ask you what I should do. I'm just letting you know what's going on in your little brother's life." His tone lets me know I've offended him.

"My bad, Carl. I'm going through some things over here."

"You all right?"

"I will be." I take another gulp of the myriad-flavored drink. Taste different flavors of life. "I'm happy for you, though."

"Thanks, Cory. She really makes me happy." He pauses, contemplation in his silence. "I hope you find that one day."

"Maybe, maybe not."

After I hang up, I pour myself another glass of J.W. Try to wash my misery away. Try to wash the dreams away. Dreams of the dead.

My hand shakes as I reach back for the phone. Hit speed dial.

"McMillian and Watson, how may I direct your call?"

"Cora Douglas, please."

"May I tell her who's calling?"

"Cory Hines."

"One moment, please," the receptionist instructs.

"Cory, to what do I owe this pleasure?" she answers with a smile in her voice.

It's been a little while since I've talked to my oldest sibling, but now isn't the time to be cordial. "I need to talk to you."

Her new tone owns no smile. "I'm in the middle of an ugly divorce case right now."

"The nightmares are back."

I hear her pen hit the paper. Lets me know I have her undivided attention. "For how long?"

"Been having them for a couple of weeks now."

She sighs. "Are they the same as before?"

In my dream, I'm dead, lying in a casket with my eyes open. The only person there is a little boy who stands over me. His eyes are gone, but tears are rolling down his face.

I reach for my glass. Need the scotch to wash away my dreams, make them disappear. "They're the same," I tell my sister.

"You need to talk to someone, Cory."

"I'm talking to you."

"A professional, Cory. This is beyond me."

I stare at the half-empty bottle of liquor on the coffee table. Hear Trish and Cole calling me out on my dependency. Now my own sister is suggesting I see a therapist.

Cora's phone clicks. Does that twice. She puts me on hold.

"Sorry about that," she says when she comes back on the phone.

"Take care of your business. I just needed to talk for a minute."

She pauses for a second. In her silence, I hear her fingers drumming on her desk. "Did I offend you?"

"A little. Feels like everyone thinks I have problems. Problems beyond my reach, beyond my own capability of handling them."

She apologizes. Speaks from her heart. "Listen, Cory. I'm sorry that you feel like it's you against the world. It's a tough crowd out here. But you've been carrying around stuff for too long. It's not fair to you. It's time to move one. Time to heal."

"Easier said than done."

"Don't give me that, Cory."

"What do you want me to say, Cora? Okay, you're right, I'm

gonna let it go." I blow out hard air. "It's not as easy as you're making it."

"I'm not saying it is, but can you honestly say you've tried?"

Her phone clicks again. Hear her struggle with the need to finish our conversation and do her job at the same time. Hear it in her staggered breathing.

"Get back to work. I'll be all right."

"Look, Cory, I know it's hard. Anything in life that has caused us pain will never be an easy healing process. I'll do all that I can to be here for you. Your brothers are trying too. You don't have to go through this alone. Just don't shut us out."

Her phone clicks again.

Again, I tell her, "I'll be all right." Hang up the phone before she has a chance to respond.

I take a long sip of my warm addiction. It goes straight to my head.

It's five minutes after eight in the evening. I'm standing in front of Patchouli, the poetry spot where I agreed to meet my new client.

I've been here for a little more than ten minutes. No sign of her yet.

A horn blows. The driver of a red Nissan Maxima waves a frantic arm out the window.

Lauren.

She pulls into an empty parking space a couple of cars over from my ride. Briskly walks in my direction by the front entrance to the lounge. "Sorry I'm running late. For some reason, my husband forgot about my outing and made plans of his own. But that's a story I'll spare you from."

"No problem."

I open the door for her to enter first.

The room is more crowded than it appeared outside. Smells warm and earthy, like the name suggests, with a hint of *We Shall Overcome*.

"Five dollars," the dark-skinned man behind the booth tells us. "We're just getting started, so you ladies made it just in time."

"Perfect." Lauren says as she pulls out a ten. Pays for both of us.

"Thanks," I say.

She blows me off. "There's a table up near the front."

On the stage is a small band. A female and a male are sitting on stools behind microphones, singing along with the band as the crowd waits for the first poet to take the stage.

"It's nice in here," Lauren leans over and says in my ear.

I nod in agreement.

"I'll have to get here earlier next time, so we can put our names on the list."

"You perform?"

"Haven't in years. Started my own poetry club in high school and college."

"Never would've known."

She chuckles. "A husband and kids will do it to you."

Handclaps and whistles surround us as a brother takes the mic on stage. Puts a cessation to our conversation.

"Welcome to Sunday nights at Patchouli. For the regulars, you already know what to expect. But for my first-timers, sit back, relax. Let the stories told on this stage pull you into yesterday and carry you into tomorrow. It doesn't get any better than this. I thank you all for being a part of this magnificent experience."

The drummer begins hitting his sticks, creating a steady beat. The keyboardist follows in. Bass kicks in on cue with a mellow tune. A female saxophonist seasons the mood with her own jazzy flavorings.

"Without further ado, coming to the stage, welcome Naadirah. The rare and precious one."

Applause.

A petite woman steps on stage. She lights up the candlelit room with her brightly colored afro. It bounces with the movements of her frustration as she speaks about losing herself within herself.

Too busy seeking external validation because, internally, I won't validate myself.

Naadirah pounds her fist into her chest.

The only vaccination…emancipation…from self.

Out of the corner of my eye, I see Lauren nodding in agreement with the poet. Makes me wonder what part of herself does she need freeing from.

The singers on stage fade out as Naadirah steps off the stage. Her afro not far behind her.

Lauren leans over. "I'm going to get a drink. You want something?"

I shake my head. "I'll pass."

"Be right back."

The MC of the evening steps back on stage. I welcome his eye contact as he stares in my direction.

"Next to the stage is a regular here on Sunday nights. Put your hands together for Simeon."

"What was up with the eye contact?" Lauren asks when she sits back down at our table.

"I don't know. Wasn't really paying attention."

"He's not bad-looking." She sucks the cherry off its stem. Sips on her Cosmopolitan.

I pick at a perfectly manicured fingernail as I watch the MC make his way over to the bar.

His walk holds no insecurity. Walks like the world owes him an apology. Regal. He has my attention. He runs his ringless hand through his textured fro. Sits down, orders a drink the color of butterscotch.

To be held…and groomed into the grooves of you.

The poet's words grab my attention, but my vision stays focused on the man in all black.

He turns in the barstool, resting his eyes on mine. Lets me know he knows I've been watching him.

I move my eyes from him. Slightly embarrassed that he caught my voyeurism.

Simeon steps down from the stage. A woman behind me tells her companion, "I sure would like to make some melodies with him," referring to the poet's sexual poem.

I smile inside. Look back for the man at the bar. He's gone.

Lauren fumbles around in her purse for her ringing cell phone. "Hey. She is? You gave her a bottle? Put her across your knees and rock her. I'm with Fatima." She looks at me. Rolls her eyes. "From the spa. We're at a poetry spot. I'll be home in a little while. She's a baby, what do you expect?" She says a few more things before flipping her phone shut.

I tried not to listen to her conversation. Tried to make small talk with the other ladies at our table, gave them business cards to the spa with a fifteen percent discount on the back. I still heard the exasperation in my new friend's voice, though. "Everything all right?"

She exhales. "My husband. He acts like the kids are my responsibility. He acts like he doesn't know what to do. Like I'm supposed to drop what I'm doing and come running to the rescue." She shakes her head. Throws the homing device back in her purse. "They're his kids too."

"Maybe you need to leave them with him more often."

She just shakes her head in frustration. Takes another sip of her Cosmo.

Poet after poet takes the stage. Men, women. Every one releasing prophetic proclamations.

A bald-headed female steps on the stage. Approaches the mic like they fed off of the same umbilical cord. She commands our attention with her familiarity.

Delusion. Illusion. My mind…a state of…confusion.

Her switch from spoken word to song is captivating. Makes me feel her words. Reminds me of the eclectic sound of Me'Shell Ndegeocello. It takes me somewhere. I grab my journal from my purse, scribble a few thoughts down. The pen moves faster than I can think.

Debating. Contemplating. Should I stay or should I go…go…go.

She talks and sings, and sings and talks of being the other woman. Lauren moves around in her seat. Sips the last of her drink.

My hand lightly touches her thigh. I lean over, whisper, "You okay?"

She looks at me with eyes glazed over. "I'm getting ready to go."

"You sure you're all right?"

She puts her purse on her shoulder. "Yeah." Her eyes tell a different story.

We wait for the poetess to finish. Wait for her applause before getting up from the table. I walk Lauren out to her car.

She leans against the trunk. "Married life is hard. Too many expectations. Sometimes I wish I could turn back the hands of time." She sucks on her bottom lip. "But if I did that, I wouldn't have my children."

I say, "Every relationship has the same expectations. Whether it's parent versus child, teacher/student, coach/player, conductor/orchestra, performer/audience." I stop myself when I notice the I-get-the-point expression on Lauren's face.

We lightly chuckle at my loss of focus.

"Got a little carried away there, didn't I?"

She nods.

"What I'm getting at is, sometimes we set our expectations too high for other people. Is it fair? No. Especially when we're not willing to set those same high expectations for ourselves."

"But, Fatima," she counters. "Never mind. I digress."

She walks around to the driver's side. Opens the door. Stands between the door and the inside of the car. So much is in her eyes. So much that she wants to say, but doesn't. Lauren sighs, gives me a hug that begs to get to know me better. "I'll call you," she says before shutting the door on her emotions. Drives off like she's on the tracks of NASCAR.

❂ ❂ ❂

All of the seats are empty at the bar. I settle myself on one in the center. People are on the floor dancing, a few are in dark corners vibing. The band is playing catchy tunes for everyone to get their groove on to.

"What can I get you?" the brother behind the bar asks.

"Hennessy and Coke. No ice."

He sets my drink down on a Patchouli's napkin. I hand him ten dollars. "Keep the change," I tell him.

He nods his thanks, his ebony skin glistening under the candle-light.

I feel like someone is watching me. Look to my left, no one there. No eyes staring in my direction to the right either. I take a long sip of my nerve calmer. Maybe it's my own thoughts stalking me. The rest of my drink goes down in one sip.

A cool breeze chills the hairs on the back of my neck. Lets me know I'm no longer at the bar alone. Arousing hints of vetiver and tender violets draw my attention to the occupied seat next to me.

It's the MC from earlier. His eyes more alluring up close than at a distance. He looks at my empty glass. "What are you drinking?"

I tell him. He orders me another round.

"Thanks."

He grabs a bottle of Johnnie Walker from behind the counter. Pours his own drink.

"Misery loves company," he says. "The name's Cory."

"Fatima." I shake his extended hand.

"So what's your story?"

I take a sip from my fresh drink. "Depends on which book you want to read."

The background singers echo their version of Jaguar Wright's melody in Jay-Z's *Unplugged* "Song Cry" as another poet does a freestyle about his loving and losing a woman who didn't mean him any good.

I move the subject away from me. "You always emcee?" I ask.

"Every time the doors are open," he answers.

I take another inventory of the place. Nod. "This is a nice place. It's magnetic."

"This your first time?"

"Yeah."

"Something tells me it won't be your last."

I run my finger around the rim of my glass. "Why is that? You sound like you want to see more of me."

Cory shies away at my assumption. Takes a long sip of his scotch. "Maybe. Maybe not."

"I see."

He says, "I saw you writing in a notebook earlier. You looked pretty intense. Figure you got a few things to get off your chest. There's no better place than the stage."

My curiosity piques. "So, you were watching me?"

"I just happened to be looking in your direction at the time." He smiles.

Our eyes connect. Brown to black. His eyes the color of onyx.

I look at my barely sipped-on glass. Do that to break the connection.

Cory looks away too.

I push myself away from the bar. Remove the strap of my bag off my knee. "Thanks again for the drink, Cory."

"You're leaving already?"

I don't answer the obvious.

"I was just getting started on chapter one." He takes a quick sip of his drink. Almost spills it as he rushes to put it back down. "Let me walk you out."

"Thanks, but no thanks. I'm a big girl."

"Didn't say you weren't. Just offering."

I press my lips together, smooth my lip gloss around. "Well—"

"Hold up, Fatima." Cory hops down from the barstool, moves so close to me I can taste his scotch. "I just want to read your books. Want to know who you are. Is that too much to ask?"

"Why?" I want to know.

"Something tells me that we have a lot in common."

I chuckle. This guy is quite a character. "Well, something tells me let's not go there."

He digs in his back pocket, pulls out a little pad and a pen. Scribbles and hands me the paper.

I toss the paper in my bag. "Good night," I say as I walk toward the door. Walk toward my car and head to loneliness on the other side of town.

The weekend came and went without any record of time. Monday morning and I'm back on my nine-to-five grind.

"Excuse me, sir. Where can I find *First Time Mommy* by Allison Chambers?"

My head immediately starts pounding at the sound of the all-too-familiar voice. I turn around as slowly as possible, not wanting to see her face. "Trish, this is my job. Don't bring drama here," I say in as low a voice as possible.

She stands back, hands in the air. If I were any closer, she probably would've pushed me. "I told you not to call me that."

"Keep your voice down. This is a public library." My voice carrying more bass this time.

"I know where I am. If you'd call me by my name, I wouldn't have to get so loud."

Twanna, my supervisor, clears her throat behind me. "Cory, is there a problem?"

I keep my attention on Trish. "No, there's no problem."

"I didn't think so," she says before walking back into her office.

Trish puts her hands on her hips. Huffs out her frustration. "Are you going to help me find the book or what?"

"Wait right here."

Instead, she marches right along with me. Her hard footsteps draw the attention of a few people around us. I shake my head. Try to locate the book as fast as I can, regretting the day I met her with every step I take.

"Is this how it's gonna be?" she asks as soon as we're in an aisle by ourselves.

"What are you talking about?"

"This. Us." Trish rubs her ever-growing belly. "Is this what I have to do to spend some time with the father of my baby?"

I grab the book off the shelf. It takes every fiber in me to keep from hitting her upside the head with the three-hundred-page book.

She keeps talking. "I've been calling you, leaving you tons of messages. You don't return my calls."

"Look, do you want the book or not?"

Her voice breaks. She shifts her weight to one leg. Shows her insecurity. "What did I do that was so wrong?"

"For starters, you slapped me."

"You disrespected me."

My jaws clench so hard it feels like my teeth are about to shatter. "This is not the place for this, Trish."

"Patricia!" she yells.

Voices whisper around me. How can I enforce them to keep their voices down when I can't control my own guest?

I grab Trish by the arm. Ignore her pleas to loosen my grip. I escort her all the way out of the library. Shove the book at her chest. "Don't ever come to my job again."

✪ ✪ ✪

I no sooner walk in the door than the phone starts ringing. Not in the mood for any more drama, I let the answering machine do the dirty work.

"Cory. It's your sister. Give me a call when—"

"I'm here, Cora."

"Oh, oh." My interruption of her message catches her off guard. "Everything okay?"

"Why do you ask?"

"Last time we talked, you were a little down. Just wanted to make sure you were doing better."

The only thing on my mind is the theatrics from work earlier today. "Having some baby mama issues."

She sighs. "Cole told me about the baby."

I figured he would. "What else is new?" I ask, not really looking for an answer. Neither he nor Cora have been good with keeping their mouths shut.

"Cory, why are you doing this to yourself again?"

"You think I wanted this to happen?" My head starts pounding harder. I walk toward the kitchen for my infamous painkiller. Black Label.

"Do you even know if the baby is yours?"

"The condom broke."

"Damn it, Cory. You can't keep doing this."

My voice raises, finger pointing at my own chest with the bottle in my hand. "You act like I planned this."

"You're the one sleeping around with all these women. Acting just like your daddy."

"You didn't have to go there," I say.

She hangs up, disconnects our call with no apologies.

The phone rings again. My sister's number pops up on the ID. I don't speak, just put the phone up to my ear.

Cora doesn't say anything either. Sobs are the only sound coming from her lips.

I put my anger aside. "Sis, what's wrong?"

"I didn't mean to attack you. I just get so upset when I hear about these women taking advantage of you."

"No one's taking advantage of me."

She doesn't hear me. She's too busy crying.

My sister has always been a strong woman. She had to be to help raise three boys. It's times like this, her moments of weakness, when I really see just how fragile she is.

"I'm a big boy, Cora. This is just another card I was dealt."

The only time she puts her guard up is when she's in the court-room. Then or when she's in some sort of emotional pain.

She sighs hard.

To hear her like this lets me know it's not about me. "Talk to me. What's bothering you?" I want to know.

The phone muffles. Hear her blowing her nose in the background. She comes back on the phone with so much pain in her voice it hurts me. "It's Mama."

It's been a while since I heard talk about the woman who birthed us. The woman who loved the letter C because her favorite teacher's name began with it, so she named all of her kids the same way. Cora, Cole, Cory, Carl. I pull out a chair, sit down at the dining room table. Prepare myself for the worst.

"Cory, Mama has cancer. She's dying."

I'm in my car. On my way to a place that holds too many bad memories.

Called Twanna last night at home. Told her I wouldn't be in for a few days. Told her I had some family issues to take care of. After my fiasco with Trish, she felt relieved not to see my face around for a while.

It takes a little less than two hours to reach my hometown. A place I swore I'd never return.

Avery, Mississippi, a town so small it only has one stoplight. I ride over the railroad tracks. My heart pounds in my chest. Saliva in my mouth grows thick as I near the desert-brown stucco home at the end of the street.

I sit in front of the house, maybe five, ten minutes, struggling with whether or not I should even be here. I didn't choose to be born. Didn't choose the upbringing I had. But I have to remind myself that she's my mom. She didn't choose any of this either. For that reason alone, I open my car door.

✪ ✪ ✪

Madeline Hines, Mattie as she was often called, holds the door open, looks at me with disdain in her eyes. "People hear 'bout the dying and come rushing. Never reckoned my own child would treat me wit' the same cowardly hospitality."

She lets the door close behind her as she walks toward the kitchen.

I open the door to let myself in.

No hugs. No long-time-no-see banter. Nothing but facial expressions letting me know that too much time has passed since we last saw each other.

Mother.

Son.

Strangers from the same blood.

"How long it's been?" she asks with her back turned toward me. "Five, six years?"

"Hasn't been that long."

"Humph," is her simple reply.

Her back stays turned as she fiddles around in the cabinets. Pulls down two coffee mugs, fills them with her back facing me. Comes to the table, hands me a cup. I push the cup away. "Don't drink coffee."

She pushes it back in my direction. "Me neither."

In the cup is a bronze liquid. The familiar smell registers in my brain. Johnnie Walker. Mama never drank coffee. She always carried around coffee mugs so we wouldn't know that she was really drinking a stronger pick-me-up.

I smile at the memory. As bad as it is, I smile.

"Cora told—"

She cuts me off. "That girl always did run her mouth too doggone much. Thas why she a lawyer. Always had ta be in er'body's bidness."

"So, why'd you tell her if you didn't want the rest of us to know?"

"I didn't," she informs me.

"Then how did she find out?"

She doesn't answer me right away. Sips a healthy gulp of Scotch. Lets it marinate on her tongue. "I ain't tell that chile nothin'. My nosey neighbor, Ms. Alice, did. She drove me up ta the doctor since I can't drive. She was listenin' in when the nurse told me 'bout chemo and her mind went wanderin'. She asked me 'bout it, but I jus told her ta keep her mouth shut. I see she ain't listen."

"Why didn't you ask one of your own kids to take you to something so important as that?"

"'Cause I ain't want y'all in my bidness then jus like now, so stop askin' me so many damn questions. Startin' ta sound like yo nosey sister. Cora, and Alice worryin' me enough."

She picks her mug up, fills it up with more of the good stuff. Strolls down the hall.

I follow her into the living room. I ask, "How are you feeling, Mattie?"

Her bulging eyes glare up at me, struggle to focus. "Let me ask you something first."

"Okay."

"You hate me?"

I almost spit my drink out at her question. "I can't believe you would ask me something like that."

"Then why I gotta be dyin' for you ta come see me? You'on even call me Mama no more." Her eyes begin to water up, but nothing falls. Her well dried up years ago.

I want to answer her. However, the words refuse to form. I want to tell her that I don't hate her. Want to call her Mama, but I can't. Too much has happened. Too many bad memories.

She sucks her teeth, the few that she managed to keep through all of the times Mister hit her in the mouth. "Thas what I figured." She confirms her own assumptions with my silence.

My mouth opens this time and words come out. "Why did you stay with him?"

She hesitates. Can see where I'm going with my question. "'Cause I loved him, thas why. And ain't nothin' wrong wit' that."

"Didn't say it was."

"Why you thank I stayed wit' yo daddy?"

I ignore her question and ask another of my own. "Did he love you?"

"What kind of question is that?" Her frail body raises from her recliner, the burgundy one I brought her the last time I was here several years ago, and walks over to the fireplace. Wipes off a frame containing a picture warped by time.

"Do you *think* he loved you?" My voice raises an octave because I want an answer.

She turns and looks at me. Gives me a look that lets me know I've struck a nerve. "People walk 'round thanking all the time, don't mean they know nothin'. I *knew* yo daddy loved me."

I stare in her flushed face as I speak. "Well, he had a funny way of showing it."

She puts her hand on her bony hip, her deteriorating body using all of its strength to stand strong. Independent. Too late for that now. I get up to assist her. Try to get her to sit back down.

The woman who gave birth to me refuses my help. "Get yo hands off me. I'on need yo help. Always did thank you was tough. Always coming to my rescue like I couldn't handle thangs wit'out you. I been standing strong forty-eight years. Now sit yo ass down somewhere."

I shake my head. Wish I had not come. Some things never change.

Mattie straggles back into the kitchen. A loud noise comes from her direction. The sound glass makes when it comes in contact with a hard surface rings in my ears.

As independent as she tries to make herself feel, I check on her anyway.

She's kneeling on the ground, picking up the broken bottle of scotch. Mumbles to herself, "I done the best I could and he gon' come in my house slanderin' me."

I kneel down beside her. Help her pick up the shattered pieces of our lives.

"I… I didn't…didn't mean to make you feel bad," I say.

Mattie stops picking up glass, hugs me. Hugs me tight. Breaks down in my arms.

Her pain is my pain.

Two lost souls just trying to live with the cards we were dealt.

I want to break down in her embrace. Want to, but don't. I can't.

She says through tears, "You know, you was always my favorite."

I pull away from her. "I was?"

A tear forms in my eye. Mattie wipes it away before it has the chance to fall. She does that like she used to do when I was a little boy. Wipes away my pain, but leaves her own, leaves her face tear-stained to make a statement. "Yeah, you was. You was the only one bold enough to protect me. You was strong, stronger than me. You came to my defense when I couldn't fight no mo'. Your strength made me hate you, made me hate myself 'cause you was stronger than me and I made you."

Her confession is the clearest I have ever heard her speak. Not as slurred or illiterate as usual. If she wasn't in front of me, I'd swear it was someone else talking.

"The same strength that made me hate you became the same strength that made me fond of you. You was my lil' protector. My lil' hero."

I see something in her that makes me wish things were different between us. Wish time could be rewound for us to do a few things over.

Mattie moves a few things around in the cabinet under the sink. Pulls out a fresh bottle of the one man we've depended on all our lives. Pours us two more cups full. We take our drinks to the front porch. Sit on the swing.

"You know what?"

"What?"

She takes a sip from her mug. Swallows long and hard. Sighs. "You know, I ain't mad 'bout the cancer."

"Most people would be," I say, taking a long sip from my own cup.

"Most, but not me. This my punishment."

I'm confused. "Punishment?"

"Yo daddy had his. This mine."

Memories of the way Mister was killed replay in my mind. One night he was out tiptoeing around with a married woman. Her husband came home, found them together. He had been waiting to catch the two of them together since the day he discovered that Mister had fathered a kid with his wife. That night, he reached under the bed, pulled out his shotgun. Killed both of them, their baby, then himself.

"He ain't love me." She brings me back to the now. "I knew he ain't the first time he put his hands on me."

"Mattie," I swallow, "Mattie, you don't have to talk about it."

"It's okay. I wanna."

Neither one of us talks for a minute. Both trying to retrace our steps so we can understand where we went wrong.

She continues, "He ain't love me. Ain't love none us. One time he told me after I had Cora if I had any mo' babies he was gon' make me watch him kill 'em. Told me he'd kill all my babies, then kill me."

I shake my head in disgust. "Bastard."

"Shoulda been my sign right there ta leave. I jus ain't know where I was gon' go. I was thirteen wit' a baby. My own family ain't want me brangin' my trouble on they porch."

I shake my head again. Take another sip of the stimulant in my hand.

"Next thang I know, I was having Cole. Two kids and a crazy husband. It was hell."

She rubs her hand over her hair. Pink rollers holding together what little wisps she has left. Takes another sip of her painkiller.

I ask, "You never tried to leave?"

"Tried after I had Cole. Yo sista was walking then. I packed up enough ta get us through the night. Hid the bag on the top shelf of the closet. We was gon' leave when yo daddy left for work. He found the bag. Made sho' we ain't try ta leave again. We ain't try no mo'."

I have a feeling I know what her answer will be, but I ask anyway. "What did he do?"

"Raped me. That bastard raped me, then went ta go lay up wit' his otha woman."

"Bastard."

Her hand finds its way to my thigh. She comforts my pain. Tries to comfort her own.

She starts slurring as she repeats a lot of what she had already told me. "Cory, son, believe me. I ain't mean for my own kids ta go through the hell I went through. Busted lips, black eyes, broken bones, I had ta walk around wit' it all. I went through hell wit' yo daddy. I was young when we got married. B'fo I knew what was happenin', yo sista was born."

She starts crying, coughing, slurring curses at the dead. It's too much for me. I go to the bathroom, bring her back some tissue. Mattie resumes her life story as if I had never left.

"Thangs slowed down for a while. Ain't thank yo daddy was gon' hit me no mo' 'cause he was nice and all. He was even nice ta ya sista and brotha. Then, one day he came home and hit all us. I heard he knocked up anotha one of his womens. He came home and took it out on all us when we ain't even do nothin'." Her eyes glaze over as she travels down memory lane.

"I was carrying a baby again myself, but I wasn't gon' tell 'im. I jus prayed I ain't have it. Bad as it sound, babies only meant more beatin's." She rubs her stomach. "I ain't want no mo' babies. I ain't want no mo' trouble."

It hurts to hear her hurt. Hurts her to say she wishes I wasn't born. I don't want to hear any more. "Mattie, please."

"You need ta hear this. Been carryin' this around too long. Let me get this off my chest. Let me let go."

Silently, I concede.

"After you was about two, I said I was gon' try and leave again. Cora and Cole was older then. I got scared, though. Zach found out. He stopped us again."

"Bastard."

She fidgets on the swing. Prepares to tell me something painful for her. "Sometimes, I let him hit y'all instead of me. I was too tired to fight. I needed a break, so I pawned my babies on him." Her eyes continue to glaze over as she releases her demons.

Acknowledgement of her selfishness is a blow to my gut. Feels like I'm in the ring with the float-like-a-butterfly-sting-like-a-bee Muhammad Ali. I'm speechless. What do you say after hearing a confession like that? Especially from your own mother.

I can't take any more. I get up from the swing. Leave the woman whom I once called Mama in her own pool of sorrow.

Back in the living room, I stare at pictures taken over time. Zachary Hines, the man whose seed fathered me, isn't in any of them. He refused to take portraits with a family he didn't want. Never wanted kids, but for some reason that didn't stop him from spreading his seeds all across town. Fathered more than seven kids before his life came to an abrupt end.

I hear Mattie enter the room. I acknowledge her by saying, "In a lot of ways, I'm just like him."

She sits down on her favorite chair. Waits for me to release my own demons.

"I never wanted kids either. Never really understood why. Guess when I was young I made a decision that I wasn't going to be like him."

"What make you thank you'd be like him? You ain't nothin' like him."

"I didn't know that. Still don't, and you don't know that either." I look at her. So many questions in my eyes. "There's no guarantee that I'd never hit my kids."

"Ain't no guarantee for nobody. We all gotta learn how ta raise our own chirren."

"But that's not good enough for me, Mattie."

"What, you wanna see it written in stone? Ain't gon' happen."

"Exactly my point."

She makes a frustrated noise with her lips. "Maybe it's best that way. Maybe you'on need no kids. I mean, we ain't gave you no good example."

I shake my head. "It's too late." I tell her about my seed growing in Trish's stomach.

"What you gon' do 'bout it?"

I sit down on the worn couch. "I don't know."

"You better come up with somethin'," Mattie tells me. "Jus 'cause you confused 'bout yo life don't mean you gotta make life confusin' for that chile."

My cell phone vibrates on my hip. An unknown number flashes across the screen. I ignore it. Let whoever it is leave a message if it's important.

I need clarity. "So you're saying I should be there for her and the child?"

She doesn't answer.

I lean back, search within myself. Wonder if what I'm contemplating is even possible. Can I be there for Trish? Can I be there for the baby?

She disrupts my thoughts. "Why this so hard for you?" she asks.

As hard as it is to answer, I speak from my heart. "I remember what it was like growing up. Remember seeing things no child should see. I never wanted to introduce that kind of world to my own flesh and blood. Some experiences shouldn't be repeated."

"Jus show you ain't nothin' like yo daddy. You got a conscience. Somethin' yo daddy ain't neva had."

I let her confirmation resonate inside me. Let it marinate. Feels good to hear positive words come from someone who I always felt thought negatively of me. Feels real good.

I look in the face of a woman who has aged decades since we last saw each other. Looks more like an octogenarian instead of a woman in her forties. She moves her chapped lips. "We all got choices ta make, son. Some good, some bad, but we all got a choice ta make. You gotta make the best one for you."

My phone vibrates again. My older brother's cell number pops up this time.

Cole tells me he's on his way to pick up Cora from the airport.

They'll be at the house of the woman who gave us all life by noon.

As soon as I get off the phone, Mattie asks another question. "You happy, son?"

For a second, anger takes over. "What do you think?"

Through my anger, she remains just as calm as ever. "Don't know. Thas why I asked."

"Are you?" I want to know.

"I'm 'bout ta be put out my misery. Wouldn't you be?"

I think about my answer. Think long and hard. Think about the years that have passed me by. Think of the ones yet to come. "I'm not happy. I'm working on it, though. I've got too much to live for."

"Then act like it."

She scoots off her recliner looking more broken than she did when I first walked in. Sits next to me on the couch, close enough for me to smell her intoxicated breath. Doesn't make eye contact. Says, "There some thangs in life we'll neva understand. Some thangs yo mama can't explain But in time, ya gon' find all the answers ya need."

She stands up, stands in front of me, bends over and embraces me. Pulls away, causing me to feel the moistness from her tears on my face.

The woman who gave me life begins walking toward the hallway that leads to her bedroom. She turns back, looks at me as if it's her last time. Tells me, "Quit walkin' 'round this earth like you already dead. If you ain't gon' live yo life, somebody else gon' live it for ya."

I watch her until her figure fades. Pick up my keys, take one more look around. So many skeletons in this room.

So many broken lives.

"Why are you here?"

"I have an appointment."

I walk him toward the back room to give us some privacy. "So, basically, you're wasting my time just so you can get some time with me."

"If that's what I have to do."

"Damn. I swear. Sometimes you act just like a woman."

"Call it what you want. I'm paying you."

David hands me three twenties. "This is a half-hour's worth, right?"

I toss the money back at him. "Keep your money and get out."

"You're turning down money just like that?"

"If times get hard, I know who to call. But today, I can do without your dollars."

He puts the money on the counter. Sits down on the massage table.

"Take your money and leave, David. It's that simple."

"Maybe for you, but not for me." He hops to his feet. Comes close to me. "Why won't you let me love you, Fatima?"

I back away, move closer to the door. "Because that wouldn't satisfy you."

"What makes you think that?"

"It never has before. Every time I give, you require more. I'm tired of giving in this category."

David rubs his clean-shaven face. Ponders his next move. "Look, just have dinner with me tonight. Let's talk about this."

"We're talking now and you ain't saying much."

"Fatima, please. Just hear me out."

The thing that pushes me away from David is the same thing that draws me to him. His vulnerability. In so many ways, we're the same lost soul searching for validity. We both need to feel needed. That's a dangerous place to be in, but I give in to his plea anyway.

"What time?"

With a voice full of eagerness, he says, "My house. Eight o'clock."

With no words, I open the door to let him out.

❂ ❂ ❂

I pull the piece of paper that Cory gave me a few nights ago out of my bag. Not ready to add another man to my list, I toss his number in the trash. Grab my keys to meet David for dinner.

Traffic is bad on the freeway. B93 announces an accident with fatalities a mile ahead at the Treeborn exit. I look at the clock. It's ten minutes to eight. I reach for my phone.

David answers, "Hey, babe. Come right on in."

I roll my eyes. "Calm yourself. I'm not there yet. There's an accident up ahead. It'll be at least an hour until they clear this up."

"That's cool. I'm about to take the lasagna out the oven, so it'll have a little time to cool off."

My mouth waters at the sound of my favorite meal. "Go, go Gadget helicopter."

He laughs. "All right, Inspector Gadget. If all I have to do is cook to get you over here, I'm making lasagna every day from now on."

I don't fall into his trap. "Yeah, well, I'll be there shortly."

Nothing good is on the radio. I pop in a throwback from Alicia Keys. Skip the CD to track number seven, "A Woman's Worth." David definitely knows my worth. From preparing my favorite meal to making me more consciously aware of my needs. Maybe that's the real reason why I keep coming back.

Fifteen minutes later, traffic starts moving. In no time, I pull up to David's condo. I walk right into his place.

"Mmm, smells good in here." I lock the door behind me.

He meets me in the hallway. Kisses me on the forehead. "That was quick."

"Yeah."

David looks good. Dressed in a button-down, khaki shirt, brown corduroy slacks. His freshly twisted locs pulled back. He leads me into the dining room. Pulls out my seat, waits for me to sit before gently pushing me up to the table. He pours two glasses of wine. Hands one to me, sets the other at his place. "Be right back."

He puts Kem's debut CD on. Kem's distinctive voice brings back memories.

One day when I got home from massage school, my neighbor was in his garage cleaning the interior of his Lexus. The sound coming from his car's stereo system drew me in. The voice was different. The words seemed to resound from his heart. *If people can go from bad to good, then so can I.* I was hooked. Mellow and honest. My neighbor gave me the name and title of the album. I went out the next day and bought two copies. Being the jazz lover that he is, I bought one for David; the other was for me.

My chef of the evening brings out a plate of spinach leaves, chopped walnuts, cranberries, feta cheese, topped with a home-made raspberry vinaigrette dressing. Places it in front of me. Goes back to the kitchen and comes back out with a plate for him.

We don't talk. Just enjoy the music and salad.

"Thanks for coming over," he says when he picks up my empty plate.

"I never turn down a free meal."

He stands still for a minute. "Why do you always do that?"

"What?"

"You just have a habit of making it seem like this is nothing to you. Like I'm nothing more than a convenience."

David walks back into the kitchen without waiting for an explanation. Brings out our dinner.

As good as the lasagna looks, I've lost my appetite.

David doesn't eat either. "Didn't mean to spoil things."

"Yes, you did," I say. "That's *your* habit."

He looks away. "Guess I do that because I want you to feel bad just like you make me feel."

"If I make you feel like that, why keep pursuing me?"

"Because I know it's an act. You try to make yourself seem so hard, so unattached, like nothing fazes you. Deep down, I see differently."

"There you go with that foolishness again." I push my untouched plate away from me. Hate that he spoiled a delicious-looking meal.

"If that's the case, why *do* you keep coming around? If it's not true, why *are* you here now?"

I bite down on my bottom lip. Try to suck all the clear gloss off.

"Quit fighting me, Fatima."

Our eyes meet.

He's trying to get inside my head, trying to see which way I'm going to go. It's not him I'm fighting, but the idea of what he can give me. I'm so weak right now, my strength fails me. My walls are crumbling quickly.

He walks over to my side of the table. I fall helplessly into his arms. He pulls me up. His persistence shows that I'm important to him.

"Don't fight me," David says again.

I remove my hands from his, place them on his face. Kiss him so hard I make him bite his own lip.

"Sorry."

It doesn't bother him. He kisses me back even harder.

My legs are weak. Feel like I'm losing control. He holds me up, lets me know he won't let anything bad happen to me.

With one arm on my back, helping me keep my balance, David uses his other hand to push the candles, food, and wine aside. Neither one of us misses a beat when we hear a plate of vegetable lasagna meet the hardwood floor. It only encourages our hunger for each other.

David takes off my linen skirt. Undresses me while I undress him. We climb on the table, him on top of me. He enters me ever so gently. I submit to his will. Our hearts beat fast, but our movements are slow. We take our time. If I didn't know any better, I'd swear he was making love to me, trying to get me to surrender and give him all of me.

I look into his face; his eyes are closed. The expression on his face is euphoric. This is the moment he's been waiting for.

I close my eyes and see Cory.

Cora gives me a call once she makes it back to Chicago. Calls me with an appointment she made for me at Dr. Bryant's office.

"I'm not going to see a shrink," I protest.

"Call it what you want, Cory. After seeing Mom, I think we all need to seek professional help."

"You thought she was that bad?"

"Cory, we've been through a lot. All of us. It's obvious that some of us are harboring more pain than others."

"So all of y'all agree I need help?"

"Do you have to ask? I mean, you're having these recurring nightmares of being dead with an eyeless kid standing over you. You need to see somebody."

I let out a deep sigh. Let her know, "Just because you made an appointment doesn't mean I'm going."

"At least think about it."

Before I can hit the end button, I hear her call out my name. "Yeah?"

"Get a blood test before you take on a lifetime responsibility."

I disconnect the call without making any promises.

◊ ◊ ◊

For a Friday night, Blockbuster is pretty empty. I can count the people, including the staff, on one hand.

I'm holding a couple of classics in my hand. *Boomerang* with Eddie Murphy and *Moving* with Richard Pryor.

The bell on the entrance door chimes.

"Good evening!" the employee behind the counter yells.

I peruse the shelves for one more movie. Not sure what I'm looking for, but will know it when I see it.

The entrance door chimes again. More and more voices surround me. The normal Friday crowd starts to pick up. Guess I got here too early.

"Hey, watch out," I tell a little kid who almost steps on my foot.

I pick up one of the new releases, check out the synopsis on the back cover. Being a sucker for independent films, I take my chances on the movie and head toward the checkout counter.

"Don't waste your money," a voice tells me.

Those eyes. I'd see those big, caramel-colored eyes with my eyes closed. "Fatima."

"Courtney, right?"

"Wrong dude. It's Cory."

The sly grin on her face lets me know she made the mistake on purpose.

I hold the movie up. "So, it's not good?"

"Not at all." She shakes her head. "The people on the cover aren't even in the movie."

I look over the movie again before putting it back on the shelf. Ask, "What're you watching tonight?"

"Probably something I already have at the house."

"Nothing caught your eye, huh?"

"You know, I haven't rented movies in a while. Blockbuster isn't cheap anymore. Makes more sense to buy than rent."

I say, "I'm the same way. Can't tell you the last time I've been in here."

We walk and peruse the other movie titles.

"Kismet," she whispers.

I look at her. "Definitely. Guess it was meant for us to run into each other tonight."

She smiles.

I smile right back. "You hungry?"

"I can eat," she says.

"Let's get out of here."

I put my movies back in their respective places. Tell Fatima she can ride with me or follow. "It's your choice."

"Where we going?"

"Chili's is right up the street."

She shrugs. "I'll ride with you then."

I open the passenger door to my 300C for her to get in. Walk around the back of the car to my own door.

As soon as I start the car, my stereo blasts the sounds of Bilal that I was jamming to on my drive here. I move to lower the volume.

Fatima stops me, her hand on mine, sending a shock of electricity through my body. "Don't. I like this song," she yells. "He's one of my favorites."

The song is talking about labeling relationships. Something that I never like to do. I bob my head to the beat.

One traffic light later, we pull up in the crowded parking lot. "It might be a minute," I tell her.

She looks out the window. People are standing outside the restaurant. "It's like a club up in there."

"It's the weekend. Nobody cooks."

I pull up to the curb. Fatima gets out, goes inside to put our name on the list. Comes back out, hops in. "The wait's not too long. Fifteen, twenty minutes."

I drive around. Find an empty space on the side of the building. Roll the windows down, let fresh air in.

We sit in silence for a minute. The street light makes her nose ring sparkle. It's so small I missed it the first time I met her. "You have the perfect nose for a piercing."

She touches her nose, smiles. Shows me her deep dimple. "Thanks."

Breeze from the outside blows her scent my way. A light, calming aroma. Not overpowering. I tell her, "You smell nice."

Fatima gives me a cut-the-BS look. "Come on, Cory. We both know there's an attraction between us. No need for all the extras."

Her attention is pulled from me and down to her hands. Sees red; feels the vibration. "Our table's ready."

We get out slowly. Loud voices approaching the car next to us makes us do that. Don't want to get caught in the crossfire.

The tall woman says to the even taller man straggling behind her, "I'm tired of you disrespecting me every time we go out."

"Calm down, Shelly. It wasn't nothing like that."

"Yeah, whatever. Tell that to your mama 'cause I ain't tryna hear it."

Their voices attract attention from others on the outside. Fatima's face and mine hold the same better-them-than-me expression.

Fatima says as she walks through the open door, "I don't have time for foolishness."

A few days ago, I didn't have time for foolishness either. But somehow, drama will make you have time for it. Whether you think you're in control or not.

The hostess leads us to a booth in the corner. "Your server will be right with you."

"Thank you," we say in unison.

"So, Fatima, why didn't you call me?"

She takes a minute before answering. "Threw your number away." She says that without taking her eyes off of me. Doesn't put up a front for me.

Her bluntness catches me off guard. Just in time to mask my rejection, a college-aged kid comes to our table. "Hey, folks. I'm John and I'll be your server tonight. Can I start you off with something to drink?"

John takes Fatima's Appletini order, then looks to me. I order a beer.

"Do you need a little more time to look over the menu?" he asks.

"Give us a few," Fatima requests.

As soon as he leaves, Fatima picks up our previous conversation. "I didn't mean to be so brash."

"You were being honest. No need to apologize for that."

"But still. It wasn't the way it sounded."

"So, why did you throw my number away?"

"It's complicated, one of those chapters I'm struggling to end. It had nothing to do with you, though."

"Let me get this straight. You're attracted to me, but you threw my number away?"

"Like I said, it's complicated."

I leave it at that, shrug, lean back in the booth with the menu in my hands. If she wanted me to know, she would come right out with it.

It takes a few minutes before John brings our drinks to the table. "Okay, folks, what can I get you tonight?" We give him our orders and send him on his merry way.

"So, tell me about you," Fatima says. "What do the pages in your diary look like?"

I can tell she's uncomfortable talking about herself. Her eyes tell me that. I begin with the basics.

"You're a librarian? Wow, never would've guessed that." She sips her martini.

"Books were my refuge growing up. I could always be found in some corner reading. It didn't matter what; anything which allowed me to remove myself from my life was perfect for me."

"I know what you mean. Writing poetry does that for me."

I'm curious. "What are you trying to escape from?"

With her pretty brown eyes, she tells me not to go there.

I honor her wishes. Put the subject back on me. "I want to open my own bookstore one day."

She takes a sip from her drink. Swallows hard. "What's stopping you from doing it now?"

"I just opened Patchouli's. Right now wouldn't be a good time to start another venture. Give me a few years."

She nods. "So, you're not just the emcee, you're the club owner, huh?"

"Yes, ma'am."

"An entrepreneur. So we *do* have something in common."

"I told you," I joke.

She smiles. Says, "Yep, I own my own business as well."

I ask, "What is your specialty?"

"Conscious Kneads. Kneading you to a more conscious state of being. I opened my own spa."

I nod. "I'm feeling the name."

Fatima combs through her crinkled locs with long, thin fingers. "You know, if you give me some flyers about Patchouli's, I'll post them up in the spa. Maybe recruit some new talent for you."

"Not a bad idea. I'll definitely do that and do the same for you."

John comes back. Places a bowl of fettuccini with broccoli and no meat down for her. Chicken and shrimp fajitas for me. "Can I get you anything else?"

"Another beer for me."

Fatima requests a glass of water.

I blow off some of the steam from my crackling fajita mixture. "What made you want to go into business for yourself?"

"Figured since I have basically been independent my whole life, why not keep it that way?"

Finally, getting past the first chapter. Very slowly, she's letting me in just a little bit. "I hear you."

My cell phone creates a jingle in my pocket. I recognize the song immediately. Trish's ringtone. *Baby Mama Drama*. Dave Hollister's voice makes me want to crack my phone in half. Don't know why, but I answer anyway.

Trish reminds me of her next doctor's appointment that I agreed to take her to on Monday. "Nine-thirty. Got it. Look, Trish. Whatever. I'll call. Okay. Yeah. I'll be there."

Fatima reads the frustration on my face. Avoids my eyes when I look at her. "Sorry about that."

"No need to be," she says.

We go back to talking about our businesses as if there was never an interruption. "When will I get to hear some of your escape method on my stage?" I inquire.

"I don't think you should be concerned about that right now."

John comes back to our table. "Dessert tonight?"

I look across at Fatima who shakes her head.

"We'll take the check now," I tell him.

He pulls out our check. Places it in the middle. Picks up our empty plates before walking off.

Fatima reaches into her bag; pulls out her wallet.

I grab the check. "Put your money up. I got this."

"This isn't a date."

"Who said it was?"

"Just letting you know."

We keep each other in check. Let each other know we're just two adults enjoying dinner. Nothing more, nothing less.

"So what now?" she asks once back at my car.

"I'm passing you the mic."

She runs her fingers through her locs; bites down on her bottom lip. "How far do you live from here?"

I see where she's headed. "Not far. About five minutes up the road."

We pull up next to her SUV back at Blockbuster. She gets out without a word. Hops in her ride, starts up the ignition. She rolls down her tinted window; licks her lips. "Follow me."

❂ ❂ ❂

Fatima pulls her Acura into her two-car garage. I park behind her. She walks up to my car. "Park inside."

I don't ask any questions. Start my engine up again and pull in next to her.

The garage door rolls shut. Seals me in. An outsider on the inside.

She bends over, picks up her shoes, and puts them in the rack on the back of the door.

I do the same.

She ushers me through the kitchen and into the living room. "Can I get you something to drink?" she offers.

"What you got?"

My hostess goes over her list of alcoholic and non-alcoholic drinks. "I make a mean Apple Martini," she brags.

A look of interest crosses my face. She takes the hint.

"Sit down. Get comfortable. I'll be back."

I do as told, sit down on the chaise, and let my eyes wander. Try to let my eyes see what her words don't say.

Fatima cuts on some music. Sounds of Me'Shell Ndegeocello surround the room. I think it's her second album, *Peace Beyond Passion*. She's singing about eyes not being satisfied with seeing, ears unsatisfied with hearing.

My loc-wearing bartender sings as she places her "mean" martini in my hand.

"Don't tell me you sing too."

"Well, you know." She sits on the sofa across from me. "I can do a lil' something."

I watch as she sips her martini first. Her eyes close as if the taste brings back fond memories.

I follow her lead. "You weren't lying." I take another sip. "This is good. Best one I've ever had."

"Chili's ain't got nothing on me."

We share a laugh at her imitation of Denzel's line in *Training Day*.

"I need to patent my shit, huh?"

The more of her I read, the more interested I become. It's more than the book cover that draws me in. The whole package is so put together it makes me want to keep turning page after page well after the book is done.

She gets up, comes toward me, eyes narrowing down. I scoot up, lean forward and wait for our lips to touch. She leans past me. Picks up the remote to the television from the end table next to me instead.

Fatima tries to hide the smirk on her face, but I see it. Something tells me she wants me to see it.

She walks over to the ottoman in the center of the living room floor, lifts the lid. "Let's see." She shuffles through her DVD collection. "What are you in the mood for?"

"Everything with a side of more."

She laughs. Almost falls over. "Movies. I'm talking movies here."

"I'm not," I say. Try to see how far I can take it.

Fatima pulls out the classic I had in my hands earlier, *Boomerang*. Slides it in the DVD player. She doesn't take her eyes off of me as she comes back to where I'm sitting. Doesn't even blink. Brings her face so close to me I can taste remnants of garlic from her meal earlier. "I don't want you to take any mercy on me tonight."

Her boldness catches me off guard. Makes the bulge in my pants swell.

She grabs my empty glass from the table. Takes it in the kitchen. Cuts off the music. Comes back with two fresh glasses.

"Where's your bathroom?" I ask. Need to put some space between us to get my thoughts together.

She points at the door under the staircase.

When I come out, she's on her cell phone. "That was a mistake," I hear her say.

I clear my throat. Let her know I'm back in the room.

"Stop sweating me. Look, now isn't a good time." She doesn't wait for them to acknowledge that fact before flipping her phone shut. Reopens it. Turns the power off. "Some people just don't know when to give up."

I nod. My type of woman. A no-strings-attached kind of woman.

Things are quiet between the two of us while we watch a movie that we've both seen more than enough times to count.

"Robin or Halle?" Fatima breaks our silence.

"Definitely Robin."

"I figured you would say that. Most men would've said Halle."

"I'm not most men."

"Well, let me rephrase that. Most men who are honest with themselves would have chosen Halle."

"Once again, I'm not most men."

That shuts her down. "Okay. So why Robin?"

"Because she's unattached. I wouldn't have to worry about hurting her feelings if I didn't want a commitment."

"So you're saying you're a no-commitment kind of guy?"

Without going into detail I say, "I enjoy being a free spirit."

"Oh, don't get me wrong. I'm right there with you. Robin's character would be me. I'm not trying to get my heart cracked. It's easier to leave than love, or get left in the process."

Fatima keeps amazing me. The independence I read in her eyes wasn't a lie. "Leave than love. I like that."

She goes on. "People get so caught up and blindsided by the idea of love to where they lose themselves. Start acting insane. Doing things they wouldn't do if they were in their right minds. I don't want to be like that."

Something tells me she's speaking from experience. She's been hurt before. "So you don't believe in love?" I ask for clarification.

Fatima stretches out, plays with a few of her locs. "No, sir."

I sit forward in my seat. "Come on, now. All women believe in love. Y'all start planning your fairytale weddings the day you snag your first boyfriend."

"I'm not all women."

I move forward in my seat. "Okay, okay. You got me there."

"Obviously you men are the ones enthralled with the 'fairytale' misconception. I can't speak for all women, but I sure as hell don't believe in love. Love is for punks. And I ain't no punk."

"Don't get it twisted," I let her know. "I'm no punk either."

"Good. We'll get along just fine then."

"Question."

She looks at me intently. "Answer."

"Why did you say most men would choose Halle if they were honest with themselves?"

She sips her martini before answering. "Because, deep down, most men want a woman who isn't afraid to be a woman. A woman who's nurturing, affectionate, attentive to their needs. A woman whom they can see growth in."

"So, you're saying a man wouldn't be able to grow with a woman like Robin?"

"As long as you're talking about his penis, yes. Other than that…" She shakes her head. "Negative."

I look at my barely sipped-on drink. Tell her, "Like I said, I'm not most men," before consuming the rest of green liquid.

With an understanding behind us, we go back to watching the rest of the movie. At least what's left of it. Even though we're both looking at the tube, I know neither one of us is watching. I look over at her, see her glance at me. We've both laid our wants on the table.

Without any words, I get up from my chair, join her on the sofa. She takes her hand, rubs her slender fingers through my messy fro. I lean over, let my lips speak to hers.

Her succulent lips part; my tongue follows her lead. Her mouth is warm with passion. I can taste leftover martini on her thick tongue. My eyes are open, so are hers. We kiss and stare. Stare and kiss.

Our kiss is interrupted by the sound of Dave belting out about his baby mama drama being enough to make him scream and holler.

I silence the call this time. Wait a few seconds and shut my phone off just as Fatima did moments ago.

She looks at me. I look at her. We kiss again. This time with more desire. Hunger. Exchange delicacies every time our tongues touch. She rubs both hands through my hair. I rub my fingers through her locs. Pull her closer. She pulls back, stands up. Grabs my hand. Leads me upstairs to the place she lays her head down.

Fatima guides us into her master bathroom.

I don't know why, but I ask, "What do you want to do?"

Her eyes become seductive. She licks her lips. "Everything with a side of more." Uses my line.

She pulls off her baby tee. Bare breasts. I take off my shirt. She slides down her jeans. Purple lace thong tantalizing me. I let my khakis and boxers hit the floor. Don't hide my growing manhood.

Her body is toned. Very toned. One of the best bodies I've seen in the nude. "You work out?"

"Ran cross-country all through junior high and high school. Still run every now and then. Guess my muscles are just trained," she tells me.

She shows me the firmness of her backside when she turns around to cut on the shower. I walk up behind her. Let her get a feel of me. She bends over, pushes her rear against me. Pulls down her panties like a pro. Steps away, opens the shower door. "Get in," she pants.

Steam surrounds us in the shower. We create more heat when our lips come back together. I lose myself in her kiss. She does the same in mine. Her hands run down my back, grab my behind. Mine do the same to her. I feel myself getting harder. Moans escape her as she releases me, reaches for a washcloth. Lathers me up, cleanses me to her standards. I repeat her actions, clean all of her.

We dry off. Find each other again in her satin sheets.

Fatima pushes me down, sits on my chest. Leans over and pulls something out of her nightstand. A scarf is in her hand. She smiles. A kinky smile. "Told you I wanted everything tonight."

"With a side of more," I finish.

She covers my eyes, restricts my sight. Makes me use my other four senses. I'm not myself with her. I have no control of me. She's the head, I'm the tail. I assure myself that this would not go down with anyone else. Fatima is different. Something about her.

Her finger finds its way into my mouth. It's wet. I savor the juices she feeds me. "Mmmm," I moan. Not being able to see, I try to visualize her every move. The mystery arouses me.

She kisses me. Wants to know what her juices taste like in my mouth. Slowly she traces my lips with her fingertip before sliding it back into my mouth. "You like?"

"Yes."

"Want to taste more?"

"Yes."

She places herself on top of me. Feel her warmth near my face. Wish I could see the expression on her face as I breathe on her. Make her warmer. Suck the air back in, cool her off. Tease her before I devour her.

"Oh, you got games," she pants in anticipation.

With my tongue, I trace the outside of her heat. Softly suck on that fleshy part of her. Hear her moan. Take her in. Palm her firmness. Let her grind her way to ecstasy.

She climbs off before reaching her peak. Removes my blindfold. Tells me, "I want you to watch."

She kisses me. Licks her juices away. Kisses; flicks her tongue against my neck. With a moan, I let her know my neck is a hot spot. She doesn't stay there long. Takes her kisses down below my waist. Stares at that growing part of me. "You're so beautiful."

That's the first time I've heard anyone refer to that part of me the way she does. She looks up at me. Lets me see myself disappear inside her mouth. I close my eyes. She stops.

I reopen my eyes.

Remember she wants me to watch.

She continues.

I want to close my eyes. It feels so damn good. But I don't. I keep my eyes on her. Feel my volcano nearing eruption.

She slows her pace. "Not yet."

She gets up. Goes to her closet. Pulls out a box of condoms. Brings one back to the bed. Rolls it on me. Positions herself on top. Lets me glide into her moistness. She starts a slow pace. Gets used to me inside her. Kisses me. Moans in my mouth. Picks her pace up. I palm her firmness again.

I feel the inevitable burning sensation inside. Fight it. Don't want to seem premature. Want to last as long as she does.

Her vibrations tell me she's nearing her zone too. An explosion steaming inside her. She's trying hard to fight it. Each of us tries to outlast the other.

A long moan escapes her lips.

I open my eyes.

See hers on me.

Realize the moan came from me.

She's not far behind. She tremors on top of me. Collapses on my chest.

She won. Pride streaks my nemesis' face. Doesn't bother me though. This was a battle I'd gladly let her win anytime.

13 / FATIMA

My back is hurting, legs are tired. Been standing, massaging all day. Think it's time for me to be the one receiving service.

I pull into my garage, walk out to the mailbox and pull out more mail than I thought the box could hold. Throw it all on the island when I get inside the kitchen. The only thing on my mind right now is relaxing.

In the bathroom, I fill the tub up with water as hot as I can stand. Pour in a couple drops of lavender oil. No suds tonight. Just oil, water, and me. Hoping to soothe my thoughts and calm my nerves.

The house is quiet. I keep it that way. Don't bother putting on any music as I strip down naked, remove my external layers. Stick my foot in to test the water. It's perfect. The water draws me in. Removes my internal layers. They say when you quiet the mind, you hear the answers.

My mind...a state...of confusion.

Words from the poetess at Patchouli's comes to mind. Somehow, I've found myself in the same state of mind. Questioning myself. Not understanding how I've allowed my feelings to consume me to the point where I can't even breathe. Not understanding how I got here. How I've become concerned with someone else's feelings.

David.

Someone I've known forever. A man who makes me feel protected. I feel safe with him. Feel like no matter what, he'll be there. He understands my moods. I can curse him out, leave in the middle of the night. Call him a week later for a minute of his time, no apologies. He'll drop whatever he's doing to give me just that and then some.

Cory.

Someone I've known a few minutes. A man who was content with what I gave. He didn't ask any questions, didn't need any explanations. Just packed up and left. Didn't need to get into my subconscious. My need was his need. "Damn." I move my fingers around in the water. Stir up the lavender. Make the water ripple like the waves in my mind. On one hand is David, on the other, Cory. Two opposites. Two men with different options. Yet, in my mind, their existence is equal. No scale tipping in either's favor.

Maybe I don't need it to. This is my life. I'm making the decisions. I can have them both.

❂ ❂ ❂

I climb out of the Whirlpool, pat myself dry. Don't bother putting on clothes, just my robe. Slide on some socks and walk downstairs to the kitchen. Fill the kettle with water, set it on the stove. Grab some grapes from the fridge.

The kettle begins a slow purr. I pull down an oversized mug from the cabinet, put an Earl Grey tea bag in it. Walk over to the stack of mail. Water bill, mortgage, more bills. A birthday card from Grandma. Box of business cards. Hmm, *What's this?* I keep the thick envelope in my hand as I walk over to the stove to remove the screaming kettle. Pour the water in my cup. Let it steep for a few.

I rip open the catalog size envelope with no return address. A book falls out. It's soft, suede. A journal. I open the cover.

My hands shake as I turn the page. The handwriting, written so hard I can feel the words without even looking at them. Feels like someone wants everyone to think they're in control, but they are really breaking apart at the seams. I don't recognize the harsh penmanship. At the same time, it reminds me a lot of my own.

March 2, 1978

It's been seven hours since your birth. I can't sleep. You'd think I'd be able to after eighteen hours of labor. But I can't.

I can't sleep.

I can't eat.

I can't do anything.

I can't even look at you.

You weren't supposed to be here. If I had had it my way, you wouldn't. Maybe someday you'll call it "Divine Intervention." For me, today, it's the beginning of my demise.

~Ruby~

✿ ✿ ✿

My doorbell rings at a quarter after ten. I open the door, let Adrian in.

"I came as fast as I could." She looks at me, sees the distance in my eyes. "What happened?"

The unknown paralyzes me. Don't remember calling her. Don't remember going upstairs to change into sweats.

Adrian pulls me into her. She holds a lifeless me. Rubs her hands across my locs. Soothes me the way a mother does her heart-broken child who was dumped the night before prom. "Whatever it is, you'll get through it."

I feel my lips open. Hear words tumble out. "You know what's funny?"

She holds me. Doesn't let go.

"I wanted this. Been begging for the key to my past. The key is in my hand and now I'm running."

Adrian releases me from her embrace. Holds my hand and leads me to the sofa. She ushers me down and sits next to me, her hand on my thigh. "Tell me what happened." Her voice is as soothing as a cat's purr.

I leave her to go get the journal from the kitchen. I pick it up from the floor where I dropped it moments ago.

"What's this?" she asks when I put it in her hands.

"Read the first page."

I lean back into the sofa. Close my eyes as she reads my uncensored reality.

"Oh, my God," slips from her lips. "I...I'm sorry." She lays the book next to her, keeping it out of my reach.

"She started it the day I was born. What a fucking welcome into this world, huh?"

"Fatima..."

I know what she's going to say. My own language catches me off guard. "I don't know what I'm supposed to feel, Adrian." I move forward in my seat. Cover my face with my hands.

"It's understandable, Fatima. You're not supposed to know how to feel."

"I mean...what the hell? That's beyond some postpartum bull shit."

I'm standing now. Pacing the floor.

Adrian gets up too. She heads for the kitchen. Comes back out with something stronger than tea. "Drink this."

The vodka goes down a little choppy. Burns my throat. Feels like I'm swallowing flaming swords.

Have to clear my throat a few times before I'm able to speak. "This ain't fair. From the minute I was born, that woman hated me. I hope she burns in hell."

"Don't talk like that, Fatima."

"Why? While I was in her womb, she wished me dead. She despised me before she even saw me. Tell me, what kind of mother is she?"

"She's your mother."

More than my throat is burning now. Feels like Mt. Saint Helens is about to erupt in me. "Why are you defending her?"

"I'm not. I'm just…you shouldn't judge her."

"She judged me." I take another gulp of my drink. Let it add more fuel to my fire.

Adrian backs off. We stare eye to eye. I see the struggle in her to keep me sane. Can see it hurts her to do so. In my eyes is pain. Pain I'm not ready to heal from.

I glare at the empty glass in my hand. All I see are those words. Keep seeing them no matter where I look. Wishes for my non-existence from the woman who is the reason for my existence. I roll the cup between both hands. A scream escapes me as I hurl the glass toward the empty fireplace. "What did I do to deserve this?!" I want to know. Need to know.

Silence.

Neither of us says a word. Neither of us makes any moves. My actions scare us both. Makes me wonder if I need to be locked up in a padded room.

I scream again. Feel like I want to pull all of my locs straight out of my scalp.

"Fatima," Adrian calls.

Right here, in the middle of my living room floor, I have a mental breakdown.

"It's okay to cry," she says.

Adrian moves to the floor, lies down next to me. Wraps her arms around me. "Let it out, Fatima. Let it out."

The tears aren't ready to fall yet. I don't want to cry. I want to fight. I want to find the woman who did this to me and beat her until she bleeds the color of her name.

I pound my fists on the floor. "I hate her! I hate her! I. Hate. Her!"

Adrian keeps rocking me, keeps telling me, "It's okay."

Water slowly drips from my eyes. Before I know it, the levees break and water covers me like the city of New Orleans.

I feel myself shaking uncontrollably in the arms of my good friend and employee.

"Just let it out," she says over and over.

My head throbs like I've been crying for hours. Shed years of pain in sixty seconds.

I cry like a newborn baby at two in the morning. Don't know what I want, just know I want something. I need something.

My nose is stopped up. I can barely breathe. Snot and tears drip down to my open mouth. Adrian gets up, brings her purse back to the floor. She digs through it until she finds a pack of tissues, hands it to me.

"Thanks." The taste of salt is now on my tongue.

She rubs my shoulder. Relaxes my mental congestion like a jar of Vicks.

My mind goes back in time. I tell Adrian, "When I was four, Daddy left. He came home late from work one night. I was in my room because Mama sent me to bed early. I didn't go to sleep though. I was in my window waiting for my daddy's headlights to come down the street."

I blow my nose, tell Adrian how it all went down.

✿ ✿ ✿

It was close to midnight when his car finally pulled up to our house. Heard Mama yelling before he could even get the front door open. I snuck out of my room, ran downstairs.

"Daddy." I ran in his direction.

"Get back to your room!" Mama yelled.

Daddy looked at her, then at me. I wanted to leap into his arms like I always did when he came home from work. He wanted to pick me up and swing me around like he always did. It was in his eyes, but he didn't.

"Where have you been?" Mama badgered.

"Fatima, go to your room like your mama said," he instructed.

I ran up the stairs as fast as I could. Felt like I wasn't moving though. Felt like the stairs were made out of quicksand. When I finally made it upstairs, I went to my room, closed the door. I didn't go in, though. I sat crouched down in front of my door and heard everything.

"Where have you been?" she asked again.

"I'm leaving, Ruby."

"What is that supposed to mean?"

"It means what it says. I'm leaving. I can't live like this anymore. I want a divorce."

My heart broke. I didn't know what divorce meant, but I knew it didn't sound good.

Daddy started climbing the stairs. Mama was close behind, yelling about him being selfish. "All I've done and you think you're going to leave me?"

They brushed past me like I wasn't even there.

It was quiet in their room for a minute. Then, all of a sudden, I heard screams. Stuff was being thrown around. Heard a lot of name calling. Daddy stormed out of the room. "I don't even know who you are anymore. Do you even know?"

"Stop saying that!" she yelled back.

He had a suitcase in his hand. "I'll be back to get the rest of my things later."

I ran to the top of the stairs. "Daddy, don't leave," I begged, tears running down my adolescent face.

I swear Mama flew up the stairs, she moved that fast. She grabbed me by the arm and pulled me downstairs with her. "If you're leaving, you're taking her with you." She shoved me in his direction.

"Don't do this, Ruby." He refused to look at me.

"You're the one who wanted her. Your *blessed* Fatima," she mocked.

"Don't do this," he repeated.

They talked about me like I wasn't there. Talked about me like I was a family pet to squabble over.

"Take me with you, Daddy," I pleaded.

He looked down on me. Shook his head. "I'm sorry, Sweetheart."

A tap at the door broke our focus. Daddy went to the door. It didn't take long for us to see what was pulling him away from us.

"You bastard." Mama attacked Daddy with closed fists.

He pushed her off. "You're insane," he said.

He walked out the door with a woman who had a swell in her belly.

I ran after them, after him. "Can I come with you?" I didn't care who this woman was. I just wanted my daddy.

He picked me up, kissed me on my forehead. "Not this time, Pumpkin." Tears were in his eyes as he placed my feet back on the concrete.

❂ ❂ ❂

I shake the bad memory from my head.

"That was the last time I saw him. A few days later, my mom left too," I tell Adrian. "What kind of parents put their child through that kind of hell?"

She just shakes her head. No words come from her lips. I understand. Doubt I'd be able to find any words if someone was telling me an equally depressing story.

Adrian leaves me on the floor, goes upstairs. Comes back with a blanket and some oil. She spreads it out on the floor, helps me out of my clothes. "Lay down," she says, pulls a few lavender candles from off of the fireplace mantle and places them around me. She lights them with a lighter from her purse.

I lie down on my stomach, just as naked as I was the day I was brought into this world.

Her hands know exactly where to touch, knows exactly where my pain lies.

I inhale the relaxing scent escaping from the candles. Feel my pressures lifting from my mental anxiety.

Adrian rubs me from head to toe. Somewhere in between, I fall asleep.

"What brings you into my office, Cory?"

I pick at lint on my dark pants. Feel like an adolescent with grown-man problems. "My family thinks I need help."

Dr. Bryant leans back in an oversized chair behind his desk, folds his arms across his chest. "And what do you think?"

Mattie's deteriorating body flashes through my mind. Years of neglect eating her alive. Wonder if I'll end up the same way if I continue to keep my burdens bottled inside. Wonder if I'll turn out the same way if I keep a bottle of scotch next to my bed at night. "I don't know. Maybe that's why I'm here."

He nods for me to continue my thoughts out loud.

Silence holds my tongue captive. I quit using my hands as a lint roller and leave the thousand pieces of lint on my pants alone. Drum my fingers against my thigh.

"What's going through your mind?" he wants to know.

I think about where I am in life at this moment. In a couple of weeks, I'll be thirty and, other than family, I have no one. It's a choice I made a long time ago, in my younger years, but I don't like that choice anymore.

I look up at the doctor for the first time. Look into the eyes of a man old enough to be my father. "Closure," I say.

He doesn't ask the obvious. Just nods again for me to elaborate.

The room suddenly becomes cold. Wish I had a coat or something to insulate my emotions. "You have something to drink?"

Dr. Bryant gets up from his chair. Walks from behind the desk. "I'll get you some water."

I ask, "Got anything stronger?"

He shakes his head. Hands me a glass of water.

I gulp it down. Put the empty glass on the table next to my seat. Move forward, place my face in my hands. Wipe my fears away. "I don't want to end up like my mother."

"And how is that?"

"Alone."

"What makes you think you will?"

"Fear." The same fear of ending up like Mister is what keeps me from being there for Trish and the baby I helped her create. The same fear that's keeping me from being a legacy to my offspring. "I push people away, don't let anyone get too close."

"Why is that?"

"Just the way things have always been," I say.

"Things may have always been a certain way, but it does not mean they have to continue in the same direction. We evolve, become stronger over time. What we could not handle yesterday is easier to digest today."

I disagree. "I don't know, Doc. My life ain't been easy."

"Depends on what side of the grass you're looking at," he says matter-of-factly. "Everyone runs across potholes in their journey. Even I have hit a few in my lifetime. However, instead of letting a bump in the road damage me or hold me back, I keep driving. It's all about choices, Cory. Some are easier to make than others. Nonetheless, they are choices *you* have to make."

His words marinate in my mind. Life is so full of choices. I'm struggling with a decision right now. The decision to let go. I say, "Doc, I didn't choose my life, didn't choose to grow up in the home of an abusive father and an alcoholic mother. Didn't choose to be this non-caring man who is afraid of commitment because of my own fears of being like my daddy."

"Do you think you're like him?"

I don't think about my answer. Just say what comes to mind first. "In some ways, yes."

My therapist wants to know, "In what ways?"

Angela. Tasha. Trish. Too many names to remember them all. Faces I couldn't pick out in a lineup if I tried. "Women," I answer.

He rubs his beard. "You're afraid to let a woman get too deep. If she does, then she sees your scars. She sees your father's blood. So, when you sense her getting too close, you pawn her off for the next woman. Am I right?"

My eyes tell him he is.

"Have you ever hit a woman, Cory?" he asks.

I sigh, make a long story short. "In college. My first real girl-friend. We had been together for maybe a year, off and on. She came to my apartment one day, crying. Told me she was pregnant. That news triggered something in me. Saw my mother; saw a weak woman standing in front of me. Didn't want that kind of woman raising my child." I look down at my hands and see destruction. "That's when I realized I truly was my father's child."

"What did she do?"

"She ran. Cried and ran."

"How did that make you feel?"

I tell him I felt like crap, felt like I was the one who was weak. No real man needs to hit a woman to feel strong. "Like hell," I say. "Contemplated suicide."

Concern shows in his face. "Are you suicidal now?"

I shake my head. "Couldn't go through with it then, wouldn't dare to do it now."

"So what's next?"

I think about Fatima, think about how different she makes me feel. The twinkle in her eye has sparked something in me. Makes me want more out of life.

Then there's Trish. She makes me want to run from life. But I can't. She has my seed growing inside her. As much as I want this to be different, changing the hands of time is impossible. It is what it is.

I answer, "I've got to make some changes in my life."

"How do you think I can help you?"

"Honestly, I'm here with no expectations."

He nods. "Good, because I don't expect to do anything for you. It's all about what *you* are willing to do. Too many times, we enter new experiences with too many expectations that go unmet, leaving us warped the next time something new comes along. If we would just take a simple approach, let nature take its course, life would be much more livable."

Silently, I concur.

The book makes a hard thud when it hits the dining room table. I stand, stare at my mother's mother. "Talk."

She slowly puts the book in her hands, opens it to the day my mother's demise began. Doesn't need her glasses to see my despondent reality.

I stand.

She reads.

My mother's mother grunts, sounds like a wounded dog still fighting for his life after being hit by a speeding car. She closes the book, looks up at me. Opens the book again. Too much to bear in one dose.

I say, "As if leaving me wasn't bad enough, she goes and drops some shit like this on me."

"Watch your mouth."

"Whatever."

She sighs, puts on her glasses to hide her misty eyes. "What do you want me to say?"

Finally, I sit. I slide my mother's confessions to my side of the table. "Let's start with where this came from."

Grandma hunches her shoulders.

I slam the book down again. "Damn it."

"You wanted answers, well, they're right there. You don't need nothing else from me," she says.

"Did you send this?"

She shakes her head.

I want to call her a liar, want to tell her I know she did, but I know she's telling the truth. "How did she know where to find me?"

"From what I hear, you can find anybody on the Internet if you look hard enough, even people who don't want to be found."

As hard as I try to stay strong, I feel my insides crumbling. "She's a coward. She has no conscience. I'm glad she's not in my life."

A hard tear lands on the table, sounds like a gavel sealing my unresolved existence. I wipe my pain away, wish I could do the same with my life.

"Ruby may not have been there for you , but she is still your mother. She is still my daughter. I will not let you talk about her like that."

"She sent a journal, Grandma. She has all of my information, probably even knows about my business. Instead of picking up the phone, or showing up at my house, she sent a cotton-pickin' journal. She can't even face me. That's a coward. I call it what it is. You need to face reality, you raised a frigging coward."

Grandma Pearl gets up from the table. Moves like her feet are made of stone as she walks over to me. Her eyes ominous.

Slap.

She does that with the same lack of sensitivity as her own flesh and blood. "Get out."

I'm stunned, dazed. Scared of what my hatred for the woman who gave me life will make me do to the woman who gave her life.

I scoot my chair back from the table so hard it hits the floor, lean on the table for support. "You're no different than her. Two peas from the same pod."

"Get. Out."

❂ ❂ ❂

My adrenaline pumps as I drive away from my shattered past and pull into the parking lot of Thai Cuisine to meet Lauren for lunch.

I don't want to be here. I'd rather be in the comfort of my own home where nothing matters but me. But sometimes we have to put our own burdens aside to help carry those of others.

She smiles when we make eye contact, waves me over to our table. We hug.

Both of us releasing our despairs in our embrace.

"This is one of my favorite restaurants," she tells me. "They have some of the best Thai food around."

Even though my appetite is nonexistent right now, my stomach growls, tells me differently. I pick up the menu, glance through it. "What are you getting?" I ask.

"Every time I come here, I get the same thing. I think I'll try something different today." She looks over the menu for a few seconds, shakes her head. "Nah, I'll stick with the Pad Thai."

My thoughts are too consumed to be trying to find a decent sounding meal. "I'll get that too," I say and put my menu off to the side.

Lauren sits back in her chair, no longer able to put off the reason for asking me here. "Isaiah's leaving me."

I speak from what I know to be true. "Doesn't surprise me. Men are always walking out on their responsibilities."

She sighs. "He told me this isn't the life he wants, at least not right now. Said everything happened too fast. The wedding, the kids, all the responsibilities." Lauren's eyes fill with tears. "Five years and two kids later, he just woke up one morning with an epiphany."

I think about when my father walked out on my mom and me. Wonder if life was moving too fast for him. I look across the table, look into the eyes of a woman being walked out on. Mom had the same anguish in her eyes. "Do you think there's another woman?"

She laughs. Laughs a hysterical laugh. Sounds like a woman losing her mind.

I don't see anything funny. I pick up my sweet tea, move the straw to the side and take a big gulp. Don't know what else to do. Want to grab my purse and get out before we both get carted off to the loony bin.

Lauren comes to her senses. "I wish it were that easy."

I don't hide the what-the-hell expression from my face. "Are you serious?"

She moves a few loose curls away from her face. "You think I'm crazy, don't you?"

I repeat my question.

"I'm not crazy if that's what you think," she reassures me. "For a couple of weeks, he had been coming home with what-am-I-doing-here look in his eyes. Looking lost, confused, distant. I ignored it. See, you have to know Isaiah. If something bothers him, he won't just come out and say it. He likes to pout or stand in your face with a big-ass smile on his face just to have the satisfaction of having you ask him what's going on. He feeds off of attention. So, anyway, I really didn't have the energy to give him 'cause I had my own stuff going on. Then one day, without warning, he came home and told me he needed a break."

"A break?" I try to soften the tone in my voice, but my attempt fails me.

"Damn, you sound like he's leaving you."

I shake my head, try to shake my emotions out of her misfortune. "Where is his *needing a break* supposed to leave you?"

Our waiter brings out our Thai entrees. The interruption gives us time to put our thoughts in perspective.

Lauren squeezes lime over her lunch, tries to put her energy in making her food just right while her marriage is falling apart. She swivels noodles around her fork, stabs a piece of shrimp. Plops the fork back down before taking a bite. "This wasn't supposed to happen. Not like this."

I give her my full attention.

"My marriage hasn't been easy, Fatima. We got married too young. We've both had to grow up together, make choices neither of us wanted to make. I got pregnant which threw everything off course."

I think about my mom, Ruby. My being in her womb threw things off for her too. Messed up her life, as she put it. "That's no excuse," I find myself saying.

Lauren moves forward in her seat, furrows her brow. "I'm not making excuses."

Our conversation is going sour fast. Her marriage is falling apart and all I can think of are my own issues. I do not want to be like this, don't want to be an it's-all-about-me type of friend.

I feel her eyes on me as I gobble down a couple of forkfuls of food. She watches me struggle with my emotions, watches me act as if everything is happy-go-lucky in my world. Like I have full control over everything that happens in my life. I know she sees things differently. She sees exactly what I see when I look in the mirror—pain.

"Fatima?"

I avoid making eye contact as I slurp up the rest of my sweet tea.

"Fatima?"

My eyes tell her I'm not ready to go there.

Lauren reaches her hand across the table, rests it on top of mine. Calms me from the outside in. "What's up? Is something bothering you?"

I move my hand, put it in my lap. "I'm good."

"Don't play me. I am a mother, a wife, and a friend. I'd like to think I can tell when someone is putting up their best face. At least trying to anyway."

Her eyes tell me she's willing to put aside her own issues to hear out mine. She does the opposite of what I did for her. I say, "I'm sorry."

Lauren throws her hand in the air. "You know, we've only known each other for a minute, but I feel close to you, Fatima. I want you to know I'm here for you. Whenever you're ready to talk, I'm here."

My head throbs, nose burns. Lip quivers as I try my hardest to fight back tears. "Hate it when this happens."

She comes over to my side of the table, kneels next to my chair. "It's okay, Fatima."

Between sobs I say, "I need to get out of here."

❂ ❂ ❂

I kick my legs out, lean back, try to reach the sky. My locs fly in the wind, hang like nothing even matters. I wish I could do the same. Wish I could fly away from this place, no worries or troubles. I kick my legs out harder, pull them in with more force than before. The bar shakes, lets me know I'm swinging too high. I get the message. Cross my ankles and swing back into reality, rest my head on the chain as I slowly rock back and forth to safety.

"Fatima?"

I'm back to ground zero, back to where I can no longer hide my instability. I say, "For the longest, I've walked around with no sense of being. Felt like parts of me were dead. Never understood why. My life just failed to make sense to me."

Lauren sits on the swing next to me. Sits and listens to me.

I turn to her, so much weight in my face. "When we make decisions for our lives, we fail to realize the toll it can take on others." I look down in my lap. All I can see is Ruby's journal, her confessions written as plain as day.

Across from us is a bench. I get up, walk toward it.

Lauren's not far behind me. "You ready to talk about it?" she asks when she sits down next to me, her hand on my thigh.

My posture shows my weakness, shows my fragility. I comb my fingers through my locs a few times, rest my palm at the back of my head. "I despise my parents. They're dead to me." I mean every word I say.

"Whoa." Lauren removes her hand from my thigh. "Don't talk like that."

"Why not? When they walked out of my life, they might as well have been dead."

"Come on, Fatima. My parents have done some pretty jacked up things during my upbringing, but I'm not about to send them six feet under for their mistakes."

I jerk my head in her direction, ignore the popping sound in my neck. "Did you really just say that?" I spit my words out so hard I barely recognize my own voice. "How dare you even compare?"

Her green eyes become brown, warm. An apology hidden behind them. "I'm sor..."

I shake my head in between my hands. Cut her off before she can take back her true sentiments.

Words leave my lips as if I'm reading the pages of Ruby's diary on stage. Soft, full of emotion. "When my mom was almost five weeks' pregnant with me, she made the biggest mistake of my life. She was wheeled into a morbid room. Said it was cold and emotionless. Said it felt like a morgue. She lay on a table waiting for the doctor to suck my life out of her. There was commotion out in the hallway, made everyone in the room nervous. No one was nervous about my life coming to an abrupt end before it even began, but the idea of Pro-Lifers coming in to end their lives tensed them all."

I feel Lauren's hand wipe away my non-stop tears.

"That commotion in the hallway was because of my father. He had found out about the abortion and ran straight to the clinic. He acted like he was my savior. Did it all like he cared and still walked out on me four years later."

"Fatima, I am so sorry." This time she wipes away her own liquid emotions.

I say, "Even though my heart kept beating, I died on that table."

Lauren's curls brush against my cheek as she shakes her head furiously. "Fatima, please, honey, listen to me." She holds my hand in hers. "You are not dead, you hear me? You're very much alive."

"I don't feel like it. I have all of this hate penned up inside of me. I don't even know who I am."

She wipes away another stream of tears from my eyes. "I know it's easier said than done, but you know what I want you to do?"

"Oh, boy."

"No, no. Hear me out." She wraps her arm around my shoulder, eases me closer to her. Leans her head against mine. Holds me close like a best friend. "I want you to let go, Fatima. You've been hanging on to the past for too long. I once heard my mom say, 'the past will last as long as you let it.'"

I tell her, "I hear you. It's just so hard. There's not a day that goes by when I'm not thinking about my parents. I have so many unresolved questions, so many feelings that I don't know what to feel. I feel so hapless."

"What would make you feel better?" Lauren asks.

"Honestly," I take a deep breath, "I really can't answer. One side of me wants to kick ass and ask questions later. The other side simply wants their existence to be washed from my memory like footprints in the sand."

She says, "I don't know why your parents left, but you know what, you've got to look in the mirror every day and be proud of who you are. Be proud of who you've become. You've come a long way on your own, despite what happened yesterday. Tell yesterday goodbye, Fatima. Sure, your parents are somewhere wishing they could do things all over again. Don't let their mistakes keep you in this unhappy place."

I look at her real good. "Tell yesterday goodbye, huh?"

I've been in the hospital with Trish since we came to her thirty-two week checkup. Her blood pressure was up. Things weren't looking good for her and the baby. Her doctor said they needed to admit her, keep an eye on the both of them. If her blood pressure didn't go down, they'd have to get the baby out for the safety of both of them.

"Need anything before I head out of here?" I offer.

Trish shakes her head.

"I'll be back later."

She mumbles something under her breath as she changes the channel on the TV. Does that like she's trying to change the programming in my brain.

"What did you say?" I ask.

She looks at me with red eyes, her voice strong and defiant. "Why bother, Cory? What's the point in coming back?"

"Keep your voice down. The doctor said getting excited is not good for the baby."

She doesn't listen. "Oh, like you care. I've barely seen your face during this pregnancy and now all of a sudden you want to act like this baby is important to you."

I slide a chair close to her bed. Think about some of the things Dr. Bryant talked with me about. "Look, Trish... I mean, Patricia.

I know I haven't been there for you. I'm not gonna lie, this isn't easy for me…"

"Oh, so this is a walk in the park for me?" she says with more attitude than before.

"How are we going to make this work if you don't even listen to me? I didn't say this was easy for you. I'm just saying it ain't easy for me. It's too late for me to change the hands of time, but I want to be here for you, be here for our child." I put my hand on her belly for the first time.

A hesitant smile crosses her face. "So you want to be with me?"

I remove my hand from her expanding stomach, push myself up from the chair. Stand next to her. "I can't be with you, Patricia. We're going to be parents. We need to get along for the sake of this baby. That's all. Nothing more."

"Well, you know what, you can save your sentimental bullshit for someone else because it is too late for me." She puts emphasis on every word. "You no longer exist to me."

"Don't be like that, Patricia."

"'*Don't be like that*,'" she scoffs. "After all the stuff you put me through."

"I'm just saying…"

"You keep saying that, but you ain't saying nothing. You seriously expect me to welcome you with open arms just because you all of a sudden had a change of heart? I don't think so. This ain't TV. If you want to be in my life, it's either all or nothing."

"I guess it's nothing then." This time, I'm the one walking out the door.

❂ ❂ ❂

I press the button for LOBBY. I'm wondering if I made the right decision. If walking out on her in her moment of weakness was the right thing to do. She wasn't willing to compromise, wasn't willing to look at things from my side. Maybe in another lifetime things could've worked. If I weren't Cory and she weren't Patricia, maybe it could've worked. Maybe.

The doors open. All of a sudden I feel like the Geto Boys. Feel like it's Halloween night and my mind is playing tricks on me. "Brenda?"

She moves back, moves out of my way. The fear is still there.

I'm at a loss for words, say the first thing that comes to mind. "I'm sorry."

"That was years ago."

"You left, didn't give me the chance to apologize."

She stands there, recollecting ten years in a matter of seconds. I stand there and do the same.

Neither of us saying anything.

A man moves from behind her, flowers and a balloon in his hand announcing his son's arrival into the world. "Are you folks getting on?"

I look at Brenda. She looks at me.

I move from between the elevator doors, let the man get on to see the new member of his family.

Brenda speaks through tight jaws. "I have nothing to say to you, Cory."

I ask, "Was I *that* bad?"

"Cory, I was pregnant and you hit me. There's really no need for me to even entertain your question."

An older couple with two little kids approach the elevators. I reach toward Brenda to get her to move to the side. She jerks her arm away at my slightest touch.

I see eyes that remind me of my mother's in her times of fear, see the fear of a battered woman. I did that to her.

Brenda touches her cheek, does that like she can still feel the imprint from my fist a decade ago. The band and diamond on her ring finger let me know I'm stepping on sacred ground.

"Look, I have nothing else to say. I really need to get upstairs before..." She cuts herself off. "I just need to get upstairs."

I step out of the present, flash back to when we were face to face ten years ago. Flash back to when my father's blood boiled in my veins. "The last time I saw you, my seed was growing in your belly and you have nothing else to say?"

We both turn our heads when the chime of the elevator announces that we are no longer alone.

Brenda watches the doors open, glances back at me, looks back at the doors. "This isn't what it looks like," she tells the husky brother who wears a glare so strong I swear he's about to kick both of our behinds.

I refuse to show any sign of weakness. "Where's my child?"

The what-is-this-fool-talking-about expression on the man's face tells me he doesn't know about me, doesn't know that I fathered a child with his wife.

She grabs him by the arm, tries to cajole him back into the elevator. "Come on, baby. Let's get back upstairs."

I don't back down. I stand my ground. "Where is my child?"

He grabs her by the arm this time, squeezes her like she's a stress ball. "You got something to tell me?"

Brenda speaks to him in a voice too low for me to hear.

Whatever she says doesn't go over well with him. She squirms in his arms, the death grip too much for her. I realize the fear I saw in her eyes earlier wasn't because of me, but because of him.

"You need me to call security?" I ask.

"You ain't gon' call nobody," he informs me.

Her eyes begin to water. I look at her and I see Mattie, a weak woman who can't stand up for herself. "You're hurting her, man."

"Let that be none of your concern."

She begs him to just drop it. "We need to get upstairs. Bernard needs me."

A chill runs through me. I feel the hairs on the back of my neck come to attention. "I have a son?"

The burly man with big hands tosses his woman, the mother of my child, to the side. Comes toward me like I just blasphemed him.

Brenda grabs him by the arm, uses all of her strength to hold Mighty Joe Young back. "Bernard, stop. Don't do this. Leave him alone."

She calls him by the same name as the person who needs her upstairs. She sees the confusion in my face, but her main concern is putting a cease-fire to the man charging toward me.

"Get off me!" he yells at her. "I'm about to put a hurting on this fool."

She lets him go, runs to the front of me. Blocks him from getting close enough to put his proclaimed hurting on me. "This isn't supposed to be happening!" she exclaims.

"You'd better start talking," he threatens.

"Bernard, please," she begs.

He stands back. "I don't know why you're protecting this dude, but you'd better start talking and you'd better start talking now," he threatens.

Two men in green uniforms approach us, hands on top of their guns. "Is there a problem?" one of them asks.

"Everything is fine, Officers. We just had a little misunderstanding, that's all," Brenda answers.

"This is a hospital." The taller officer points to the chapel door on our right. "We got folks in there grieving. I suggest you take this little 'misunderstanding' outside."

We all nod our compliance.

As soon as we make it out of the hospital doors, brother man tells Brenda, "I'm waiting."

Brenda turns her back to me, asks him to give us a moment alone.

He shakes his head. "Hell, no. A man should never leave his wife alone with another man. If you can't talk with me right here, then you don't need to be talking."

She focuses her attention back on me. I hear the uneasiness in her voice before she even speaks. "*Our* son..." She grabs her husband's hand to emphasize that the boy is theirs. "...is upstairs in a coma. He was hit in the head by a baseball at his game a week ago. He hasn't made any signs of improvement. The doctors don't think he's going to make it. Now, if I come across as insensitive to how things turned out with us in college, you can understand where my concern is right now."

"You told me you were pregnant and then walked out without saying anything else. Now, you tell me I have a son who is barely hanging on to life. I deserve to be up there by his side just as much as you do."

Brenda's husband stands there and ingests everything. The vein throbbing in his forehead tells me that this is all news to him. Lets me know that he has had enough.

She senses his fury, yet she does nothing to put the fire out. "Cory, my son does not know you as his father."

"Don't recall that being my cross to bear."

She sighs, becomes just as frustrated as her companion.

"I won't let him go out without knowing who I am," I say and turn toward the sliding glass doors to head for the elevators.

No footsteps follow behind me.

"Go up there if you want, Cory. It won't change a thing," Brenda says.

I stop, turn back around. "It might not, but at least he'll know that it wasn't me that kept us apart."

"Damn it, Cory." Desperation stains her voice. "Just leave things the way they are. You've already complicated matters enough."

The big man has his own questions that need answering. "Why does he think my son is his?" His tone rages, lets me know Brenda will have hell to pay later.

"Why shouldn't I?" I want to know.

Brenda looks up at her husband, then back at me. Her eyes are just as glossy as they were the last time I saw her many years ago. "Look, the reason I left wasn't because you hit me. I left because I realized I wasn't carrying your baby. Bernard Jr. is not your son. He never was."

"You don't look so good. Something happen?"

"Something is always happening."

"Want to talk about it?"

I shake my head. "Not really."

I look up at Dr. Bryant. Wonder what he thinks about when he looks at me. He probably thinks I'm just wasting my money.

"Okay. Well, what would you like to talk about today, Cory?"

All I can think about are Brenda's words. *Bernard Jr. is not your son. He never was.* I never thought hearing those words would bring so much pain to me, especially since it was something I had not wanted. "Has somebody ever given you something that you didn't want, but when they took it back, you found yourself wishing you still had it?"

He nods, says, "I can think of a time or two when that has happened."

"How'd it make you feel?"

"Where are you going with this?" he wants to know.

"You asked me what I wanted to talk about. Just hear me out, okay?"

He concedes.

I ask again, "How'd it make you feel?"

"I'd say I felt cheated, slighted in some way."

"Did it make you mad at yourself?"

His body language shows that he's uncomfortable being on the other side of the table, but he answers my question anyway. "I guess I could say it did. When I think about it, I was mad at myself because I wasn't grateful or appreciative enough to receive, causing it to be taken away. Made me feel like I was selfish."

"That's what I'm feeling like right now, Doc."

"Want to tell me about it?"

I tell him what went down at the hospital a couple of hours ago. "I never wanted to be a father. When Brenda told me she was pregnant, I became someone I never wanted to be; I became my father. But while I was standing there as she told me I never was her child's father, I felt like someone had ripped out a part of me. Felt like someone had carved out a piece of my heart."

Dr. Bryant writes a few things down on his tablet. He sits still for a few seconds before sharing his thoughts. "Cory, are you familiar with the Law of Attraction?"

I nod in the affirmative.

"Keeping that in mind, have you considered the fact that you might be giving what you do not want too much power? Everything that you did not want has manifested in your life. Fatherhood, being like your father... What *do* you want?"

His question throws me off guard. Don't know if I know the answer. Been spending so much time focusing on what I *don't* want that I haven't given what I *do* much thought. I tell him just that.

"So, what do you want, Cory?" he asks again.

"Clarity." I nod at my answer. "Yeah, for now, I want clarity and peace of mind."

"Okay, now, focus on those two things and everything else will fall into place. It may take some more barriers coming down, but you will learn the true desires of your heart as long as you keep seeking."

✸ ✸ ✸

Fatima steps to the stage. Her face disconnected from life. She looks how I feel.

Your message has consumed me with hatred...a contaminant that can't be replaced with contentment or some facet of acceptance.

She's standing up there, revealing her pure emotion. Words that breathe the story of my life.

I watch her, want to go up there, hold her and rub my fingers through her locs. Want to whisper "This too shall pass" in her ears. I want to do all of that, but I can't. Hate is the same toxin running through my veins. Hatred of circumstance.

Fatima is escorted off her platform with a thunderous applause, makes a few wish they had written the poem themselves. She moves to the bar slowly, moves like her feet are heavy, like her burdens are weighing her down.

I try to get her attention, but some woman with a lot of hair is all in her face. She seems to be doing most of the talking because Fatima's lips aren't moving.

Finally, we make eye contact. She calls me over with her irises. For a minute, the only words between the two of us are with our eyes. We're both in a place we don't want to be in right now.

The woman with the curly blonde hair clears her throat. "I'm Lauren," she introduces with her outstretched hand.

"Cory." I reciprocate her warm handshake. "I've seen you around here before."

"I'm a frequenter," she says.

Fatima enters the conversation, "Yeah, Lauren's the one who introduced me to Patchouli's."

I wink at my loc-wearing fondness. "I'm glad she did."

A smile crosses Fatima's face, lets me know she is as well.

The time on the oversized clock behind the bar tells me I don't have time for chit-chat. "Excuse me, ladies, work calls. It was nice meeting you, Lauren."

I leave the two of them, step back up to the stage, grab the mic. "It's time to turn down the lights, sip on some wine, snuggle up close, and caress the mind." I turn to the band. "Drop the beat."

The band kicks it with a funky groove. Sounds like a Raphael Saadiq track.

Neither Fatima nor Lauren are at the bar. I open the front door, see them standing by a red car off to the side. I feel like a voyeur watching them wipe each other's tears away.

I walk back inside, ready to pack it up and leave this place myself. Head home to wipe away my own tears. Mourn the loss of a life that was never mine.

Fisher, my man who tends the bar, slides me over a glass of my favorite. The moment the bronze-colored drink touches my lips, it burns, melts away my emotions. Makes me numb to anything past or present.

A light tap touches my shoulder. Her signature lavender scent awakens my senses. "Hey," I say before I even turn around.

Fatima looks at me, grabs and hugs me. I hug her back, tightly. Give her emotion I didn't know I had.

We hug for what feels like hours, searching each other's embrace for what words can't say.

She pulls away, sits down next to me. Grabs my sipped on drink, sniffs, takes a sip herself.

Her face contorts, mouth all balled up like she has no teeth.

"You alright?" I ask.

"This will mess somebody up." She coughs, chokes. "Man, the smell is deceiving. Smells sweet, light, like rum cake. But once it hits your lips, it's a whole different story. Can't taste anything else."

We laugh.

I tell her, "The first time I had some, I was young. My mouth went numb, my chest burned. Thought I was dying. I ran to the bathroom to try and make myself throw up. Didn't do anything but make me feel worse."

"And you're still drinking it because…?"

"I tried it again, let it burn the second time. Felt like I had been given a lethal injection for a murder I didn't commit. My whole body went numb. I laid in the middle of the floor and stared up at the ceiling. I couldn't feel anything, couldn't hear anything. Everything was a blur. Been drinking it ever since."

"How old were you?"

I take another sip of my addiction. "Nine."

She doesn't act shocked, looks at me with genuine concern in her eyes. "Was your childhood that painful?"

I look at Fatima, but I can't see her or anything in the room. Feel like I'm not even here. "I saw a lot of things a child shouldn't see."

She rubs her hand up and down my thigh, rubs like she's trying to rub away my bad memories as well as hers.

I put my hand on top of hers. "Your poem tonight, wanna talk about it?"

Silence is her answer. She bites down on her bottom lip, chews on it like it's her last meal. She sighs. "Not here."

I nod. Felt like I was saying too much in here anyway. "Let's get out of here."

"Your place this time," she says.

☯ ☯ ☯

Twenty minutes later, we pull up to my apartment unit. Fatima parks her car in my spot, walks over to where I parked, shaking her head. "Let me get this straight. You have a full-time job, own your own business, and you're still living in an apartment?"

Her comment does not offend me in the least. "Owning a house is too much of a commitment for me. Feels like a marriage. When I'm ready to leave, all I got to do is turn in a sixty-day notice. No breaking contracts or pockets. It's as simple as that."

Inside my place, she looks around. Tells me my place reminds her a lot of her own.

"In what way?" I want to know.

"It appears as if you're in this world alone. No pictures, no nothing. Just furniture and four walls. No existence in your life other than you."

"Does that bother you?"

She nods. "Never thought much about it until now. Seeing your place makes me realize that my life is void of feeling."

Fatima sits down on the couch. I tell her I'll be right back.

In the kitchen, I grab a couple of coffee mugs from the cabinet, remember Mattie as I fill them with scotch.

I hand her a cup of liquid pain killer, then sit on the other side of the sofa.

"I'm an official Bag Lady," she says.

I tell her, "Who doesn't have issues?"

"Not like mine." She sighs. "I've been in a struggle for as far back as I can remember. A draining battle. There have been times when I wanted to call it quits, but the little voice inside kept pushing me to continue my journey. Right now, I feel stuck, feel like I'm fighting just to live."

"What would you say if I told you I feel the same way?"

"Do you?"

I nod. "I don't even know who I am any more. Just as soon as I take a step forward, something pulls me two steps back."

She gives me an understanding look. "Do you think your childhood has a lot to do with what you are going through right now? Is that why you have commitment issues?"

"No doubt. If I hadn't seen half the things I saw, I would definitely be standing on the opposite side of the tracks right now."

Both of us sit in silence. Nothing but the sound of our throats burning as we drink the numbing elixir.

Her voice fails to hide her vulnerability as she speaks. "I like you, Cory. Like you a lot. And it scares me."

I'm taken aback by her confession. "Why does it scare you?" Need to know if her fear is the same as mine.

"Because it gives me a conscience, gives me a meaning to my being here. But at the same time, it confuses me. Don't know if my attraction to you is authentic or if it's your pain that draws me in."

"So if we weren't both hurting in some way, you don't know if the attraction would be there?" I ask for clarity.

She nods. "These feelings are new to me. I haven't felt like this in a long time. I'm just...I don't know, I'm just confused and scared all at the same time."

"Is that how you really feel?"

Fatima rubs her hand across her forehead a couple of times. "I really don't know what to feel. I'm being pulled from so many directions right now and I can't quite stop spinning."

"What is it that you want from me?"

Her hand trembles as she holds the drink in her hand. She takes a big gulp, face scrunches up as the liquid blisters her emotions.

"I'm going through a lot these days. What I said on that stage tonight is a true reflection of where my head is at. Being near you doesn't make things any easier."

Her words earlier were etched in pain, anger. Wanting to cut life short. "I've been in the same place. Truth be told, I'm swimming in the same pool right now," I say.

"What do we do about it?"

I take the glass out of her hand, place it on the table. Kiss her like my life depends on it.

Fatima reciprocates my kiss, just as strong. Unlike the first time, neither of us denies what we feel. "I want you in the worst kind of way. I need to feel you inside me," she pleads. "Take away this feeling I'm feeling."

Her wish is my command. I grab her by the hand, lead her down the hallway to my room.

She cuts the light on. Says, "I want to see tonight. I don't want nothing hiding in the dark."

I hesitate for a minute. The last time a woman stood in my room with the lights on, I saw something I never wanted to see. Saw my seed growing in her belly. But I oblige Fatima anyway.

She comes to me. We stare eye to eye. She rubs her fingers through my hair, pulls my face close to hers. Inhales, then kisses me. Exhales inside my mouth.

This time with Fatima is on a different level than the first time. We had passion then, but nothing like right now. Tonight, we are passionate about each other. We have opened the lines of communication, crossed the boundaries of what is sacred.

We undress each other, stand together butt naked.

"I don't want to think about anything tonight. I want to be numb to everything outside this room," she says.

Silently, I concur.

She sits on the edge of the bed. I stand in front of her. Fatima's thick lips graze across my abdomen. She wraps her arms around me, pulls me close.

Wetness runs down my leg. I gently separate her from me so

I can see her face. "What's wrong?" I ask when I see her pink, watery eyes.

"I'm sorry." She doesn't wipe the tears away. "I don't know what's wrong with me."

I sit on the bed next to her. "We don't have to do anything. Let's talk. What are you feeling?"

"What I'm *not* feeling is more like it. I just feel overwhelmed."

"Is it me?"

She shakes her head, scoops her locs, rests them on her shoulder. Scoots back and sits Indian-style in the middle of the bed. "If you had a fucked-up past, would you run from it or act as if it never existed?"

"Since you learned that I started drinking scotch at the age of nine, I think you already know the answer to that."

Her eyes tell me to save my sarcasm for another day.

My response was serious, but I take it back to her level. "Is that what your poem was about, your past?"

She nods.

Thinking about my own past causes me to go soft. I *did* have a fucked-up past. Watching everyone except my dad get knocked around didn't leave me with pleasant memories. I say, "Sometimes, when you run from the past, it has its way of catching up with you. Sometimes, you get tired of running."

"So, what would you do?"

I'm uncomfortable. But I answer anyway. "I'm still running."

Her eyes reconnect with mine. The fog from her past clears from her eyes. She's back in the present. She kisses me with such intensity that it hurts. Hurts because I feel the same pain. I'm just as intense.

She breaks our kiss. The need for answers persists. "Have you ever wanted something so bad that you couldn't rest until you got it?"

I nod. "Everybody has at some point in their life."

"How long would you wait?"

"Depends on the search."

I wait, wait for her to unleash her struggle.

Fatima twists a couple of locs around her fingers. Contemplates whether she's telling me too much.

"You uncomfortable?" I ask.

She pulls back the covers, climbs underneath. I do the same. Our backs up against the wall.

"Tell me something good."

I search my brain, try to find something good to say, but come up short.

Fatima leans her head against my shoulder, her breathing heavy. "I was hurt really bad when I was younger. Both of my parents walked out on me. No explanations. They left me like I was a stray cat on their porch begging them for some affection. Growing up with that on my conscience has not been easy. But it makes me who I am, you know. At the same time, I can't even say that I like who I am."

I lean my head back against the wall, try to lighten the load from my own emotions. My voice is carrying the pain of both of us. "It's hard to be who you are when you don't even know who you are."

She lifts her head up, looks up at me. "Exactly. I mean, like you said earlier, I try to take a step forward, try to find some balance, some meaning, and then I get a blow that sets me back another decade." She hits her fist against her thigh. "Damn, where's the reciprocity?"

I wonder the same thing.

Her hand is in her lap, I reach for it, intertwine my fingers with hers.

"What's your pain?" she wants to know.

My eyes close, her hand still in mine. "My father."

"I take it y'all aren't close."

"He's dead."

"Oh, I'm sorry."

"I'm not."

Surprisingly, I remain neutral. Maybe seeing Dr. Bryant was a good investment after all. I tell Fatima, "Someone once told me, 'A scab is only the beginning of the healing process.'"

"Do you believe that?"

I evaluate my life, reflect on where I was weeks ago, before I sought professional help. Compared to where I am now, I realize I *am* different. Maybe my scab is falling off and making room for new skin. "Yeah," I admit.

"I see."

"I hear doubt."

She says, "I guess I can kind of understand, but that pessimist side of me wonders what happens when your wound heals and then something happens and you have to wait for that same wound to be healed all over again. Or what happens if you get a fresh injury that hurts more than the previous one? How many bruises and scabs does it take to heal?"

I dig. "Are you speaking from experience?"

"That's the only language I know. Can't speak from anyone else's experiences. Only my own."

I tell her that I do not have all of the answers.

"I don't expect you to. I'm just voicing my thoughts."

Our hands are still intertwined, heat from our chemistry making them moist. Her eyes travel up to mine, see me looking at her. A smile from the corner of her mouth, shows me that deep dimple.

I smile back. Rub my thumb back and forth across the back of her hand. Her skin is so soft, feels like I'm rubbing my thumb across satin sheets.

"I used to have nightmares." My voice is low as I tell her about my dreams of death and a little boy with no eyes.

She doesn't say anything.

"Shortly after I met you, they stopped."

She lets go of my hand, rubs her fingers over her eyebrows. "You think your dreams were trying to tell you something?"

"Maybe. I guess when I think about it, those dreams were triggered by my fears. Fears of the past, fears of the unknown. After meeting you, some of those fears have tiptoed away. I kind of feel like I'm not scared of certain things anymore. I'm ready to see what's behind the door. Discover who I am. See who I can be."

"So, you think I had something to do with you not having those dreams anymore?" she asks.

"Could be a number of things, but, yes, I do believe it's partially due to you."

Fatima's eyes stare at me blankly.

Makes me feel like I've said too much.

"I'm glad you're not having those dreams anymore," she finally says.

"Me, too."

She gives me a quick peck on the cheek. "I've got to tinkle. Which way is the bathroom?"

I point her in the direction of the closed door out in the hallway.

❂ ❂ ❂

Minutes later, Fatima walks back into my bedroom with one coffee mug in hand, so much confidence in her stroll. Makes me wonder if she's the same woman who was crying on my shoulder moments ago. Makes me wonder if she's the same woman I just confessed my nightmares to seconds ago.

She eases the cup up to my mouth, gives me a sip, then turns it up to hers before putting it down on the nightstand. She straddles me, tells me, "You arouse me in the worst way."

"What way is that?"

"You make me lose my mind, make me insane."

"I could say the same about you," I confess.

Fatima nibbles on my tongue, sucks away any traces of liquor. Slips her tongue into my mouth and lets me return the gesture.

Both of us keep our eyes open, stare into each other's soul. Finding out things about each other that we'd never reveal.

My cell phone rings from my slacks on the floor. The voice of Dave Hollister letting me know who it is without having to look at the caller ID. I refuse to interrupt kissing Fatima for any of Trish's foolishness.

Once it stops ringing, my house phone rings. "Sounds like somebody's trying to track you down. Maybe you should get that," Fatima suggests.

"It's not important." As soon as I say that, Dave starts ranting again.

My lady friend hops off of me, grabs my pants from off the floor, hands them to me with no words. Her eyes tell me enough.

I dig my phone out, cut it off. "Now, where were we?"

She lays on top of the comforter, spreads her legs wide open.

I lick my lips, get ready for the meal she put on the table.

The house phone rings again. Whoever it is finally gives up and leaves a message on the answering machine.

"Your no-good ass is probably laid up with some other chick while my sister is in this hospital fighting for her life to have your baby. You better get up here…"

I'm at the hospital with Cory. He asked me to come, so I'm here. We didn't say much en route. In fact, we didn't speak at all. Both of us trapped in our own thoughts. Both disturbed by the message left on his answering machine.

No-good ass.

What have I gotten myself involved in? Cory and I haven't known each other long, not long at all, but that's nothing new to me. I've slept with many men I barely knew. I never felt anything for them, so their pasts, presents, and futures were of no concern to me. With Cory, things are different. I'm feeling him. In a bad kind of way at that. The kind of way that has me worried. Concerned. I don't want to be hurt, not like this. Just as soon as a I take one step forward…

We're a couple of doors down from the room where his child is being born. I pull Cory by the arm. I want him to slow down. "I shouldn't be here," I tell him.

The sound of a baby making its first request to the world is heard. He wants to go back into the warm womb where nothing else really matters. I don't blame him. That's probably the same way I felt when I met my mom's cold welcome.

He looks at me. Fear crosses his face. His lips move. "Neither should I."

Take his fear, add my confusion, and the result is a very bad equation. Can't combine oil with water and expect to make chocolate milk.

He moves closer to the sound of the crying baby. I follow slowly behind. He wants me here; he needs me here.

A woman with panic in her eyes approaches us. She looks at me and says, "Just what I thought." Directs her attention to Cory, "You have some nerve bringing *her* up here. What was my sister thinking? I told her to leave your no-good ass alone a long time ago."

"I didn't come here for this." He pushes the stocky woman out of the way. Anger is in his every move as he pulls me closer to the crying sounds.

"Fool, she's not in there," the lady tells Cory.

"I don't have time for games, Candace. Which room?"

Her arms are folded, she looks me up and down. A disgusted scowl on her face makes me feel like *I'm* the irresponsible baby's daddy. She keeps her hard eyes on me as she spits her venom at Cory. "If you cared anything about Patricia, you would've been here. I guess you were too busy with…never mind." She looks at him, points toward the elevator. "She's in ICU and she's not trying to see you."

Cory stands and stares, stares and stands. He looks lost, like he doesn't know which way to go.

I ignore the heat coming from my right, and turn to my left. "You okay?"

He looks at me with weary eyes. "I'm going up there."

I grab his hand, lead him to some privacy. The protective sister huffs out her discontentment, but neither Cory nor I care. "Earlier, when I told you that my feelings for you scares me…" I try to swallow my fears, feels like I swallowed a bag of flour. "Well, this is one of those times. I don't like what I am feeling, Cory. I'm uncomfortable and I should not be here."

With both hands, he brushes my locs back from my face, rests his hands on the back of my head. "I'm uncomfortable too, but, right now, my irresponsibility is forcing me to make a tough, but responsible decision. I have to be here. As much as I don't want to be, I have to be."

I step back, step as far away from him as possible. His hands fall from me. "I don't," I say.

He turns and heads for the elevators. He ignores the tears in my eyes before the elevator doors close him in.

❁ ❁ ❁

I drive as far as I can until my ride comes to a stop in front of the park Lauren brought me to a few days ago. The same park my daddy used to bring me to before he bailed out on me.

It is after hours; the park is closed, but I still get out of my car and walk over to the swings. The chains are cold to my touch, just like the world—a place where no one cares about anyone but themselves.

As I did that day with Lauren, I swing beyond the swing's comfort zone, try to make myself a permanent fixture in the sky. Wish I was up there with the stars. Then I would not feel this way, wouldn't feel anything at all.

My cell phone vibrates in my pocket, jars me back to reality.

Damn my mom, damn my dad, damn Cory. Damn them all for doing this to me. They all saw me in my moment of weakness and still turned their backs on me.

I leap from the swing without waiting for it to stop. My ankle twists, makes me lose my balance. I hit the sand, pick myself up, dust the dirt off. I hear laughing around me. I look around. No one is here but me. "I'm losing my mind."

My phone vibrates again in my pocket, reminds me that I have a message. I pull it out, see I have a text message from Cory.

Before I know it, I find myself driving in the opposite direction of home. I am on my way back to the hospital.

Candace is standing outside smoking a cigarette when I step off the elevator. Her nerves were bad earlier, but the nicotine appears to have calmed her down some.

"Can I get one?"

She glares at me, blows smoke in my face. Her lips are black from years of sucking toxins through her mouth.

Again I ask, "Can I get one?"

"Why are you still here?"

"I have a right to be here just like everybody else."

"Stop the bull, Cory. Don't act like you care."

"What is your beef with me, huh? You've had this attitude toward me since day one. You mad 'cause I picked your sister over you?"

She laughs like I just delivered a knee-slapping joke on the stage of *ComicView*. Her face straightens, lets me know she's dead serious. "You ain't all that."

"Then what's the problem?"

"You ain't been here all this time. You brought some nappy-headed chick up here while my sister is on her deathbed and you want to know what my problem is. You're crazier than I thought."

I get up in her face. "You don't know nothing about Fatima, so keep her out of this."

"Man, back up. I call it how I see it." She says that and walks away from me. Walks over to a bench, pulls out another cigarette.

I sit next to Candace.

She lights the cancer stick, takes a long drag, then holds it in for a few seconds. Exhales slowly like her thoughts consume her. "I don't know what my sister ever saw in you."

My focus is no longer on the cigarette, but on my nemesis' face. "I pity you."

"No need. You need to feel sorry for yourself. Oh, my bad, my sister did that for you. Now look at her. She pitied your sorry ass too much. Now she's up there using a machine to breathe."

"I had nothing to do with that. She brought that on herself. Trish…"

"Damn it. Her name is Patricia. How many times you gotta be told that?"

Candace shakes her head, gets up, moves away from me.

"Look, I never misrepresented myself. She knew where I stood from day one. I never begged her to be with me, didn't have to. She never gave me the chance to."

"So, you're saying my sister forced you to be with her?" Her anger is showing again.

I stand in front of Candace, don't want to look weak by keeping my seat. "All I'm saying is that your sister didn't give me time to sweat her."

She gets so close to me that I can smell her harsh breath through her nostrils. A smile of defeat crosses her face. "You just don't know how disappointing it is to hear you say that."

"What is that supposed to mean?"

Her black gums and yellow teeth are showing. "Nothing. Don't worry about it."

I grab her by the shirt, keep her from walking away from me.

"Fool, you better keep your hands off me." She slaps my hand off of her. "I don't know who you think you are."

My angst gets the best of me, brings out the Zach side of me. I throw my hands up, back off.

"Don't you ever put your hands on me again."

I back off a little more, wave my invisible white flag in the air. "Tell her I'm sorry."

"I know you are. You're a sorry excuse for a man. Patricia was right when she said you were heartless. You're pathetic."

"Just tell her I'm sorry," I repeat.

"I'm not telling her nothing. And I better not hear of you trying to contact her. She doesn't need your too-little-too-late kind of sympathy. In fact, she doesn't need you at all."

The chain smoker pulls another Newport out of the box, fires it up, passes her addiction on to me, then leaves.

❂ ❂ ❂

Fatima sits down on the bench next to me, takes the burning cigarette out of my hand. Throws it on the ground, suffocates it under her boot.

I don't smoke, never have. Just wanted to feel powerful for a minute. Smokers always seem so in control, like nothing plagues them. I was wrong.

I tell her, "I was too late."

Fatima sighs a pained sigh, struggles with her words. "What happened?"

"The baby didn't make it."

She wraps her arm around me, tells me she's sorry.

"Just when I took a step forward..."

"I'm sorry," she repeats.

"Guess those are the breaks."

The sound of hurried steps takes the focus off my sorrows, puts them on the husky, black man running after his fleeing wife.

Brenda and Bernard.

My anger rises, that ugly part of me I thought I had laid to rest.

They see me.

I run after them, Fatima not far behind me. Her heels clicking against the concrete comforts me.

"Cory, what's going on?" she wants to know.

I cannot answer her right now.

Brenda turns around, sees three people running after her. She screams, trips over her own two feet. Hits the pavement.

Her husband towers over her, doesn't help her up. Stands there with his hands on his hips, trying to catch his breath.

Fatima pulls me back, moves me out of earshot. "Maybe we should call the police."

I take the phone out of her hands, shake my head.

Her eyes grow dark toward me. Looks at me as if she never knew me. Walks with a quickened pace toward the woman on the ground.

I walk just as fast.

"Are you okay?" Fatima asks.

Brenda makes eye contact with me, then looks in her husband's direction. "I'll be alright," she says. She rubs gravel from her hands and with decreasing strength, she slowly lifts herself from the pavement. Blood drips from her nose. She wipes it away like it's just a runny nose. Does that because her nose was bleeding before the fall.

Bernard doesn't say anything. He stands back, away from the scene of the crime.

I reach out to Brenda. She turns away. "I don't need your help."

"Well, I need answers," I say.

"Cory, please," she begs. "Just let it go."

Bernard invites himself back into the picture, puts his hand in between his wife and me. "Man, right now ain't the time."

"Will it ever be?"

"Look, man, I'm feeling the same thing you are right now, but this ain't the time," Bernard warns, his voice more adamant.

Fatima grabs my hand. Her touch calms me down enough to back down for now.

Bernard goes after his wife. Wipes his evidence from her face.

Fatima holds my hand tighter, gives me just enough strength to get one last word out. "Why did you let me carry a burden that was never mine to begin with? All these years, Brenda? All these years?"

Brenda stops walking. She refuses to turn in my direction, refuses to look me in the face and tell another lie. Nothing falls from her lips. No apologies, no condolences, no nothing. With her head down, she simply resumes her step.

"Do you want me to stay?" I ask Cory once we get back to his place. "I won't go if you don't want me to."

"I can't believe this shit," he says again. Those are the only words I've heard come out of his mouth since we left the hospital.

I know it's messed up. He knows it's messed up. No point in validating what we both know to be reality.

He fails to let me know if I should stay or go. I take his silence as his way of asking me to stay without showing his need for me to stay. He walks to the kitchen, I assume to fix himself something to calm his nerves. I debate if I should just leave, but I need a drink myself. Plus, he shouldn't be left alone, especially not at a time like this. If the shoes were on my feet, I doubt I would want to be left alone either.

Cory comes back out with a bottle in his hand. No cup. Pain riding his eyes like he has not slept in three lifetimes. I don't ask, just take the bottle out of his hands. Down a few sips to calm my own nerves.

Silence lives in his living room. Nothing but the sound of scotch burning the lining out both of our throats.

He fails to look at me when he speaks. "You know what kills me?"

I don't say anything. Let him talk once he finds the words.

Cory sighs, leans back on the sofa. Lets the cushions swallow him as he holds the bottle tightly with both hands. "I knew I wasn't the only one she was sleeping with. I always knew when she had been with someone else because she would act different. She'd be more emotional, more clingy. It was like she was trying to get me to feel for her what she felt for me, so she could stop cheating. She wanted me to respond to her the way her other lover did. But I couldn't. No matter how hard I tried, I couldn't."

I finagle the bottle out of his hands, take one long sip, put it back in his hands without him missing a beat.

"I never wanted to be a father. Didn't want to be like my poor excuse of a father. Sometimes I still wake up in the middle of the night and feel his hands on me. There's no way I would bring that energy into another life, but I was willing to put all of that aside. Not once, but twice, and for a child that wasn't even mine."

Piece by piece, I try to put things together. "Are you talking about the woman in the parking lot?"

"Can you believe she made me think I had a child out there for over ten years? What kind of woman does that?"

"Maybe she was doing what she thought was best."

He looks at me like he can't believe those words came from my lips. "That's a load of crap and you know it."

"Well... I can't really speak for her."

"Speak for yourself then. Would you have told me the truth?"

I'm caught off guard. Not sure if he wants to hear my real answer or one to satisfy his needs. "If I was sleeping around with more than one person and found out I was pregnant...hmmm." I think about it for a minute. Say, "I'd be honest and tell all parties involved. It's not just about me. And it's not just about the father. It's bigger than the both of us."

"You say that now, but I'll bet you'd do just like Brenda did."

"I beg to differ." I shake my head. "What she did is inconsiderate and selfish."

He swallows the last drop of the butterscotch liquid.

I sigh, feel lightheaded. "I'm going to be honest with you, Cory. More than likely, I would get an abortion. Even in the womb, babies can sense things aren't right. No sense it bringing it into the world to add to the confusion."

"Wish Brenda would've done the same."

Deep down, I wish my mom would have done the same too. Then I wouldn't be so messed up. I would't even be here.

Cory stumbles back into the kitchen. There's a loud noise. The sound of glass being thrown against a wall almost causes me to snap my neck in panic. Slurred obscenities fly out of his mouth when he steps his bare feet on the shattered scotch bottle.

My heart pounds against my chest. Rapid. Hard. I feel the pores in my forehead and underarms open. Fear leaks from my pores. I want to leave, leave this rabid man before he lets his frustrations loose on me.

As if he has read my mind, he storms out of the kitchen. "Fatima, you'd better leave." Destruction lives in his red eyes. Reminds me of the bull in *The Last Unicorn*.

My mind tells me to grab my shit and get out of there. Another side of me tells me to stay.

Cory comes toward me. His pace is mission-driven. He grabs my bag and jacket. "Leave. Now." Pushes me toward the door.

With my stuff being shoved at my chest, I don't move. I can't. I can't leave. Not like this.

"Fatima, please," he demands. "I don't want you here. Forget you ever met me."

"I can't do that."

He contemplates his next move.

"I'm not lea—"

He shushes me with his lips. Kisses me with the familiar, painful intensity. I kiss him back with that same pain.

Cory loses his balance, causes us to hit the floor.

The fall doesn't stop him. He gets up, helps me up, and marches us into his bedroom. He pulls his clothes off, then tackles mine. No kisses, no foreplay, no nothing. He inserts that hard part of him inside of me with a hesitance that lets me know this isn't personal. His strokes are long, deep.

"Harder," I instruct.

He does just as told. Takes his frustrations out on that soft part of me. Creates a space inside of me just for him.

Cory's quickened pace, the steady *thump, thump, thump,* from his chest lets me know he's reaching his peak. His point of no return.

I close my eyes, feel that salty liquid run from my eyes and into my ears. I open my eyes. Realize the tears aren't mine.

"What did I do to deserve this?" he sobs.

My lips are void of words.

He pulls himself outside of my rawness. I ache on too many levels to count. Can still feel him inside of me. Inside my head and my thighs.

Cory moves across the room. That hard part of him now soft. He has let his guard down. Shown me that vulnerable side of himself.

He swings his arms in the air, fights a battle with no opponents. Maybe life is his opponent in this case. He curses and swings some more. Does that for like five minutes.

"Fuck!" he yells. With both arms, he sweeps everything off the top of his dresser. Cologne bottles, books, any and everything go crashing to the floor.

I ignore the pain in between my thighs. Let the madman continue his tantrum as I grab my clothes with a quickness. He refuses to look in my direction as I pass by him. I trip over my shoe in the darkness, fall to the floor. "Damn."

His hand touches mine. "Sorry."

"It wasn't you. Tripped over my shoe."

He helps me up. Tells me he was apologizing for the way he took advantage of me seconds ago.

I put my finger up to his lips. Hush him because it was something we both needed. He needed to pass on the pain he was feeling. And what I needed was for him to make me hate him. I needed him to make me feel like nothing, so I would feel nothing for him.

That's what I wanted, what I needed.

But not what I got.

It has been weeks since my life took another plummet down south. Wish things were different, wish my life was different. Feels like I am back to square one. No matter how hard I try, I cannot get out of this quicksand.

Fatima.

Can't stop thinking about her. As if her life wasn't screwed up enough, I had to go and drill the screw even further.

"Uncle Cory?"

"Yeah?"

"Are you okay?"

I look across the table at my little nephew. "What makes you think something is wrong with me?"

He points at the four green houses. "That's the second time I landed on Boardwalk and you missed it."

"Cole, take your sister upstairs," my big brother tells his overly excited son.

"But, Daddy, look at…"

My sister-in-law intercedes, "Cole Jr., your daddy didn't ask you, he told you. Now get your behind up those stairs and take your sister with you."

With his head hung low and shoulders slumped, he does as told. "Yes, ma'am."

"I'll let you two talk," Dawn tells us. She kisses her husband on the lips. "It was good seeing you again, Cory. Don't be a stranger," she tells me before excusing herself from the room.

My brother doesn't waste any time reading me. "It's just me and you now, little brother. I know when things aren't right with you. 'Fess up."

As if on cue, the emotional wall that I had built inside breaks. Crumbles. Tears fall from my eyes as I tell my brother what I've been going through. "To know that I tortured myself all these years for nothing. I put myself through hell."

"You ever stopped to think she might've been going through hell right along with you?"

I cut my eyes at him. "I couldn't care less. To do some foul mess like that to a brother gets no sympathy from me. She should've had her facts straight before she told me I was going to be a father. There's no excuse for a lie like that."

"Cory, listen to me." He moves forward in his seat, makes a fist, pounds it into his palm. "What this Brenda woman did was wrong. I don't condone what she did at all. But, at the same time, you got to look at why she did what she did. Sometimes, you can be heartless."

I shake my head in disapproval, refuse to listen to this. "What are you trying to say?" I get up out of my seat. "You trying to say I deserved this? That's bullshit and you know it, Cole."

"I've got kids upstairs. Watch yourself."

"Naw, man. I'm not gonna have you saying I brought this all on myself."

"That's not what I'm saying at all," he refutes. "All I'm trying to say is that you have got a reputation with these women. Screw 'em and leave 'em. Nobody can catch feelings for you without having the door hit 'em in the ass on the way out."

"You've got kids upstairs, remember?"

He pulls me by the shirt, throws me back into the couch. "This is not a game, Cory. You cannot play with women's emotions like that. If you don't plan on getting emotionally involved with these women, stay from in between their thighs or this type of thing will keep happening."

I grab my keys off the coffee table. Look at my brother and shake my head. "I'm out of here."

"Cory—"

I snatch my arm away from Cole's reach. "Why do you always have to do that?"

"Do what?"

"Forget it. I'm out of here." I march straight to the front door without so much as a good bye.

Cole pulls me back, pulls anger out of me that I never knew I had for my own brother. I turn around, push him so hard he stumbles into the coffee table. The Monopoly board crashes to the floor.

I'm so heated, feel so out of control. My nostrils flaring, blowing out steam. I'm ready to charge at him, ready to rush him into the next lifetime like a bull kicking up dirt waiting for the *forcado* to wave his red flag.

I prepare for battle.

He moves closer. I see my father in his eyes.

I move back.

He keeps moving closer, he's closing in on me.

I'm up against the wall.

I put my fists up, prepare to do whatever I have to do to protect myself.

He doesn't blink, doesn't flinch. Fact is, he's stronger than me and he knows it, he knows that I know it too. He wants to fight me, wants to kick my ass. Wants me to see things his way, it's in his eyes.

"Hit me," I tempt him.

Again, he refuses to flinch.

We stare eye to eye, I see my reflection in his stare. See a weak, unstable little boy who couldn't save himself even if he wanted to.

Cole yanks my fists from midair, draws me in to him, lays my head on his shoulder, and wraps his arms around me. Hugs me so tight I can't breathe. Suffocates me with his love.

"I'm not your enemy, Cory."

I break down in his embrace. Cole gives me what I longed for my father to do. He gives me love.

"*I need to see you.*"

That was what the message on my voicemail said. Listened to it more than ten times. His words did not change. What I heard in his voice did not change either. He needed to see me just as much as I needed to see him.

Everybody and then some is out at McGlenn Park this afternoon.

I search the crowd for that man with the messy afro. Two ladies push their strollers away from the front of a bench by the sandbox, create space for my eyes to connect with the man I've been searching for.

He knew I was here, saw me coming before I saw him. His eyes already on me. Cory watches me walk toward him. My hips let him know I know he's watching.

We hug.

He smells of Right Guard and Shower to Shower.

Our hug does not last long. Both of us are uncomfortable.

I speak first. "Put enough powder on?"

He laughs, breaks our nervousness. "It's getting hot out here. Don't want to offend anybody."

"I see." I nod at the bench. "Wanna sit or walk?"

"I've done enough sitting."

"How long have you been out here?"

"Long enough," he tells me.

"It's nice out today," I say, not ready for our conversation to get heavy.

"Guess that's why so many people are out here."

I look at Cory. I don't know why, but I smile.

His eyes twinkle and he smiles back.

The familiarity evident in our eyes.

I ask, "You come here often?"

"Not really."

"So why'd you suggest we come?"

He looks away, says, "The last time you were in my presence, I showed you a scary—"

"Cory, you don't have—"

He stops me mid-sentence. Stops my stopping him.

We move up on the sidewalk, five or six people in tights and tank tops run past us.

He lets a group of noisy teenagers pass us before continuing. "When you agreed to meet me here, you said we would be real. Agreed for us to be honest with each other. Are you changing your mind? 'Cause if you are, you can turn around and walk back to your car."

I cross my arms over my chest. Tell him, "I'm not the indecisive one. Once I agree to do something, I follow through." Voice reeking with attitude. "This is the second time I agreed to meet you, remember?"

He keeps an arm's length distance between us, hands stuffed in his back pockets. Cory doesn't let us get too close. "Now that you've got that out the way," he pauses, rubs some sweat from his brow, "Can I apologize now?"

I turn from him, start walking back toward the hill. "Just let it go."

Cory doesn't move, he stands still where I left him. "Maybe it's easy for you to do, but I can't let it go. I showed you a side of me that you never should have seen. I'm not comfortable with that. I can't live with that."

I walk up to him, put my hand on his face. "Cory, I'm not scared of you. As much as you want me to be, I'm not."

He looks past me, walks away shaking his head.

"Did you hear me?" I catch up to him, get in his face. "I just told you I'm not scared of you." My voice rising with my desperation.

"I am, Fatima. I'm scared of me."

His truth jars me. Leaves me speechless.

Cory's eyes glaze over. He's not crying, but his eyes look as if they are drowning in a bad memory. "I've been scared of myself ever since I was seven."

"What happened?" My voice now soft and soothing.

Everyone at the park vanishes. In my eyes, it's just me and Cory. Us and our skeletons.

He takes the blanket from my arms, spreads it out on the grass. I follow his lead, sit down in front of him so I can read his face.

He doesn't speak right away. Neither of us say anything for what feels like a lifetime.

Slowly, his lips move. "I was in third grade. My class was outside for recess. A couple of the boys and I were on the monkey bars. We made a bet to see who could hang upside down the longest. The first one to let go had to do the winner's homework. This girl, Regina, came over with some of her girls. She liked me, one of her friends told me so. I didn't like her though. Didn't like girls."

He notices the that's-your-business expression on my face. Tells me, "It wasn't that kind of party."

I put my hands in the air. "I didn't say anything." Wave my hand for him to continue.

He does.

✪ ✪ ✪

We all lined up on the bars. I told Regina to keep count for us. She gave us the go ahead and upside down we went. As soon as my body flipped down, I felt stuff slipping out of my pocket. I hopped down to grab it before anybody could see what it was. I didn't care if I lost the bet, school work was what I lived for; just didn't want anybody to see what I had. Damn Regina got to it before I could.

She picked it up from the sand and held it in the air. "Why you got a doll in your pocket?"

"Give it back," I demanded.

The other boys jumped down. They didn't care about the bet anymore either. I had a doll in my pocket and everyone wanted to know why.

Regina ran around the playground with my doll. Kept yelling, "Cory plays with dolls. Cory plays with dolls."

I caught up to her. Told her to give it back.

She put it in my face, pulled it back. Called me a sissy. "Boys that play with dolls are sissies."

I defended myself. "I'm not a sissy. My mama gave me that."

"Cory's a sissy, Cory's a sissy," she kept yelling.

Recess was at a standstill, everyone was watching. I refused to be made fun of in front of the whole school. "You just mad 'cause you like me and I don't like you back."

She said, "I don't like you. You're a sissy. I don't like sissies." My classmates started laughing at me.

I thought about why I had the doll. It was a little stuffed black doll that could fit in the palm of my hand. Mama gave it to me one morning before I left for school. She knew that I worried about her when I wasn't around. She told me that if I kept it close, Mister wouldn't hurt her. As long as the doll was with me, she'd be okay.

The doll was no longer with me. I could see it, but it wasn't in my hands. That meant Mama was in trouble. I had to get the doll back.

Something came over me. Had to save Mattie. I ran straight for Regina, pushed her down. She scratched up her knee. Started crying when she saw the blood. None of that fazed me though. I jumped on top of her. Hit her in the face. Did to her what I saw Mister do to Mama.

Regina threw the doll at me. Teachers were running in our direction, yelling, "Get off of her."

I got off my rival before anyone had the chance to pull me off. I had my doll. Mama was okay.

❀ ❀ ❀

"In the back of my mind, I knew what I did wasn't okay. Regina had the same look in her eyes that Mattie would have when Mister hit her," Cory tells me.

"But keeping your mom safe was most important to you at the time. There's nothing you can do about that."

He nods. "And that's the scary part. What happens the next time I need to protect someone close to me, or myself for that matter? Knowing that I'm capable of reaching that point, as long as I live, something or somebody will push me to that point and I'll remember that day—the day I put fear in Regina's eyes, the day I put fear in my own life. It's hard to live in that fear."

I understand his fear. Saw him reach that point the other night. The night he found out Brenda didn't include him in the big picture. That's why he wanted to meet me in a public place, for my own peace of mind. "You don't want to be like your dad."

"Fatima, there wasn't a day that went by when he wasn't hitting on Mattie. He would hit her just for waking up. He hit his own kids because we were born. I hate him for that, hate Mattie for letting him."

"Why didn't she leave?"

"Said she tried." He shakes his head. "I don't know why she didn't try harder."

I think about Lauren's situation. Wonder if people stay in unpleasant situations for the sake of kids. Sacrifice their own well-being and the well-being of their kids because they feel they're doing the right thing by keeping their family together.

Cory interrupts my thoughts. "I'd rather die than continue that cycle."

"Don't say that."

"It's how I feel. Living like that ain't fair for nobody."

He jumps when I put my hand on his thigh. On impulse, I jerk my hand back. "Sorry."

Cory grabs my hand, puts it back on his thigh, puts his hand on top of mine.

I smile inside. "Can I ask a question?"

He nods.

"Why do you call your dad Mister?"

He rubs his free hand through his fro. "I started calling him that after watching *The Color Purple*. He was just like Mister in the movie—mean, had no compassion. Seemed like he hated everyone around him except his mistress."

"That had to hurt."

"You know what hurts more? The night after the fight at school, my dad came home and beat me so bad I ended up in the hospital. Mattie told the doctors that I got jumped by some jealous kids in the neighborhood. To hear her defend him while

I was laying up in a hospital bed took every last ounce of respect I had for her. She let him beat me for the same thing I saw him do to her. The pot calling the kettle black." He shakes his head. "That's when I stopped calling her my mama." He looks at me. "How is that for pain?"

My eyes can't take the hurt in his. I look away, flick a grasshopper off our blanket.

His fingers find their way in my hair, he uses those same hands of destruction to calm my spirit. He finger massages my scalp, rubs my worries away.

"That feels good," I tell him.

Cory guides my head toward his, his lips touch mine. I open my eyes, watch him watch me as our tongues make harmony.

He pulls away, searches for answers without asking questions. The reality is, we both need each other. We need each other to validate our existence. We need each other to survive.

"Where do we go from here?" he wants to know.

I shrug. "Who says we have to go anywhere?"

"Guess I'm just feeling you more than I expected and I don't want to stop what I'm feeling."

"What makes you think you have to?"

"I don't know. I never did ask if you had somebody."

David. I have put him on the back burner since I've been dealing with Cory. But then again, that was over before it even began. "What you see is what it is. I'm not with anybody," I say.

He smiles, nods. "How about you and me then?"

I blush enough to let him know that I am flattered. But I tell him, "Let's just stay where we are for now."

"We've already put our feelings on the table, Fatima."

"And that wasn't easy for me, Cory." I put some distance between us. "Now you're asking me to act on that."

"It wasn't easy for me either. I'm going to be honest with you, Fatima. I have never had feelings for any woman before, so this is new for me. I'm always the one being pursued, now I'm trying to get at you."

"Wow."

He continues. "I am not asking for us to be in a relationship. Not asking for nothing more than companionship."

"Isn't that what a relationship is? Companionship?" I debate.

Both of us mentally search the dictionary for the meanings of the two words. There is a difference between the two. A relationship means a bond, connection, link. Companionship is nothing more than friendship.

"All I'm asking for is your company. Be here when I need you. And I'll be there when you need me. Nothing more, nothing less."

I wonder where this companionship will lead to. Wonder if in time the companionship will move more toward him wanting a relationship. David tried that same mumbo jumbo on me years ago. However, I find my lips mouthing, "Okay," to Cory.

"Change is inevitable, Cory. You cannot run from it." Dr. Bryant walks around to the front of his desk and sits on top of it. "Why do you think it scares you?"

"Guess I'm afraid of let down."

He rubs his graying beard. "What did I tell you before about expectations? Change is about going into something *without* expecting anything from it. What would be the point?"

I argue, "Doc, we're talking thirty years of disappointment here. I can't change overnight."

"Okay." He leans forward, rests his elbows on his knees. "Coming here was a major adjustment for you, correct?"

I nod strongly.

He nods back. "My point exactly. You have been coming for more than two months now and I would say you have fared pretty well. Your apprehension is gone, you don't hide behind that wall built by self anymore. Is that something to be afraid of?"

"Guess not."

"Progress." He smiles. "See, change is about growth, evolving. Becoming the opposite of who you no longer want to be. It is a part of life that a lot of people miss out on because of fear. Those same people go to their graves unaware of how much they missed out on. I do not want that for you, but, ultimately, that choice is up to you. Everything is up to you."

He gets up, moves back behind his desk. My time is up.

He's right. I am making progress. Can't remember the last time I had a nightmare. Haven't even found a need to pick the bottle up either. And Fatima... Here I am crossing that bridge and making commitments to being there for her. Yeah, maybe I am evolving.

❂ ❂ ❂

It's close to nine by the time I pull up in the parking lot of Conscious Kneads. I whip out my cell, tell the owner I'm out front.

The lights on the inside cut off. A few seconds later, I hear heels clicking on the pavement.

"I *know* you didn't stand up in those all day."

She looks down at her three-inch heels, bends over, looks me in the face through my rolled-down window. "I may be insane, however, today is not one of those days."

I laugh.

"Just wanted to be girly for a few." She kisses me on the cheek. "I'm following you."

Fatima trails me back to my house. I see her xenon headlights in my rearview mirror. I can't stop from smiling.

My companion.

It was hard for both of us to admit to what we were feeling, but we put it out there. No turning back now. No turning into a pillar of salt like Lot's wife in the Old Testament.

She speeds up on my bumper, gets in the lane next to me, pulls up to the driver's side of my ride, window down. Yells, "Change of plans. We're going to my place."

I wink.

Now I'm following her.

❂ ❂ ❂

I pull in the garage and park next to her just like I did the first time. Again, I'm closed in with this intriguing species.

"Get comfortable," she instructs.

It takes me a minute to do as told. This time, I actually evaluate my surroundings, take in the loneliness I failed to see the first time. I let her know just that. "I see what you mean. Your place *is* a lot like mine."

"Told you." She looks around herself. "What the hell is wrong with us?"

Don't know why, but we both laugh, look at each other and laugh even harder.

"We're pitiful," she says.

I grab Fatima, pull her close. "We will be alright."

She buries her head in my chest. "You think so?"

I kiss her on her forehead. "I think we will."

We stand there and hold each other like our future depends on us making this work. What *this* is, I'm not quite sure, but we hug each other that long and hard.

Fatima slides her hands down from my back to my ass, grips me firmly as she plants a wet kiss on my lips. "There's more where that came from."

Both of us blush like it's prom night and we are about to have sex for the first time.

"Sit," she says. "I'll get us something to drink. I've got some of that Black Label."

I think about what Johnnie Walker represents in my life, what it stands for. Think about why I began drinking it almost two decades ago, think about who introduced it to me. "I'll pass," I find myself saying.

She sits on the couch by me in slow motion. "Damn, why the screw face?"

"Guess I'm just surprised. I never turn down a drink."

"Hmm," she says, hops off the arm of the couch and goes into the kitchen. Comes back out with two glasses of green tea.

I tell her, "It has been weeks since I last had a drink."

She snuggles up on the couch next to me. I pull her feet up and place them in my lap, rub the stress away. Do for her what she does unselfishly for others every day.

"Do you ever wonder how different your life would be if your parents never ran out on you?" I ask.

I'm not sure if she closes her eyes from my touch or because of my question.

"That's all I used to think about. Thought about it so much it tore me up. Couldn't focus on anything else."

"Why do we do that? People in general, not just us."

Her eyes are still closed. "Good question. I guess we like to torture ourselves. It feels better when we can blame others for our shortcomings. All I know is, had they not left, my life would definitely be different. How different, I don't know, but it would be different."

I say, "If Mister wasn't abusive, if he had loved us the way a daddy should, I probably would be married with a ton of kids by now."

My admittance opens her eyes, her feet tense in my hands. "You think so?"

"No doubt. My problem isn't with kids. It's my fear of what I'd do to them. If they refused to listen, would I use my hands to shut them up? If my wife pissed me off, would I beat her to make things right in my mind? All of that scares me away. Keeps me from making commitments in my life."

"Gotta be hard."

"I look at my brother with his family, want that for myself. Want to come home and feel like my hard work is well worth it. My sweat worth every drop."

Fatima gently touches me on my shoulder. "You can have that, Cory. If it's what you want."

I shake my head in disagreement. Ask, "What's kept you from starting a family?"

"Not sure I know what a family is. I mean, I remember my dad loving me. Remember us going on trips. Something was missing, though. At a young age, I could feel that things weren't right. Everything I thought family stood for dissipated when they walked out on me. These days, everyone is either cheating, living apart, or heading to divorce court before the ink on the marriage license dries. No one cares about family values anymore. We're both evidence of that."

I watch her take her locs down. Watch them cascade over her shoulders.

She gets up, turns the lights down. Lights a few candles, burns a couple of sandalwood incense. She moves as if her life doesn't make sense. Confused. Being pulled in many directions.

"You know, you're the first man to come into my house," she tells me as she falls back into the couch.

"For some reason, that doesn't surprise me."

"You know me well."

"But why?" I want to know.

"Never wanted to bring strangers into my place. Didn't want them to look around, see the absence of life here. Didn't want them to ask questions, learn more of me than I wanted to give."

My interest piques. "Why me?"

"Because, as we've said before, we're a lot alike. We're both victims of circumstance. We didn't have a choice in the way we were brought up. Didn't get to shuffle our own deck of cards. But we are here."

"Our past is what connects us to the present, the here and the now."

"Exactly."

Through the luminescent light, I see a flood forming in her eyes. I move closer to her. Wrap my arm around her shoulder.

She hits her fist into the couch. "I have got to get over this. I'm ready to get off this emotional rollercoaster."

I rub her arm, wish I could rub her pain away. "Don't rush it, Fatima. It will happen when it's time."

Tears fall from her vacant eyes. I don't know where she is, don't know if I can bring her back, but I do what she did for me weeks ago in my moment of weakness—I stay by her side.

She blinks, comes back into the present, lays her head across my lap. "Hold me, Cory. Just hold me."

I do just that. Hold her and let her know that I am not going anywhere. I hold her until the sun comes up.

❂ ❂ ❂

My eyes open. Feel softness around me. Realize I'm in Fatima's bed, alone.

I get up. Go to the bathroom to set my bladder free.

Fatima's in there. One hand holding her locs back. The other clutching the toilet rim for support. Her head is halfway in the toilet bowl. Remnants of the last thing she ate dripping from her lips.

"You okay?" I help her up.

She rinses her mouth out with water, pats her mouth dry with a towel. "Yeah, pushed the toothbrush too far down my throat when I was brushing my tongue."

"You scared me."

"Scared myself. I do that all the time, but that's the first time I actually threw up."

Now that I know she's okay, my bladder decides to remind me why I came to the bathroom in the first place. "Can you give me a second?"

She walks out without a word, closes the door behind her.

I handle my business, dilute my morning breath with some water, rinse the sleepy boogers out of my eyes. Go back into the bedroom for my clothes.

Fatima is sitting on the foot of her queen-sized bed. "Thanks for last night."

I kiss her on the forehead. "No need. You feeling better?"

"I'm good." She gets up to leave the room. "Want me to fix you something to eat?"

"What time is it?"

She looks over at the digital clock on her nightstand. "Seven-seventeen."

I decline her offer. "Maybe next time. Gotta be to work by nine."

She walks me out to my car in her garage, gives me a hug before I get in. Fatima trembles in my arms. "You sure you okay?" I ask again.

She gives me an unconvincing nod.

"If not, I can always call in sick."

That deep dimple pops when she smiles at me. "Thanks. I'll be okay."

❂ ❂ ❂

The number two flashes in my face as soon as I walk through my front door. Two messages.

I hit play.

"*Cory, it's your sister. Give me a call as soon as you get this message,*" Cora instructs.

"*You know who this is. Call your family.*" Cole's message sounds more like a threat than a checking-up-on-you message.

The phone rings before I have the chance to cut the shower on. I don't answer. Got things to do.

"Cory, are you there? Pick up the phone. Cory... Cory."

The clock is still ticking, I'll just have to call her back on my cell on my way to work.

Phone rings again, stops me in my tracks. Grab the cordless off of my bed, notice the Chicago number on it.

"Damn Cora. You calling me like I owe you child support."

I laugh.

She doesn't find anything funny. "Cole told me everything."

"It is what it is." Don't know what else to say.

"Why didn't you tell me?"

"Look, Cora, I'm just getting home. I need to hit the shower and get to work. What's so urgent?"

"I'm worried about you."

Last time she told me that, she made an appointment for me to see a therapist. "No need to worry. Dr. Bryant says I'm making progress." My voice drips with sarcasm.

"Don't be a smart ass."

"Hey, you're the one who sent me to him. I'm just letting you know you don't need to worry. Everything is under control."

She doesn't buy that. "Then why'd you try to beat up your own brother?"

"Like I said, I need to get ready for work."

"I know you are *not* trying to brush me off. I barely talk to you anymore. You make me feel like I'm one of your women when I am your sister."

Her comment offends me and she knows it. Makes me wonder if she said it on purpose. "I don't know why you would even say something like that to me."

"That's how I feel sometimes."

"You are my sister, my flesh and blood. You will never come second in my life. Believe that."

I hear a smile in her voice. "Awww, you do love me."

"How could you ever think that I didn't?"

She says, "I love you too," but hesitates like she's debating something else heavy on her heart.

I don't let her form the words, time won't let me. "I'll do better, Cora. Y'all are all I got."

"Thanks for coming with me."

Adrian says, "Told you I'll always be here for you."

"I know, but…"

"But nothing. Are you going to be okay?"

"This isn't a good time."

"Never is."

I silently agree with that reality.

"Fatima." Adrian says my name so sweet, soft like chocolate cashmere. "Is having a baby such a bad thing?"

It's hard for me to swallow that question, let alone give an answer. Pregnant.

My hand moves across my evolving belly. I think about when my mom found out she was pregnant. The same thoughts about ending my pregnancy cross my mind as they did hers.

"This really isn't a good time. Cory and I are just getting to know each other. This will change the dynamics of everything. Plus…never mind. Timing's just not right."

Adrian opens the driver's side of my Acura, moves out the way so I can get in, I close the door, shut her out temporarily. Start the ignition, roll down the window.

Her focus is on me. Stares at me so deeply that I have to look away. "Don't look at me like that," I tell her.

"Promise me, Fatima. Promise me right here, right now that you'll think hard about it before you do anything drastic."

"Why is it such a big deal to you?"

"Just promise me you'll think about it."

"I've already made my decision."

I pull out of the parking lot before I have a chance to change my mind.

❂ ❂ ❂

A car is blocking my entry into my garage.

"How'd you know where I live?"

"You've been avoiding me. Not returning my calls. What was I supposed to do?"

"Damn it, David. This is a violation of privacy."

He leans against my SUV, makes no attempt to get back in his car. "Did you really think I was going to give up just because you said it was over?"

"So you're stalking me now?"

"If that's what I have to do to get you to understand where I'm coming from?"

I shake my head. Can't believe I'm having this conversation. "Come on, David. Be grown up about this. We just aren't going to work. Why is that so hard for you to understand?"

I put my hands on my hips. Not wanting to hear his answer, I wait anyway. I already had my closure. Maybe this is his.

"Because I want to marry you."

My jaw drops. Don't attempt to hide my shock.

"I do, Fatima. Felt that way for a while now."

"Whoa, David." I put my hand up. "This is getting too deep."

He reaches for my hand, intertwines his fingers with mine.

"I'm not going to let your fear become mine. I'm not scared to express how I feel. I'm not scared of love, not scared to say it either. I love you, Fatima."

I snatch my hand back. "I don't love you and I wish you'd leave me the hell alone."

His eyes open wide. "You don't mean that."

"I do. I mean that with every fiber of my being."

"Humph. You were signing a different tune a couple of weeks ago when you were in my bed."

Damn him for reminding me about that night. I couldn't get Cory off of my mind. I needed something, needed someone to take the edge off. I needed to feel something different, other than what I was feeling for him. David was my only rescue.

I stare him straight in the eyes so there is no confusion. "That was a mistake. I wasn't thinking clearly. I can see just fine now. Me and you will never happen again, David."

He reaches for me.

I move away from his touch, move toward my front door. "If I see you on my property again, I'm calling the police."

Not long after David finally decides to remove himself from my property and from my life, I find myself driving to Patchouli's. I need to see Cory in the worst way.

The chime to the door rings as soon as I open it.

"I'm sorry, we're not open yet."

"The door was unlocked."

Cory looks up at me, tries to hide his happiness to see me in his eyes. It's too late. I saw him just as I'm sure he saw the excitement in my own eyes.

"Wasn't expecting to see you. What brings you by?"

I'm void of words. I lock the front door, make sure nobody else can sneak in behind me.

Cory steps from behind the bar, looks in my eyes, senses my mood. My desire for him cannot be denied. That warm part of me throbs in between my thighs, craves for him like Jada Pinkett did for Allen Payne in *Jason's Lyric*. Got me standing at the door with a dress on and no panties. I want Cory to lift me up on the counter just like Jason did Lyric. Want to feel him grow inside me insanely.

I move closer to him, feel the heat radiating from his body. I don't kiss him, he doesn't kiss me, but our lips touch simultaneously and we kiss each other like there's no tomorrow.

His tongue penetrates my lips. My breathing grows heavy.

I feel so good right now. Feel like nothing else matters, but at the same time everything matters. Confusion plays tug of war against desire. Questions that I already have answers to burn tiny holes in my head. Something about this moment makes my need for validation heavy like my breathing. Can't move forward without it.

I pull away, slow our pace. "What are we doing?" My breathing steadies, no longer gasping.

"We can go in the back," he offers moving his lips back to mine.

I turn my face, let his lips meet my cheek. Turn back to face him, keep my eyes closed. My tone is soft, barely audible. "I mean, really, Cory. What are we doing?"

His hands loosen around my waist. He pulls away without letting me go completely. I can tell he's annoyed. Can't see his face, but I can feel the distance in his embrace.

Cory takes a deep breath, exhales slow and long. Remnants of spearmint and watermelon Jolly Ranchers form a cloud around my nose.

"Look at me," he says.

"Can't." Uncertainty holds my eyes hostage.

He pulls back closer to me. He wants to understand. "Where is all of this coming from?"

This time I pull back, turn my back to him. Grab his arms, wrap them around my shoulders.

I'm no longer afraid because he can't see me. My emotions no longer have an audience. I open my eyes, let the tears fall.

There's a vibration on my backside. Cory's cell phone. He slides his arms from around my shoulders. Says to the person on the other end of the phone, "My bad, Cora. Things have been hectic on my end."

His conversation gives me the chance to wipe the evidence from my eyes.

"What's wrong?" Cory's voice reeks with concern.

I move away, give him and me both some space to regroup.

"I'm on my way," I hear him say.

"Let's go."

"Where are we going?" Fatima wants to know.

That was my sister on the phone. She's at the airport, needs me to come pick her up. I tell her the same thing Cora just told me. "Mattie has taken a turn for the worse."

Fatima doesn't say anything. Either that or I'm too busy locking up shop to pay her any attention. Feel like I'm in a daze. Too many emotions coming from too many directions.

As I lock the front door, I hear Fatima's heels clicking in the direction of her vehicle. I run to her, grab her hand. "You're coming with me."

Once again I'm dragging her into my life. But, just like the last time, she doesn't kick or scream. No objections.

The car is silent. Neither of us has anything to say. Too many thoughts traveling around in our heads. Mine are on Mattie, my brothers and sister. Wonder what they are feeling at this moment.

Never been big on silence, makes my mind wonder too much. Got me in a lot of trouble as a kid. Right now, there's too much to think about, but I don't want to think. I reach for the radio, want something to take my mind away from everything going wrong in my life.

Fatima grabs my hand, stops me from adding any outside influence to our inside silence.

"Why'd you do that?" I want to know.

"You're not missing anything. Nothing on the radio with substance anymore anyway."

She has a point. Ever since they took "Vibe for Life" with Akela and Jay-Love off of WKPI's afternoon lineup, I haven't heard anything worth listening to on the radio lately. They played music that had meaning, music that made you feel good. You mostly heard from artists that are kept silent on the recycled music stations. The Vibe Team also had poetry segments and mind-stimulating conversations that made you think about what direction your life was taking versus what new position you tried in the bedroom last night.

Fatima pulls me from my thoughts. "What are you thinking?"

"Nothing," I lie. Don't want to talk about the lack of wholesomeness on the airwaves right now. Could talk about it all day any other day, just not today.

Out of the corner of my eye, I see Fatima turn her head away from me. Her attention is focused outside of the window. Nothing but trees out there. "Where are you at?" I decide to ask. Maybe talking for the next ten minute drive will keep my thoughts off of what's to come.

"Nothing," she says.

"I don't buy that."

"You weren't thinking about anything, so why can't I?"

"'Cause I'm a man. Just because we're quiet doesn't mean we have stuff on our minds." I pull a bothersome eyelash from my eye. "Women…y'all are always thinking."

I hear a smile in her voice when she says, "It's funny how men and women are so different. Read in *Men Are From Mars, Women Are From Venus* that men can sit still and not have one thought roaming through their heads. That baffles me because I can't fathom not thinking. My thoughts are what get me through the day."

"Silence is golden. Sometimes you have to silence the mind too."

"Listen to you."

I ask again, "So, where were you a minute ago?"

Fatima plays with her colorless fingernails. "About the future."

"In what sense."

"Just thinking about how certain actions from my past have caused certain reactions in my present. Makes me wonder how things will be in the future from the way I'm living right now. What will be my consequences from the choices I make."

I'm not sure if she wants a response or not, which is a good thing because I'm at a loss for words. Maybe I should have left her wherever she was. Like Mattie used to say, *"Sometimes you don't want to know what's on grown folks' minds. Let they thoughts be they thoughts."* Fatima's words remind me to do just that. Let her thoughts be her thoughts.

A group of people are standing near the entrance to the airport. Looks like they just came back from Cancun. Their sombrero hats and overly tanned complexions give it away.

"Can't believe it's summer already," Fatima says. "Where has the time gone?"

One of the women in the group of vacationers pulls out her cell phone. She stands out from the crowd because her business suit clashes with everyone else in beach attire.

My phone vibrates against my hip. I pull up to the curb, pop open the trunk.

The woman in the suit walks over, drops her bags and hugs me like it's the last time she'll be able to.

"Good to see you," I tell her while still in my arms.

She releases our embrace, looks me in the face. "Just wish it wasn't on these terms," she says, tears in her eyes.

During our hug, Fatima gave up her shotgun seat and relocated to the back. I open the passenger side door for my sister to get in.

I introduce them before getting in. "Cora, this is Fatima. Fatima, this is my sister, Cora."

Fatima reaches her hand out. "Nice to meet you."

Cora cuts her eyes at me before shaking my new found companion's hand. "And you're Cory's what?" she questions.

"Don't start, Cora."

I look in the rearview mirror at Fatima. She diverts her scowl from me, closes her eyes, and leans her head back on the head rest. Something tells me I should've let her get in her car back at Patchouli's instead of dragging her into this nonsense.

"Well, who is she to you?" Cora asks me instead.

"Does it even matter?" I inquire.

"If she's in this car, riding with us to go see our mother, who, might I remind you, is on her death bed, then, yes, it does matter."

"Hello. I am in the car," Fatima interjects. "Cory, please just take me back to my car. This is family business. I don't need to be here."

"She's right, Cory. She shouldn't be here," Cora adds. "I don't want any strangers looking down on my mama."

"She's my mama too."

"Then act like it." Her voice grows more emotional with every word. "Don't do my mama like this. She doesn't deserve this."

I take a quick glance over at my sister. This isn't like her. She's in attorney mode. Her defenses are up, arms folded across her chest. Swear I see her heart pounding through her blazer.

I reach my hand over, touch her shoulder. "You alright?"

She stabs the air with a sharp thumb. Points it toward the back of the car. "I don't want her here."

I hear Fatima sigh in the back.

I've had enough. "What's going on, Cora? Where is all of this attitude coming from?"

Silence.

We're not far from my older brother, Cole's house. All of us are meeting there before we head to Mattie's. There is way too much tension in this car. It would look bad showing up like this.

Up the road on the left is a closed down BP gas station. I flick my blinker on and turn into the lot.

"Why are we stopping?" Cora questions.

"Because something's not right. We are not going anywhere until you tell me what's going on."

She slaps her hands on her thighs, doesn't hide her frustration. "We don't have time for this. Mama is waiting for me."

"What's going on, Cora?" I ask again. "Talk to me."

She covers her face with her hands. Has a breakdown in my front seat.

I get out, go to her side of the car, open her door, squat down next to her. "Talk to me, Cora." I pull her hands from her face, make her look at me.

"I'm scared, Cory. I am so scared." My big sister wraps her arms around me, pulls me close.

It all makes sense. This is about fear, not Fatima. Has nothing to do with her.

I hug Cora tight, rub her back with my hand. Give her more comfort than I can give myself. Tell her everything will be all right.

✹ ✹ ✹

The minute Cole sees the pain in our oldest sibling's eyes, he beckons her with open arms. "You okay?"

"Just ready to see Mama," she tells him.

"Me too, sis. Me too." He keeps his arm wrapped around her as he walks her inside the house without acknowledging my presence.

I walk back to my car, open the door to the back seat opposite Fatima, feel her frigid energy, but get in anyway. "I'm sorry about all of this."

A sniffle is the only response I get. She wipes a stream of tears from her puffy eyes. Her voice barely above a whisper. "Will you please just get me out of here."

I respect her wishes.

Outside the car, I give Cole a call on the cell. Tell him to head on over to Mattie's. "I'll be there shortly."

"Make it quick," he instructs. "We're a family. We're doing this together."

I flip my phone shut. This isn't the time to debate. That would only waste time, and there might not be much of that left anyway.

The car is silent on the way back to Fatima's ride. Through the rearview mirror, I see her eyes glazed over. I want to say something, want to know what she's feeling. Want to comfort her like I did my sister minutes ago. Wrap my arms around her and tell her that everything will be okay. If only life were that simple.

It feels like hours have passed before we make it back to the parking lot where Fatima's SUV awaits her. It's only been forty minutes though.

She doesn't hesitate getting out once the car comes to a stop, slams the door behind her before I have a chance to put the car in park. "Hold up, Fatima."

Her feet keep moving, heels keep clicking. She gets in her own vehicle, starts up the ignition.

"Fatima. Please," I beg through a tinted window. Fumble with my key ring as I wait for her to roll down her window. "Please, just give me one minute."

I can't see her, but she can see me. The intensity is so strong you'd think we were staring eye to eye.

"I'm tired, Cory. I am really tired," she tells me through a half-rolled down window.

"Take this." I hand her a spare key to my apartment.

She rolls the window down all the way, tries to give the key back. "This is too much, Cory."

I throw both hands in the air, refuse to take the key back. "It's just a key. I'm not asking you to move in. I just want you to be there when I get back. I need you to be there."

I'm irrational right now, my thoughts aren't clear. I'm desperate.

Fatima gives me an I-don't-understand-what-the-hell-is-going-on look.

I sigh, feel seconds ticking away in my head. "Right now, you need me, at the same time, my family needs me. I can't be two places at one time. Just be there, please, I'm begging."

"This is too much," she repeats, tries to hand the key back again.

"Please, Fatima."

A frustrated tear rolls down her cheek, making a statement on her shirt. "I'm not making any promises."

I watch her pull off. Her brake lights come on a few feet ahead. She backs up. We're face to face again.

My key is in her hand. She tosses it from hand to hand. Bites down on her bottom lip, her nervous habit. Contemplates if she should use the key or lose it.

Neither of us speak. Don't think we know what to say.

I clear my throat.

It jerks her from her subconscious.

She tosses the key in my direction. The sound of metal hitting concrete rings out like a flatline.

My siblings are all in the living room, impatience etched in their faces.

Dawn says, "They were getting ready to leave you."

I look at my sister-in-law; she's the only one who speaks to me. The clock above the entertainment center lets me know I've been gone close to three hours.

Cole gets up, gives Dawn a kiss on her lips. "I'll keep you posted," he tells her. He grabs an overnight bag from the corner by the front door, walks out the door still refusing to acknowledge me.

Dawn and Cora walk out to the car together. My sister is barely able to keep it together.

"You might want to stay clear of Cole," my younger brother warns. "He's not too happy with you right now."

"Is he ever?"

"I'm just saying."

"What's he gonna do, Carl? Beat me?"

"I don't know. I'm just saying," he warns again.

"And I'm just saying. He can't do nothing to me that hasn't already been done."

Carl picks up two bags from the same place Cole had his bag at, his girlfriend picks up a third. They walk out together.

I watch Cole pack all the bags in the trunk of his Expedition.

Everyone has a bag except me. Plans were made that didn't include me.

Tameka rubs her hand across Carl's face. He reaches for her hand, kisses it, kisses a diamond ring on her ring finger. She hugs him. "I'll be here praying," she says.

Dawn and my future sister-in-law walk back toward the house. Cole Jr. is in the doorway waving bye.

Carl sits in the backseat with me. The somberness in the car is congesting. I hit my little brother on his thigh playfully. Try to loosen the tension. "So, you finally did it?"

He rubs his facial hairs. "Been with her for two years. Marriage makes sense."

"I guess."

He keeps his voice low. "Who's your new conquest?"

"Why you say it like that?" I feel myself riding the defensive line. "You say it like I run around with a lot of women or something."

Carl shrugs his shoulders as if to say I do.

I speak loud enough for everyone to hear me. "Fatima is different. I like her."

Cora turns around. "You barely even know her."

"I know enough," I debate.

"Give me a break, Cory. These women are just out here to hurt you. This Fatisha chick is no different."

"Fatima."

"Well, whatever. She doesn't care anything about you."

"You don't know that," I argue.

She turns around, all I see is red in her eyes. "When are you going to learn your lesson? All of these women are the same. They manipulate you into believing that they care so much about you, but when it all boils down, they have their own agenda which does not include you. You need to wake up, Cory, for real."

"Alright, Cora," Cole butts in. "Just drop it."

I speak up. "Naw, man. Let her talk. Let her get it out of her system."

He looks in the review mirror at me, tells me the same thing he just told our sister. "Drop it."

Carl adds his two cents. "Look, everybody needs to calm down. We're just wasting time and energy on something that doesn't even matter right now. Mama is breathing her last breaths and y'all arc up here fighting about some foolishness. Arguing over stuff that can't be changed. Just selfish."

That shuts us all down, makes silence the only argument.

As much as I hate to admit it, my younger brother is right. Our selfishness has shifted our focus from the most important to the less trivial. There will be plenty of time to discuss who I date and how I've been played, but right now isn't that time.

We ride for what feels like days, everyone trying to find comfort in their own thoughts. The truck comes to a stop in front of the railroad tracks. The house we grew up in is within eyesight.

✪ ✪ ✪

Carl gets out first, opens the door for Cora. Cole isn't far behind. I am the last to get out, the last to face reality.

One by one, we walk to the front door. One by one—the way we entered the world—the same way we enter the house of the woman who gave us life. Ms. Alice opens the door to let us in. "She's waiting for y'all," she tells us.

Mattie lies in a bed of white on her back. Total peace written on her face. If it weren't for the rise of her chest, I'd swear she had already left.

"She's been like this since I called," Ms. Alice speaks again.

Cora makes a pained sound. Sounds like the life is being sucked out of her. Cole stays by her side, wraps his arm around her. It's too much for Carl to take; he leaves the room. I want to leave the room behind him. I can't. My legs are numb. Wouldn't be able to move if my life depended on it.

"We appreciate you being here, Ms. Alice," Cole says. He's the only one strong enough to talk.

"It's the least I could do. Your mama's been a good friend to me." Cole nods.

Cora shifts away from Cole and closer to our mother. She puts her hand on top of Mattie's. "Oh, Mama. Don't leave me."

Blood circulates back into my legs, gives me the strength to go to my sister. Cole puts his arm out, blocks my efforts. Shakes his head at me. "Let's give her some time."

Ms. Alice overhears and leaves the room first. Cole glances at Cora, then at me. "We'll all get our time."

Outside the room, Carl is standing by the fireplace.

"You alright?" Cole asks.

He doesn't answer right away, the pictures where our father is absent keeps his lips shut. "She had to fight every day of her life to survive, but that wasn't enough. Now she's fighting to breathe. Just ain't right to me."

Cole puts his hand on our brother's back, consoles him in a manly way. Carl breaks down.

I go to his side. Tell him, "This is the way Mattie wanted it. She's okay with this."

"Mattie?" Carl wipes his tears away. "Man, that is our mother. Quit calling her by her name like she's your first-grade teacher or something. She brought you into this world. She deserves more respect than that."

"Damn, what is this, Attack Cory Day?"

"Get off of yourself, Cory…"

"Alright, Carl. That's enough," Cole orders.

"Naw, man. Somebody needs to tell his ass."

My fists tighten, feel the need to come to blows on the horizon.

Cole sees the preparation for battle in my eyes. "Both of y'all need to knock it off." He directs his angst toward me. "And you need to be ashamed of yourself. Mama ain't even gone yet and you're up here trying to bring the same destruction into this house that Daddy did. I am not going to let that happen. This family has been affected enough. We are all we got now, so stop bullshitting around."

Cole stares at me until I let my defenses down. Turns to Carl and does the same.

Carl opens his mouth to speak. "All of us have been through the same crap, Cory. We all lived in this house together. Quit acting like you're the only victim."

"That's enough," Cole tells him.

"Let him talk," I tell Cole. "He obviously has a lot to get off his chest."

Carl throws his hand in the air. "I've said all I need to say." He leaves the room without another word.

❂ ❂ ❂

Once again, I am staring in the face of the woman who gave me life, the woman who took that same life away from me because of her own inabilities.

I sit on the edge of the bed, watch the staggered rise and fall of her chest. Put my hand on top of hers, struggle with my words. "Why did it have to be like this?"

She doesn't answer. Hasn't spoke in days. I'll never hear her voice again. That shatters the little boy deep down inside me.

My voice is just as shaky as my hand. I close my eyes and speak from my heart. "Mama."

Her chest stops in mid-breath.

This is it. This is how it ends for her.

My heart beats fast, almost like a timpani drum at the climax of a movie. I feel desperate, not ready for her to leave; not yet. "Mama."

As if on cue, her chest deflates and slowly rises again. It does that a few more times before my heart beats at a steady pace.

I lay down in the bed with her, wrap my arm around her chest, place my head on her shoulder. My emotions form a block in my throat, feels like I'm trying to swallow a cup of cornstarch. "Mama." I rub my hand back and forth across hers. "I wish things would have been different, wish I could take back all of the years I wasted resenting you. It was just hard for me to understand how my own mother could allow harm to come my way. You let him break me and you turned around and broke me too. That hurt. And I've been carrying that animosity around all of these years. If only time could rewind.

"You remember when I was seven and you gave me that doll to carry around whenever I was away from you? I felt so special. Just to know that you were trusting your safety in my little hands. I was proud to know that my mom looked at me as her hero. Yeah," my voice cracks, "I wish we could go back to that day and start all over from there."

I inhale long and hard until my lungs can't expand any further and hold my breath right there. Every bad memory, every negative thought I have of my mother, every ounce of hate that I manu-factured over time, releases from me in my exhale. I lean my head over, kiss her on her cheek. "I love you, Mama. Always have, always will."

My feet feel lighter as I walk to the door to let my brothers and sister back in the room. We all hold hands and surround the bed as we count the final hours. Alice is in the room too, sitting on the bed of her lifelong friend.

Mattie's mouth opens, looks like she's trying to say something. She doesn't. Her chest rises and we all know that she has taken her last breath.

"Are you sure you want to do this?"

My lips are pressed together, hard, refuse to let me speak.

Lauren rubs her hand up and down my thigh, says, "It's not too late."

"This is for the best," I finally say, *my* decision made.

A nurse walks from the back, a clipboard in hand. Her face blank as she calls my name. She doesn't recognize me from when I made my appointment just two days ago. I'm just another face to her, another paycheck. Another woman not owning up to the mistakes I made.

I follow her down the long hallway, refuse to look back when I hear Lauren call out my name.

The nurse rushes me into a room in the back, shoves a paper cup with pills, another with water, in my face. "Take these." She forces the anti-anxiety pills and pain killers down my throat like she doesn't want the opportunity for a change of mind to arise.

I don't ask any questions. Just do what I need to get this over with as quick as possible. She makes sure the pills are gone before she leaves the room.

I wish I had a bottle of Johnnie Walker right about now. Anything with the ability to numb me from here to eternity would do.

My mind drifts to the words in Ruby's journal. I have switched places with her. I am the one with the decision of life or death weighing on my subconscious. Wonder if she felt as nervous as I do right now. Wonder if she regretted it before she even had the chance to go through with it.

Outside the door, I hear hard footsteps. The nurse with the blank face bursts through the door like a chimpanzee on crack, scares the hell out of me. "Let's go," she orders.

For some reason, the staff has turned off their friendly charm and replaced it with total disdain for anyone who walks through the door with their hard earned cash in hand. When I came the other day to scout the place, everyone wore smiles and spoke with the softest voices. Thought I was in a convent instead of an abortion clinic.

She takes me into a room where about twelve other women are sitting in chairs, waiting. I can hear a few sniffles throughout the room. Regret for what's to come already settling in.

I find a seat in the corner to myself. Misery doesn't love company today.

In the back, I overhear two young girls running off at the mouth.

"I hope this don't take all day. I got things to do."

"I know that's right. You done this before?"

"Yeah, girl. This my third one. I told my man he need to start wrappin' it up or he gon' keep having to give me money."

Damn, did I just hear that? Is this really what the world has come to?

I refuse to turn around and look in the faces of the heartless culprits. Then again, am I really any different?

An older woman with years of displeasure wearing on her face like a bad memory walks to the front of the room. It's obvious that an introduction is pointless when she refuses to give one. She hands out a paper to each one of us, then splits us up into three groups. I am in group number one, the first to say sayonara to the burden growing in our bellies.

She goes on to brief us on what's to come. I blank out, mentally remove myself from the room until I hear my name being called.

I get up from my seat and almost fall back down. My legs become weak, I grab the back of the chair for support. The young girl in the back that has things to do laughs, has a good throaty laugh like this is all a big joke. I shake my head, look past her like she doesn't exist.

A new nurse escorts me to another room. She opens the door. Death hits me in the face. The room is cold, lifeless. Chills me to my core. I move away from the door, try to find warmth in the hallway.

"It's okay," she tells me. "It'll be over in no time and you can go on with your life as if this was never an issue."

Her attempt at comforting me chills me more than the room does. Makes me want to grab the little bit of gumption I have left and run as fast as I can away from this place.

"Take everything off and put this on." She hands me a paper robe. "The doctor will be in shortly."

I take my clothes off slowly, fold them up, and place them in a chair by the door. The room looks like a normal doctor's office, except for white sheets covering the machines. Guess they don't want us to see what crime we're truly committing by having life sucked right out of us.

My movements are mechanical as I climb up on the table. What I feel right now is nothing like I have ever felt before. My heart betrays me, makes me question my decision. "I am doing the right thing," I reassure myself.

Nausea waves over me, makes me more consciously aware of the changes going on within me.

I think about Ruby again. Realize that this moment makes me no different than her. My hate for her was purely spawned by this exact predicament, so, in essence, I hate myself.

"*It's not too late.*"

Maybe Lauren was right. I don't have to be my mother's daughter. I no longer have to carry around this feeling of being cursed. I can stop it all right now, right?

Wrong.

Why did this have to happen? Hasn't my life been unfair enough? Cory and I are in no position for this baby. We're barely able to stay afloat with the life support we've been given, let alone raise another drifting human being.

A hurried knock at the door jars me from purgatory. I pull my gown back down, take my hand off my belly.

Two nurses enter the room followed by the doctor. He looks just as unattached as I feel. "I am Dr. Ubu and I will be performing your procedure today. I am going to do an ultrasound to make sure you are no more than eight weeks. If you are, the charge is more and I cannot continue until paid in full."

Wow, talk about straight to the point.

All I can do is close my eyes and wait for this moment to be over.

❂ ❂ ❂

Lauren looks up into my bloodshot eyes, grabs and holds me tight. She rubs my back, soothes me like a hot cup of Theraflu.

In between snot and tears, I stutter, "Get me out of here."

She grabs her purse off of the chair I occupied less than an hour ago. Holds my hand as we walk out the front door of hell.

As soon as she closes the car door, I let the dams burst again. My emotions so out of control.

Lauren pulls some tissue from a box and places a few in my hand. She keeps a few for herself to absorb her own tears. Both of us too emotional to say a word.

We sit in the parking lot in silence for a few minutes before the ignition is started and the car is put in reverse.

The ride back to my house feels like forever, swear we're driving down roads I never knew existed. To the left, I see buildings I've never seen before. To my right, I see the same. Up, above the sky is the bluest I have ever seen; down below, the grass looks like it came right out of a European movie.

"You okay?" Lauren asks, drawing me out of my internal reflection.

"Either the world changed while I was on that table or I am seeing things much differently."

She makes a sharp right, then another right onto my street. "What makes you say that?"

She pulls up into my driveway, puts the car in park, and shuts the car off. Turns toward me with a big question mark written on her face. "Are you okay?" she asks again.

I don't know why I start crying again. Tears flow so hard, to the point I don't think they'll ever stop.

"Awww, Fatima." She rubs my back with so much patience. The drained look in her eyes pleads for me to stop crying so she can stop, but, regardless of how she feels, she refuses to leave my side. That alone lets me know she is a true friend and makes me cry even harder.

My emotions overwhelm me, cause me to hyperventilate.

"Breathe, Fatima. You've got to breathe."

I take a deep breath, try to gain some composure. Try to put my emotions in check, exhale in spurts. My eyes move to the window, see a pink stork posted up in my neighbors' yard announcing the birth of their daughter. How ironic. I close my eyes, inhale long and hard, exhale soft and slow. Put my hand on my stomach.

"Did they give you any meds to take for pain?" Lauren asks.

"I didn't do it."

It takes a minute for my words to register to her. It takes me even longer.

"You what?"

"I didn't do it," I repeat, this time sounding more sure of myself.

Lauren hesitates from reaching for me. The life that comes back into her green eyes lets me know that she's pleased with my decision not to cut life short, but I can tell that she doesn't want to come off judgmental. "What happened?"

I turn in my seat, back up against the window. Face Lauren so I can't run from my truth.

She turns and does the same. Wants to face my truth head on.

My voice shakes as I fight back more tears. "When I found out I was pregnant, I was literally torn. I didn't know whether I wanted to have this baby or run straight to the clinic without passing go. I was so confused. Part of me wanted a new life, a life that I never had and I wanted to give that to this baby, but the selfish side of me saw this as the end-all to all I had been going through. My life has never been easy and to have a baby was only going to compound to the hell I'd been through."

Lauren sits quietly, listens with so much compassion. She doesn't rush me or slow me down. She listens like we have been friends for two lifetimes.

"I would be at work massaging a client and it would feel as if I was smoothing out my own problems. Things started to make sense. I felt like having a baby was giving *me* a second chance at life. It was then that I decided to have this baby."

Lauren hands me some more tissue. I take a minute to blow all of the congestion from my nose, making my breathing just as clear as my conscience.

"I told myself that I wasn't going to tell Cory. Raising this baby on my own seemed like the best solution for me at the time. Plus, he was going through some things and a baby was the last thing he needed. But, when I went to see him to cut things off, my want and need for him in my life became so apparent that cutting him off was the last thing I wanted to do. Just as I was about to tell him, he got a call on his phone which changed everything. In the moments to follow, I lost my strength and desire to continue being a part of him. He made me doubt my own capabilities. So, that's when I made an appointment to cut the ties."

Lauren asks, "What made you change your mind at the clinic?"

"Ruby."

"Your mom?"

I nod. "As I waited for the doctor to come in the room, I lay back on the table. When I looked up at the ceiling, the words from her diary haunted me. I blinked a few times, closed my eyes and counted to ten. When I reopened them, the words were still there. It was some kind of subliminal message. I have never wanted to be anything like I remember her being, let alone find myself in the same predicament she was in. Feeling the connection to her was enough to make me change my mind. Those feelings of resentment that she had are nothing like what I feel."

I flail my hands in the air, say, "Forget all of that. Ruby is in my past, my dad is in my past, and Cory is in my past. Nothing that happened yesterday can be redone, you told me that. All that matters is here and now."

Lauren flinches, runs her fingers through her curls. "Fatima,

I'm not trying to throw a wrench in your plans, but what if your parents find their way back into your life?"

I don't respond right away. Wondering what that has to do with anything holds my tongue.

"Don't answer that," she says. "Forget I asked."

"Why did you ask?" I want to know.

She says, "I don't know. It just seems that, with your mom sending her journal, that there might be a possibility that she's trying to come back some kind of way."

"You know, I thought about that too." I hesitate, swallow the possibility like a gulp of cold water. "She'd be wasting her time, and if my dad tried to make a guest appearance, he'd be wasting his time too. There is no excuse for any parent to walk out on their child. Not one."

"So you're okay with having this baby?"

With all the confidence in the world, I say, "Yes."

Lauren turns her head and looks out the window. She looks back at me. "Can I use your restroom?"

I laugh.

"What's funny?"

"Nothing. Just the look on your face seemed so serious. I wasn't expecting you to ask to use my bathroom."

She smiles an uneasy smile.

I grab my stuff from the floor of the car, tell her. "Come on."

My house feels different to me. Feels warm and cozy. I look around, it holds a whole new meaning for me. This is home.

Lauren comes out of the bathroom, her steps labored.

I ask her the same question she's been asking me since we left the clinic. "Are you okay?"

She plops down on the sofa, her eyes red. "No."

I quickly come down off of my high. "What's wrong, Lauren?"

"When I was sixteen," her voice cracks, "I had an abortion."

I sit on the sofa next to her, tears forming in my eyes, yet refusing to fall.

"Isaiah and I were both seniors in high school. He manipulated me into believing that a baby would ruin life for the both of us. He said I wouldn't be able to graduate and he would lose his football scholarship. I knew how much he loved playing football and there was no way I was going to be a high school dropout. He kept reassuring me that we would have more kids when we got married. So I conceded. I thought I was doing the most sensible thing for both us. We both put our money together that we earned with our part-time gigs at the mall and headed straight to the clinic three days later. I found out I was five-and-a-half-weeks pregnant before they performed the procedure. The staff convinced me that it was just a mass of tissue. They said it didn't even have a heartbeat yet. It was all lies," she says.

I hold her as she breaks down in my arms.

"No matter how many kids I have, I will always remember how I felt when my baby was ripped from me."

There is nothing I can say. I almost made the same mistake.

She sits up, wipes her tears away. "When I went with you today, my heart ached. Not just for me, for you, too. I wanted to stop you from going through what I am still to this day going through, but the harder I tried, the more I realized that I had to let you make your own decision. If I got in the way, it would have been for my own reasons and not yours, so I backed off."

"Oh, Lauren. I never would have asked you to be there if I had known. For you to go through that…that wasn't fair."

She puts her hand up. "I'm just glad you thought enough of me to even ask me to be there for you. You could've called anyone, but you called me."

"But still…"

"But nothing. Don't worry about it. I needed to be there today. In many ways, it was a means of closure for me. I'll never forget what I did, but at least now, I can slowly heal from it."

"I'm sorry, Lauren."

"It's okay." She smiles and rubs the top of my hand. "I just want to make sure you're going to be alright."

I smile back with a nod. "I think I can do this."

"You can and you will," Lauren reassures. "And I will be here for you every step of the way."

"Thanks, Lauren." I hug her. "I know it's not going to be easy. It's good to know that I'm not alone."

She shakes her head. "I never want you to feel like you are in this all alone. Day or night, if you need me, you better pick up that phone and call me."

"I will."

Lauren gets up. I follow her to the door and ask her, "Are you going to be okay?"

Instead of an answer, she hugs me and gives me a kiss on the cheek.

Three days ago, Mama's ashes were spread across the waters of Lake Bushwell, five miles north of her house. It was a place she often found refuge, a place where nothing bothered her. She wanted her earthly place of peace to be her final resting place.

My mother, my father...that part of my life is no more.

No matter how I look at it, no matter how dysfunctional my upbringing was, to know that the two people responsible for my being here are gone, hurts. My foundation has been uprooted and replanted on the other side of the soil. Mister's death was abrupt, untimely. One minute he was here, the next he was gone. Mattie succumbed long before her diagnosis of cancer. She was dying slowly the moment she met my father. Together, they both rushed their ending.

In different ways, I mourned them both. My contempt for Mister wouldn't let me cry. His selfishness, his need to be with a mistress and love child instead of with us, made me want to dig him up just to shoot him again. It wasn't until years later when I realized that I needed a father. Whether the man was abusive or not, I needed him in my life. At twelve was when I finally grieved over him.

I mourned Mattie every day of my life. For every black eye, every broken bone, every drop of blood she shed because of Mister, I mourned her. The day I cut myself from her, I mourned her. The day I found out she had cancer, I mourned her. All the way up until her last breath was taken, I mourned her. While we stood by the lakeside, all that was left of her flesh lay in our hands, I rejoiced for her for she would never have to feel pain again. As I sprinkled her flesh across the water, I made a vow that I would be the man that my father never could be.

I would be that man for Fatima.

❂ ❂ ❂

Her SUV is parked in the back of her spa. I pull up, send a text message to her cell phone telling her to come out back.

Ten minutes pass, no Fatima. I flip my phone open, type her another message.

Still no Fatima.

The last time I saw her, she tossed my key out in the middle of the street. Her eyes told me she needed me, but her actions told me she needed to get rid of me. That day, I felt like I was being pulled in so many directions. My family needed me, Fatima needed me, but I had to realize that I needed me too. I got desperate trying to please everyone and still lost.

As much as I want to stay, I refuse to be a fool.

I put the car in drive, head to where, I don't know. I just drive. My mind racing just like my speedometer. Going nowhere fast.

My cell vibrates in my lap. Fatima was with a client, but is free now.

I flip an illegal U-turn, head back to the place of consciousness.

She's standing out back, her arms folded, leaning against her truck. She looks different. A newness registers in her face. Looks like she found the key to her existence.

"Almost didn't recognize you," I say, hand her a single red rose.

"Thanks." She inhales the rose with her eyes closed, exhales and shows me that deep dimple. Fatima rubs her thin, long fingers across her freshly cut hair. "I'm still trying to get used to looking at it myself. Had the locs for so long to where I forgot what I looked like without them."

I look her over again, love what I see. "Change is good."

She stands holding the rose in hand, waits for me to move on from the small talk.

"Look Fatima, I just wanted to apologize for the last time you were in my presence. Things were chaotic. I was stuck between a rock and a hard place."

Her guard is down, doesn't hide her vulnerability. "Cory, before, when I told you that liking you scared me, I meant it, and the other night proved why. You put me in an all too familiar position, you left me with no choice but to reject you, to run away from you." She rubs her hands through her hair, hesitates when she remembers her locs aren't there. "I haven't been able to stop thinking about you. Something inside of me won't let me forget. But it's just so hard and I don't know which way to go. You have so much going on in your life. It's so evident that you don't have room for me."

I reach for her, put my hands on her shoulders. Make her face me. We stare eye to eye. "I want to be with you, Fatima. I want to right the wrongs in your life. Shit, I want to right the wrongs in my own life. It's going to be hard for both of us, but does that mean we can't try? We can't give up, we've come too far."

She wavers, steps back. Doubt in her brown eyes. "You talk a good game."

I move closer. "Nobody's playing."

"But—"

I put my finger up to her lips. "But nothing. I'm tired of running,

Fatima. I'm tired of denying myself the possibilities of life because of fear. Somebody told me fear simply means false evidence appearing real. That's not how I want to spend the rest of my life. Let me be the pleasure in your life, let me be your blue sky."

"Cory, there are some things—"

I close her lips with mine, quiet her insecurities. Feel her melt in my arms and feel my heart skip a beat.

We pull apart when we hear footsteps approaching behind us.

"Sorry to interrupt," the woman says, "but your one-thirty is here."

Fatima covers her mouth. "Oh, my goodness. I lost track of time. Tell him I'll be right there, Adrian. Thanks."

I walk Fatima to the back door, tell her, "I didn't mean to cut you off a minute ago."

"Don't shut me down like that again. Alright?"

"So you didn't like my kiss?"

"Your kisses are the death of me."

We chuckle.

"I'm gonna let you get back to your client." I pause for a minute. "About cutting you off, know that we both have some stuff, but there is nothing in your life that I'm not willing to handle. I just want to be a part of your life and I want to you to have a part in mine. Is that too much to ask?"

She winks at me, her reservation still apparent. "Meet me for dinner. We'll talk about it then."

✲ ✲ ✲

I pull the chair out for Fatima to sit down.

"Thanks."

When I sit in my seat, I tell her how much I really like her hair.

"It brings your features out more. I thought your eyes were mesmerizing before, but they're down-right hypnotic now."

"Stare into my eyes, tell me what you see." She exaggerates her eyes like she wants me to see down to her soul.

Her comedic face cracks me up.

Fatima says, "My hair grows on me more and more every day."

"What made you cut them off in the first place?"

She rubs her hand over her barely there hair. "Long story."

"We're not going anywhere."

"Guess not." She scoots her chair closer to the table, leans in like she's about to share a deep secret. "When I turned twenty-one, I cut out my relaxer and made the decision to loc my hair up. My hair was a statement of my independence. I didn't need any person or any chemical to define me. I was going to stand strong all on my own. It wasn't until recently that I realized how misguided my thought process was. I was successful in my own right, but emotionally I was a failure. I had nurtured my locs with so much negativity, so much pain and hate. All that I had put into cultivating my hair was starting to weigh me down, my burdens became too heavy to carry. Locs represent growth, but it became painfully obvious that I was not growing. I was still stuck in the past. I felt like a contradiction, a hypocrite. Who wants to live like that? I no longer did. For my well-being, I knew I needed to shed me."

"That's deep." The whole time Fatima spoke she kept her voice low, never taking her eyes off of me.

Our waitress comes over, fills our glasses with ice water. "Are you ready to order?"

"Give us a few minutes," Fatima tells her, then puts her attention back on me. "It's not about being deep. It's about being honest with yourself and if you can handle that, then you can handle anything."

"I hear you." I slide the paper off of my straw, take a long swallow. "You thought about what I said earlier?"

She puts her elbows up on the table, places her chin in her hands. "I did. Long and hard."

"What did you come up with as a solution to my proposition?"

"You know what? The last couple of days has been a revelation to me. I've come to the understanding that I can't bear another's fears. My life is what it is. If I can handle me, that is all that matters. And as you can see, I'm learning how to handle a lot these days."

"That's great, Fatima, but you didn't answer my question."

She stares me in the face. "I'm pregnant."

Life vacates me. Heart stops beating, no breath escapes me. Feel dizzy, lightheaded. Swear I'm in the clouds staring face-to-face with Zach and Mattie.

"Cory, did you hear me?"

She knows I heard her, no need in telling her so.

My heart starts beating, pounds against my chest like a gavel. My sentence has been made. My eyes burn like hell when I finally blink. Feels like my eyelids have a million paper cuts on them.

"I know what you're feeling. Trust me, I felt the same way," she says.

I want to tell her she doesn't know how the hell I feel, but the acceptance in her eyes makes me keep my thoughts to myself. "This is a tough pill to swallow, Fatima."

"Maybe it's not for you to take."

I shake my head, try to clear out some of the clutter. "What?"

"Look, I wasn't going to tell you because I know what you've been through and because I plan to raise this baby without you. I want you in my life, Cory, probably as much as you want me in yours, but it's obvious that this wasn't meant to be."

I don't know what to say. In my silence, my thoughts shift to the promise I made to Mattie. "Never make promises to the dead," she once told me. Wish I would've listened.

Fatima gets up from the table. "This was a big mistake," she says before walking out of the restaurant.

"Fatima, hold up," my voice carries across the restaurant louder than I'd like. Folks glare at us as if to say black people don't know how to act in public.

I run after this woman who makes me forget about my problems, the woman who made me realize there's more to life than misery and scotch. "Fatima. Wait."

She stops running, looks around the parking lot for her car. I slow my pace. I've got the upper hand, I drove.

"Talk to me, Fatima," I beg.

"I tried to talk to you, you shut down. I'm pregnant and I am okay with that. You're not. There's nothing left to talk about."

My chest feels like it's caving in. I wipe sweat from my forehead, wipe my hands on my pants.

"Just take me home."

I want to say something, want to soothe the situation with my words. Nothing comes to mind. Nothing at all.

"This is exactly why I didn't want to tell you. You kept pushing, kept calling me, sending me text messages. I tried to forget about you, but you wouldn't let me. I am not going to let you make me regret having this baby."

"I don't want you to."

She stands strong, hands on her hips. "I am not going to kill my baby." She stresses every word.

"Don't put words in my mouth. I would never suggest something like that to you."

She lowers her hands from her hips, turns her back to me and walks over to my car. "Take me home," she orders again.

I take my time getting to the car, my brain doing somersaults in my head.

When Trish told me she was pregnant, I thought my life was over. I felt like taking her straight to the abortion clinic right then and there. I did not want a baby and if I were to be a father, she was the last woman I wanted to be the mother. I honestly wanted to kill the both of them with one bullet.

Damn. It's moments like this that make me want to crawl back into my mother's womb, separate Mister's sperm from her egg and cease to exist.

Fatima stands by the car, her strength disappearing by the minute. I want to tell her that I can handle this new opposition, that I can conquer my fear with her. Want to tell her I'm willing to accept whatever flaws, insecurities, whatever she has that makes her who she is. Want to tell her all of that and then some. If only I could.

I walk over to her side of the car, stand there and hope I can find the words to dissolve this tension I've created. "I'm sorry," is all I can come up with.

She pushes me away. "Keep your sympathy. It's too late."

"It's never too late."

She pulls on the door handle a couple of times before giving up. "Will you just open this door."

I try to get her to look at me. Turn her face toward mine. She turns it back every time I try.

I click the remote, open her door. Close it behind her. Refuse to take my eyes off of her as I walk around to my side. "How can I make things right between us?" I ask once inside.

"By taking me home," she answers without so much as a thought.

She shifts to the far edge of her seat. I watch her out of the corner of my eye, see how uncomfortable she is. Notice tears forming on the rims of her eyes.

"Cory." She pauses. Avoids making eye contact. "Like I said, don't think that I'm asking you to be a part of this baby's life. I plan to raise him or her on my own. I know enough about you to know that fatherhood is not an option for you."

"So you're taking away my choice?"

She turns in my direction. "No, you took that choice away when you told me you didn't want kids. I'm not putting words in your mouth. You've made that fact well known and clear."

"You're right."

"Good, now take me home."

"Listen—"

"Look, Cory. Quit avoiding the inevitable. We just won't work."

I refuse to let her dictate this. "We will work. I just need a little time."

"Forget this." She opens the door, gets out of the car. Pulls her cell phone out of her purse.

Fatima walks a few feet away from the car. I get out. Walk up behind her. Ask her what she's doing.

"Since you don't want to take me home, I'm calling a cab," she tells me.

"Hang up the phone."

"I don't have time for this, Cory."

"Just hang up the phone. I'll take you home."

She flips her phone shut, walks back over to the car. Doesn't wait for me to open the door for her before she hops in and fastens her seatbelt.

"Do you hate me?" I want to know.

"Hate doesn't live here anymore."

"Are you disappointed in me?"

She turns to look at me. "To be disappointed in you would mean that I had expected you to play a part in my child's life. So, no, I am not disappointed in you. Being pregnant is not my burden. It's my gift."

Despite my reaction to our under-the-cover action, her eyes still hold so much passion for me.

I reach my hand over to her side of the car, rub my thumb across her soft lips, my fingertips trace the outline of her face as if I'm seeing her with my eyes closed. She doesn't flinch, doesn't move away from my touch.

Deep down, I wonder if maybe, just maybe, I *can* handle this.

For the second time this morning, I find myself leaning on the toilet for support. "This morning sickness is for the birds." What strength I have left I use trying to lift myself up from the floor.

There is a light knock at the door. "Fatima, you okay?"

I jump when I see my reflection in the mirror. Look like I just woke up from death. Eyes swollen and dark, skin all parched. Lips ashy like a crackhead's. "Pitiful, just plain pitiful."

Whoever it is on the other side of the door knocks again. This time more determined. "Fatima?"

I swing the door open. "What's a girl got to do to use the bathroom in peace?"

Adrian takes one look at me and says, "Whoa, who you been fighting with?"

"My breakfast."

She bursts out laughing. "Morning sickness is a beast, ain't it?"

"Girl, is it. I wish somebody would've warned me." I chuckle remembering the visual I saw in the mirror a minute ago. "Was it this bad when you were pregnant with Marcus?"

"Let me tell you, when I say I couldn't keep nothing down, I couldn't keep nothing down. I threw up just from swallowing my own saliva."

We walk down the hall to the break area. "Are you serious?"

She nods. "I lost so much weight that I had to be put on an IV to make sure the baby wasn't being deprived. I looked like I was anorexic."

"That's hard to believe."

"Oh, you got jokes."

We both laugh.

"I may be a little on the healthy side now, but I was under a hundred pounds in my first trimester."

"Wow."

Adrian grabs her purse out of her locker, digs through it for a few seconds before pulling out an aluminum box. She pulls open my hand and dumps a few Altoids in it. "Since you got jokes, take these, chew 'em up, sip on some water and gargle. If you go out there talking to clients with that kind of breath, you just might put us out of business."

"That's foul."

"No, your breath is."

She doubles over in laughter. She doesn't care that I'm not laughing because she's too busy entertaining herself.

My feelings are hurt, but watching her laugh with tears running from her eyes puts a smile on my face. Next thing I know, I'm laughing just as hard as she is. I laugh so hard I start snorting like Steve Urkel.

"Fatima, you have a call on line one," Danielle, the receptionist, pages in the back.

"This isn't over," I tell Adrian before picking up the phone line. "This is Fatima."

Dead silence is on the other end of the phone.

"Hello?"

No one answers. The dial tone screams in my ear like lightning at the crack of midnight. I slam the phone back on the hook and march straight up front to the receptionist. I wait a minute for Danielle to finish ringing up a client.

"Have a good day. We'll see you next month," she tells one of our regulars.

I don't waste any more time. "Who was holding for me?"

"They didn't say, just asked for you," Danielle says.

"Was it a male or female?"

"If it was a female, she had a really deep voice. But then again, I don't know. It was a bad reception on the phone."

I lean on the counter, rub some excess oil from my face. Try my best to wipe away any evidence of worry. I want to yell, "I don't like it when people play on my phone," just like the crazy chick from *Chappelle's Show*, but I don't. I am the owner of this establishment. I need to at least act like I have some sense.

Danielle notices the perplexed look on my face. Guess my attempt to wipe it away was unsuccessful. "I'm not trying to get in your business, Fatima, but is someone trying to track you down or something?"

"What makes you ask me that?"

She puts her hands down on the desk, moves in closer to me. Keeps her voice low like she holds the secret to KFC's recipe. "This isn't the first time they've called. I've heard that voice before."

Danielle is right. This is the third time in the last week that someone has called my place of business looking for me only to turn around and hang the phone up in my ear once they hear my voice. "What exactly did they say?" I want to know.

"All they said was, 'May I speak to Fatima Scott?'"

Scott.

The name I dropped years ago.

❂ ❂ ❂

My car shakes as a car zooms by me so fast I question if in fact it *was* a car. I put my foot on the brake to get control of my vehicle back, get control of my life back.

I make a left into Grandma's carport. All the lights are out, appears as if no one is home, but I know differently. Grandma doesn't like light. Maybe that's why she's always depressed. Darkness does nothing but keep you trapped, and the longer you sit in gloom, the more dreary life becomes.

I use my key to let myself in. The dark, murky house reminds me of why I lived so miserably for so many years.

This is not a home.

It is so dark in here that nothing is visible, but I know everything is in the same place as it was while growing up. I walk through the living room and down the hallway with the familiarity of a blind person. Walk until I hear light sobs coming from a room in the back of the house.

The door is partially open. "Grandma?"

She doesn't respond.

I hesitate moving closer. This is the only room in the house I have never seen. Grandma kept it locked. Any time I asked questions about it, she shut me down quickly. This room was never to be entered nor talked about. I left it alone.

"Grandma?" I call again.

Still no answer.

Slowly, my feet carry me into the forbidden room. The further I move in the room, the more uneasy I become. It's a feeling that I can't even explain, almost like this room is haunted.

"Grandma?"

She jumps back, my presence startles her.

In the dark, I can see her wipe tears away. She doesn't think I see them, but I do, and I let her know. "Why are you crying?"

She shuffles to her feet, moves from the corner of the room to the bed. Every year of her age showing in her hesitant movements. "How did you get in here?"

"Used my key." I feel around the wall for a light switch.

"Don't. Leave it off."

Even though I don't like the eerie feeling in here, I do as told. I ask again, "Why are you crying?"

Light from the moon peeks through the blinds. I watch Grandma slowly sit down on the twin-sized bed. "How many times I got to tell you to stay out of grown folks' business," she says with no ounce of question in her voice. She needs me to respect her privacy just like she always has. Today is no different.

I sit down on the bed with her. Back against back. Neither of us ready to talk.

The bed bounces with nervous movement. I put my leg up on the bed, turn slightly in Grandma's direction. Lay my hand on her shoulder, feel her shaking. I slide off the bed and walk around to her side, place my hands on her knees. "Talk to me, Grandma. What's wrong?"

Tears fall on my hands. She still shakes underneath me.

Waiting for her to talk is impossible. I have never seen her like this. Never seen her shed one tear in my whole life. Something has really got to be wrong for her to be so despondent. "Grandma, what's wrong?"

She struggles to breathe through a stuffy nose. Hyperventilates for a second before pushing herself up from the bed. Leaves me on my knees by the edge of the bed. Walks out of the room and shuts the door behind her.

I want to go after her to find out what the heck is going on, but curiosity keeps me where I am. It's possible that this room holds answers to my many unanswered questions.

I raise myself up from the hardwood floor, my knees begging me to rub the life back into them. The light switch is between the door and the closet.

Grandma bursts through the door just as I am about to cut the light on. Her eyes the color of fire. "You shouldn't be in here."

I flip the switch upward. "Too late."

The walls are painted a deep shade of red, somewhere between sunrise and sunset. Above the bed is a black-and-white picture of a woman with her hand buried in a huge afro. Her eyes glow with such intensity, draws me in, almost hypnotizes me. I stare closer, squint my eyes to make sure I am seeing right.

"She was seventeen," my grandmother informs me.

I have only seen a few pictures of Ruby and not one of them compares to what I am staring at right now. Her eyes hold the compassion I never saw growing up. For the first time, I see some form of emotion in her eyes. Makes me wish I was the one taking the picture. Makes me wish I was the one she was looking at with all that love in her eyes.

The room becomes dark again. Grandma cut the light off.

Ruby's eyes still pierce through me, tugs at a piece of me that I never knew existed for her. Through the darkness, I see a side of her that makes me want to be a part of her.

"Come on, Fatima."

Grandma closes and locks the door behind me. Tucks the key in her robe pocket. "Want some tea?"

I nod.

"Good. Make me a cup while you're in there."

She goes on to sit in her favorite rocking chair, the one that looks like it's been here since the beginning of time.

I cut the faucet on, let the temperature warm up while I grab two cups down from the cabinet. Fill the teapot up with water and place it on the stove.

"No sugar, just creamer," Grandma yells from the living room.

I never understood how anyone could drink tea with no sugar, especially with creamer. Even tried it to see what all the hoopla was about. I almost gagged. That was some of the nastiest tea I've ever had. Never again for me, but I fix hers the same way she's had me fix it for years anyway.

She takes the cup out of my hand, takes a sip. "Now that's tea."

I sip from my cup. A smile crosses my face as I savor the taste of honey.

"You cut your hair."

"It was a time for change. Felt my hair was holding me back."

"Y'all women always doing something drastic with your hair when things ain't going right, like cutting your hair gon' make it all better."

I fill my mouth with tea to prevent from saying what I want to say. Instead I tell her, "I'm pregnant."

Grandma throws her head back, mouth wide open. Laughs so hard you'd swear I just performed a Richard Pryor skit.

"What's so funny?"

She ignores my question and asks her own. "What do you know about raising a baby?"

"I know a lot more than your daughter knew." My words grow bolder by the second. "And obviously a hell of a lot more than you too."

"Who do you think you're talking to?" Grandma says, rising up from her rocking chair with one hand on her hip, the other trying to balance the teacup and saucer.

I keep my seat. No need in both of us standing, raising blood pressure and all of that. "I'm just telling it how it is. If what I said offends you, then maybe it's some truth to it."

"Is that what you came here for, to shame me?"

"You started it."

"*You started it,*" she mimics, shakes her head while *tsking* me. "And you're about to be somebody's mother."

Her questioning my ability as a mother jerks my ego, causes me to bite down on my cheek. The taste of metal, the bitter taste of despise overrides the engaging flavor of honey that coated my palate seconds ago. "What is your problem with me?"

She gives up her balancing act and places the cup down on the coffee table. "What makes you think I got a problem with you?"

Her answering-my-questions-with-her-own-questions routine is getting on my last nerve. "As far back as I can remember, you've had this cynical attitude toward me. I was just a child whose parents deserted her and even though I was living in this house with you, I felt deserted by you just the same. You always brushed me aside, treated me like I was this big burden for you."

"I was done raising kids."

"Regardless. I was your blood and you neglected me like a stray dog."

My mother's mother gets in my face, gets so close I can smell what she had for breakfast over twelve hours ago. "You never appreciated anything I did for you. I gave you a roof over your head, fed you, clothed you, and this is the thanks I get."

"You treated me like a stranger. I was…I *am* your flesh and blood."

She throws her hands in the air. "What do you want me to do, Fatima? I can't change time. What happened is what happened how it happened. Can't change none of that."

I stand up, put a little distance between us. Turn my body back toward her once there is enough space separating us. "Okay, we can't go back, but what about now? Where is the love now?"

Behind her eyes lies so much that hasn't been said. Probably words I will never hear her share.

"Never mind. Forget about it. It is over, Grandma. I am finally in a happy place in my life. I am tired of going back. This is it." I take my key to this house off of my key ring, place it on the dining room table.

I look in her eyes one last time for any sign to change my mind. The longer I look into those hard eyes, the more I see nothing. No need for me to continue to be a part of her life anymore.

"This is it," I reiterate.

She turns her back toward me.

With the part of my life that I am growing content with, I pick up my purse and leave the part of me that kept me trapped behind.

"Don't leave," she whispers.

My feet keep moving, a few more steps and I won't have to feel any of this ever again. Hand is on the doorknob, ready to turn my life in a new direction.

"Don't leave me, Fatima." Her voice broken from her own disappointment. "I need you."

I hear soft sniffles behind me. The doorknob in my hand turns anyway.

"I'm sorry to hear about your loss, Cory."

"Thanks, but I don't really look at it as a loss, Doc. My mother's passing signified the beginning for me. It has given me a new outlook on life that I never would have seen had she still been here."

Dr. Bryant looks at me with raised eyebrows. "In what way, Cory?"

I move forward in my seat, elbows to knees, hands posted up under my chin. "I always saw my mom as a weak woman. She let her circumstances manipulate her better judgment. She lost who she was. Nothing mattered to her, not even her life. My mother was the definition of weakness to me. It wasn't until I laid on her deathbed with her that I realized that I had become what I despised about her. I had allowed my circumstances to narrow my own judgment. Seeing her at her lowest made me realize that I needed to make some changes in my life or I would end up swimming in the same body of water with her."

"Tell me about some of these changes," the good doctor says.

In my seat, I relax, let my barriers fall down. "I want to start with my brothers and my sister. I have sabotaged my relationship with all three of them and I want to make things right." I smooth out a wrinkle in my shirt. "Other than memories, my brothers and my sister are all that's left from my past. They are all I have."

"So, at one time, things *were* good between you all?"

I nod. My mind flashes back to how things went down the night our mother left us. The fuel had been poured long before that night. "Everything changed when Mister was killed."

"Mister?" the therapist asks, confusion spread across his face.

That slipped. I refuse to continue speaking of my parents as if they were some strangers I read about in the paper. They were my blood, my mother and my father. To refer to them other than what they represented in my life makes their presence non-existent. And if that were the case, I would not be here either. "He was my father."

His thick eyebrows straighten back out. "Okay. So how did his death negatively affect your relationship with your siblings?"

"I couldn't understand why Mama left Cole in charge. Yeah he was older, but Mama trusted me with her safety and I felt like I should've been left in charge. Being shut down like that made me distance myself from everybody. For years, I tried to make sense of her decision." At this moment, I feel just as unsure about myself as I did back then, but I keep talking. "Guess I've been carrying that around all of these years."

"Does Cole know you feel that way?"

"No."

"You've got to be honest with your feelings. Telling your brother is the first step in mending the relationship. It's actually the way that you are going to have to handle all of your relation-ships. Be upfront and honest."

I toss my hands behind my head, lean back with bad posture. Get comfortable in my resurfaced doubt. "I don't know, Doc. Once something has been damaged, it makes it real hard to fix."

"Your relationship might be on the sour side these days, but damaged, I don't think so."

A deep sigh screams my frustration. "Tell me this, why out of the four of us, am I the only one who turned out this way?"

"And exactly what way is that?"

"Look at me, Doc. Take a good look." I point my finger toward my chest. "Isn't it obvious?"

"Cory, listen to me when I say this, and listen with your ears, not your emotions," he says moving forward in his seat. "There is nothing wrong with you. Two months ago, when you first walked through my door, it *was* obvious that you were in need of help. But that was yesterday. Today is a different story."

"Was I that bad?" I laugh even though I don't see a thing funny.

He shakes his head, no smile etched on his face. "Your only problem is that you use Cory as an excuse, as a scapegoat."

I rub my sweaty palms on my pants, feel hot like I'm in the frying pan.

"The first step in anything is acceptance. You have made that move; now it is time to move on from there."

"So, basically, I am the one holding me back?"

His head bobs up and down. "You tend to play the 'what if' game instead of focusing on what actually is. If you allow life to take its destined course, you will find that all of your worry has been in vain. Life is what it is, my friend. What has happened cannot be reversed, nor should it negatively mold us into beings afraid of taking steps out of the box that our adverse upbringings have placed us in. This is your life, Cory. Think about what you plan to do with what's left of it."

I run my fingers through my hair, try to manually process all that he is giving me.

"Do you like your life?"

I give an honest answer. "No."

"Okay. Let me ask you this, say one Sunday afternoon, you're sitting in front of the TV and you flip the channel to a movie that's just beginning. The title really piques your interest and you're already coming up with your own scenarios of how it's going to be in your head. But, a few minutes into the movie, you realize that it's not what you thought it was going to be. What do you do?"

"I'd change the channel, of course."

He claps his hands like I just answered the million dollar question. "That's right, you change the channel." He leans back in his seat as if he has nothing else to say. A big smile spread across his face.

"Um, okay," I say, my face in an I-don't-get-it expression.

The good doctor moves back forward in his seat, arms crossed on top of the desk. "Change the channel, Cory. Just like when watching television, if you don't like what you see, you change the channel. Take the same action with your life. If you don't like what you see when you look at your life, change it. Life is about perception. You can look at an object, but how you *see* is what makes all the difference in the world. How you perceive your life is how you live it."

Dr. Bryant's words marinate in my thoughts. It makes more sense to me now than it ever had before. Seems so basic, so easy. Instead, I added my own formula to the equation; one plus two didn't equal three for me. I forced myself into believing that, no matter how things added up, I was still destined to follow my father's history. All these years, my reaction to the actions of another plagued me like chickenpox on a five-year-old.

"Cory," he clears his throat, "I do not see a reason for you to continue with our sessions. I am confident that you have what you need to live a prosperous, most fulfilling life." He taps his pen on a tablet of paper. "What are your thoughts about that?"

My head throbs, the room suddenly suffocates me. I try to keep my composure, but my right leg rocks back and forth, giving my air of confidence away. Feel the anxiety creeping back in. "What if you're wrong? What if I'm not ready to go at life alone?"

The man old enough to be my father sits silently as he writes a few things on his tablet. "Do you believe that you are anything like your mother and father?"

I search deep within, think about everything I have been through. The abuse, the lies, the tears, the hate, the regret. I think about all of that. Think about Fatima and when she told me she was pregnant, hitting her was the farthest thing from my mind. Every time my dad found out about another baby, my mother paid the price. And every time my mother had a baby, she stayed in the same place; never left. I don't want to be like either of them. With all the certainty I can muster up at the moment, I shake my head. "Can't say that I am."

"Then what are you afraid of?"

My biggest fear, yet again, echoes from my lips. "I'm going to be a father."

The pen falls out of his hand, he sits back in his seat with his arms strapped across his chest. "Whoa. I was not expecting that."

"And you're always talking to me about expectations."

"Yeah, I know." His lips form an uneasy smile. "So, obviously this was not good news to you, especially after your situation with Brenda and then losing the baby with Trish."

I frown at the mention of both of their names. "Let's not go there." I dig my finger through my afro, searching for the spot giving me grief. When I find that itch, I scratch it hard enough to draw blood.

"How did you end up getting Trish pregnant again?"

The doctor is well aware how I feel about Trish. "I met someone."

"Oh, I see." He flips a few pages in a folder on his desk. I assume the folder is mine. "Considering what happened with Brenda, are you sure this one is yours?" He throws that question out like asking me if I want cream in my coffee.

With all of the confidence in the world, I nod.

"Okay, now that that is settled. Does this woman know your stance on fatherhood?"

I nod again. "It's all messed up now, Doc."

"Well, pull out the iron and steam the wrinkles out."

"It's not that easy."

He picks his pen up again, scribbles some more stuff down on paper. "So what are you planning to do about it?"

I tell him the same thing I keep telling myself. "I want her, I want to be in her life." I wipe my hand down my face. "Given my history, what would you do in this situation?"

He looks at me with disciplined eyes. "I can't make your decisions for you, Cory. My job is to help you, to lead you in the right direction." He scratches his graying beard. "In a situation like this, you have to do what you feel is best. If you want her in your life like you say, you have to be able to accept her and all that she comes with. Baby or not. But ultimately it *is* your call."

Fatima means a great deal to me. Losing her would be like losing part of myself, even though I barely know her. I just can't see going on without her being part of my world. "I want her," I say again.

"Well, you know what you have to do to make that possible."

First things first.

As hot as it is outside, a cold chill passes over me. Makes me shudder with anticipation as my hand reaches for the doorbell.

A few seconds pass, no one comes to the door. I wait a few more seconds before I ring the doorbell again.

The wooden door opens slowly. Cole stares at me through the glass door before letting me in. "Cory."

I walk in, shutting the door behind me.

"You been out there long?" he asks.

I follow his lead to the living room, sit down across from him. "Maybe five minutes or so."

"Samantha had me up all night with a bad cold she caught from one of her classmates." He rubs sleep from his eyes. "Been dozing in and out all day."

"She feeling better?"

"Her temp was pretty high last night, but Dawn and I doped her up and brought it back down. She's sleep now."

"Good. How are you holding up?"

He yawns. "Tired. Seems like we just got back from Mississippi, now this. Dawn hasn't been feeling good either. Rest is the last thing a brother is getting around here."

"What's wrong with Dawn?"

Cole's eyes are sunken in, swallowed by his expanding cheeks. "We're about to have an addition to the family. She's six weeks pregnant."

The news of a new niece or nephew for me catches me off guard.

He laughs. "You look just as shocked as I did when she showed me the plus sign on the pregnancy test."

His laugh brings a smile to my face. Making amends with my family wasn't such a bad move after all. "I thought you said y'all were done after Samantha."

"I did too. You know how that goes," he says with half-squinted eyes.

"Don't I."

Our eyes connect, his eyes asking me what brings me by, mine confessing what my mouth can't quite make out, at least not yet. He kicks his foot up on the coffee table, leans back in his recliner.

"Daaaaaaddy," a voice calls from upstairs just as Cole gets comfortable.

"It's been like this all night," he tells me in between a yawn. "Duty calls."

As Cole walks up the stairs to comfort his ill daughter, I see him in a different light. He no longer represents a man trying to rule my life. It was not his fault that our mother wanted him to be in charge. He was the oldest male and it was that technicality that prepared him for his role now—a father.

He jogs back down the stairs shaking his head. "That child called me like she was in pain or something. Had me running up there 'cause she wanted some cotton-pickin' ice cream." He sucks his teeth as the recliner welcomes him back. "That's your niece, though."

"Let me go check up on the little miss."

"Watch out. She's in one of her talkative moods. She might keep you up there all day," he says with an I'm-glad-to-get-a-break tone in his voice. "Yesterday, she had me doing her Barbie's hair."

"Quit playing. She told me she stopped playing with dolls when she was six because she was too old."

He laughs. "All right. You've been warned."

I discard Cole's advice and head up the stairs anyway. At the top, I turn toward my left, push open the door with the pink ribbon on the handle. My niece lies in a bed of fluffy pink, looks like a bed of cotton candy. Her face a burnt shade of pale.

"Uncle Cory," she exclaims. Her voice excited and stuffy.

I walk up to the bed, lips spread from ear to ear. "How's my favorite niece feeling?" I give her a warm kiss on her even warmer forehead.

She wraps her frail arms around my neck, whispers in my ear, "That's 'cause I'm your only niece."

Kids are too smart for their own good. "You're right, but you would still be my most favorite." I sit down on the bed next to her.

"Mommy might be carrying a little girl in her belly. You probably gonna tell her the same thing, I bet."

Her awareness to the addition to their family doesn't surprise me. There is not too much that goes on around here that she doesn't know about. "So, you're ready to be a big sister?"

"Yes." She wipes her runny nose while looking around the pink room. "I hope it's a girl, so she can have my room. I'm getting too old for pink anyway."

That cracks me up.

She looks at me out of the corner of her eye and joins in my laughter.

"I don't know what your parents are going to do with you." I give her another kiss on her forehead before getting up from the bed. "You need your uncle to get anything for you?"

My too-grown niece lowers her voice to a whisper. "Can you bring me some ice cream?"

"What?"

She sucks her teeth. "You heard me."

"Why are you whispering then?"

Her eyes divert toward her bedroom door. "See, Daddy's mad 'cause he's getting bigger, so he's trying to put the whole family on a diet. That's not fair, right?"

"Tell you what, I'll see what I can do."

"Thanks, Uncle Cory."

Closing the door behind me on my way out of her room, I can't help, but laugh. That little girl is too much for her own good.

❂ ❂ ❂

Cole is snoring deep when I get back down stairs. I grab my keys off of the coffee table, head toward to the front door. I should've called before I came.

"I know you ain't leaving, Cory," he states before I can get out the door good enough.

"This wasn't a good time for me to just drop by. Get some rest. I'll call you."

"Sit down," he orders.

I shut the door behind me, find myself back on the sofa across from him.

His eyes remain closed as he speaks to me. "We haven't talked since we left Mama's, barely talked while we were there. You haven't picked up the phone to reach out in weeks and now you're in my living room. You came out this way for a reason, now speak."

Dr. Bryant said that in order for me to move on, I had to let go. If I keep holding on to my animosity of the past, I'll never see who I really am. "What happened to us, Cole?"

His hand reaches to the side of the recliner, pulls the lever to bring him to the upright position. He opens his eyes, stares at me. "What makes you think something happened to us?"

I see what he is doing. He wants me to talk, for me to answer my own questions. "Look at us, we barely talk anymore."

"We've been that way for years, Cory."

"I know, but why?"

He shrugs his shoulders.

My lips are dry. Licking them doesn't help, doesn't give me the satisfaction I need. A tube of Carmex is in my pocket. I pull it out, glide a little on. It burns, but anything is better than them feeling all dry and cracked. I put it back in my pocket, fiddle around with the magazines on the coffee table.

"If you don't start talking…"

I toss the *Essence* magazine back on the table, don't know why I'm stalling. "Look, man, I'm just trying to make sense of a lot of stuff in my life right now. The way I have been living ain't right."

"Quit using words that aren't in the vocabulary," he interrupts.

"You use the word, why can't I?"

He moves forward in his seat to get my attention. "Because you know better."

"If I know better, then you do too." I clear the nervousness from my throat. "What's your problem with me?"

"I don't have a problem with you. I just know you know better. You're educated, you shouldn't talk less than such."

"I guess."

"You guess? You have always been intelligent, always been too smart for your own good. Maybe that's where your niece gets it from, 'cause she sure didn't get it from me." His face grows more serious. "I don't know if you remember my struggle with making good grades through high school. I barely graduated. My failure brought disappointment to Mama's eyes, but when you showed her your all A's, her eyes would light up bright enough to illuminate the whole world. You were her trophy child. That was hard on me, especially since I was the one keeping food on our table and clothes on our backs. If it weren't for my sacrifice, Lord knows where we'd be. So I made myself try harder, I was going to get Mama to look at me the same way she did you. I never accepted less of myself and it kills me that you do."

I am taken aback by his confession. "Wow, I never knew that."

"How would you? Your head was stuck too far up your own behind to see any differently. You saw what you wanted to see then, just like you see what you want to see now."

Again, I grab my keys from the table. "I did not come here for this."

"Then what did you come for?"

"I came to try and make things right between us."

He stands up, reaches for the keys in my hand. "You're not leaving until we let go of all this tension time has built between us."

We stand, eye to eye. Neither of us letting go of the keys in my hand.

My head nod acknowledges the fact that he is right. It's time for me to quit running, plus, this is what I came for. I came for us to be brothers and not remain strangers.

The grip in my hand relaxes, we both take our seats; the threat is gone.

"I've been jealous of you," I confess unable to look him in the eye when I say that.

"Why?"

"In my eyes, I saw *you* as Mama's prized possession. She left you in charge, made you the ruler of Zamunda."

Cole can't disguise the smile on his face, but he tells me to keep my focus. "We're having a serious conversation here."

"You're right."

"Cory." He pauses to dig a fallen eyelash out of his eye. "My position in the household was nothing for you to be jealous about. I didn't have time to be a kid. I had to get a job, put all my dreams on hold. Friends were unheard of for me. My teenage life was taken away from me. I felt like all of the responsibility was put on me. That was too much pressure."

I tell him, "None of that mattered to me. I wanted to be the one to take care of the family. Mama made me feel like Superman and putting you in charge was like giving me a shot of kryptonite. That made me feel like a failure."

"Sounds like we were both jealous of each other."

I absorb the warmness in this house, look at pictures of my

brother and his happy family all around his house. "Yeah, well, at least one of us refused to let their jealousy affect making a better life for himself."

"Having pity parties for yourself won't give you a different outcome, so stop having them."

"You sound like my counselor."

"Probably because he sees the same potential I've seen in you since day one. You just need to see it in yourself. That's all Carl and I were trying to get you to see back in Mississippi."

I bob my head as if an old school hip-hop song is on repeat in my head, bite down on the inside of my bottom lip. "It *has* been a struggle, but every day my sight becomes clearer. When I think of how Cora went off to law school and found her soul mate and married him, then you and Dawn and the kids, and now Carl is about to make that step, I can't help but feel incomplete, like my life hasn't added up to anything. Like all the tears were shed in vain."

He clears his throat a couple of times, making it clear that his fatigue is hitting him hard. "That's because you keep comparing yourself. Live your life, Cory. We all have to take different paths to get to the same destination. Some longer than others, but we all eventually get there." He yawns long and hard.

"I want to make it, I want what you all have."

He says, "If you want it you can have it."

I nod in agreement. Fatima's deep-dimpled smile comes to mind. She is who I want to have it with. "I'm going to get it," I tell him while rising from the sofa.

He follows my lead and gets up from his recliner. "I was never trying to be your father, Cory. I apologize if you ever felt as if I was. I could never be him."

"And I apologize for being the family headache."

Cole pulls me in to him. "You always were a meathead."

We laugh in each other's arms, giving each other a hug so tight it signifies that everything is going to be alright.

"So, we good?" he makes clear before separating our embrace.

I deliver an ultimatum. "On one condition."

He pulls back and looks at me with a raised eyebrow. "Which is?"

"You let me take a bowl of ice cream up to my favorite niece."

31 / FATIMA

Leaving Grandma Pearl was the last thing I wanted to do, but I had to leave for me or else I'd be stuck trying to clean up her life right along with mine.

First order of business once back at my place is cutting on the shower as far to the left as possible, well, as far as I can stand it. As the steam swallows the bathroom, I step back out into my bedroom, grab a bottle of Women's Own Massage Oil that Adrian gave me as a gift months back from a friend of hers who sold Warm Spirit before they closed the company.

My reflection in the full length mirror in the corner of my room catches my attention. Up until this moment, I had never realized how much I favor Ruby. Minus the afro, I am the spitting image of the picture that hung above her bed. From my big eyes and long, curved eyelashes that need no mascara, to the deep dimple in my left cheek and tanned freckles on the tips of my nose.

I am part of her.

She is part of me.

With the bottle of oil in one hand, I use my other to copy the pose my mother made in her photograph. I push my chin out, lean my head back. Softly poke my lips out like I am about to give someone a kiss, shrink my eyes to tiny slits. "No, that's not it," I tell my reflection. I look more like I'm trying to seduce someone.

I relax my chin a little, slightly curve my lips upward, open up my eyes more. "Nope, that's not it either." Need my face to look more natural.

I close my eyes, try to recapture a picture that meant a thousand words. Wonder what she was thinking about when the picture was snapped.

My eyes open and travel down to my unbuttoned jeans, jeans that can no longer be buttoned; my stomach won't allow it. I unzip them and let them fall to the ground, step out of them and my panties at the same time. Raise my black baby tee up over my head, unfasten by bra. My attention is drawn to my belly on which I rub my hand in circular motions. Brings a smile to my face just thinking about the life growing inside of me. Run my fingers through my barely there hair.

Cory.

Warmness pulsates through my veins at the thought of him. The same warmth I feel when he rubs his hands through my hair.

My hand travels from my hair and strokes the softness of my cheek, the fullness of my lips. Never take my eyes off my reflection as I pour oil into my hand, put the bottle down on the floor. My imagination makes me believe Cory is standing behind me, his hands massaging the oil into my skin, penetrating places that I could never reach. He is so gentle with his touch, gives me butter-flies. His fingertip traces the outline of my face, my lips, my nose, my eyes. His fingers dance in the curls on top of my head as he pulls my face toward his, and whispers sweet-nothings in my ear.

I breathe for him.

He breathes for me.

A smile creeps across my face, not on the surface, but one deep beneath the surface as if I am trying to prevent my excitement from showing.

My reflection refuses to lie to me.

In the mirror, I see a face of love.

In the mirror, I see Ruby.

❂ ❂ ❂

"Good morning, Ms. Fatima." The petite woman extends her hand to me. "I am Dr. Nguyen. How are you feeling today?"

I shake her moist hand. "Better, now that my morning sickness has let off some."

"That's always good." She sits down on a rolling stool in front of me. "With my first child, my husband couldn't keep me out of the bathroom. If it weren't for the bulge growing in my stomach on my second pregnancy, I would not have known I was pregnant."

"I wish." Her big ring on her ring finger catches my attention. Having someone to share this experience with would make my life so much easier to deal with. Nonetheless, I am content with my aloneness.

She flips through my chart. "I see this is your first baby."

I nod.

"And you are in your tenth week?"

"Yes."

She smiles.

I smile back.

"Other than the morning sickness, are you experiencing any other bothersome problems?"

I shake my head. "Can't think of anything. Just tired a lot, but I know that's a part of the program too."

"Yes, it is." She looks back in my chart. "Since you are a new patient with us, I am curious to know what made you leave your previous physician."

"Well, actually, I haven't seen anyone since I found out. I was going through a few things at the time and wasn't sure if I was going to go through with this." I swallow hard. "I want to do right by my baby."

Dr. Nguyen stands and gives me a comforting pat on my shoulder. "Take a deep breath," she instructs before putting the cold piece of metal to my back. "And again."

So far, everything that she does reminds me of a normal doctor's appointment.

She wraps the stethoscope around her neck and flips back through my chart. "Have you felt any burning or irritation when you urinate?"

I think about my answer. "Just a little, but I thought it had something to do with my upgraded hormone levels."

The African-American woman shakes her head. "Your urine sample shows you have a little bit of a urinary tract infection. A woman's chances of developing a UTI is increased during pregnancy, anywhere between her sixth and twenty-fourth week. Basically, as the uterus grows it puts direct pressure against the bladder that can block the flow of urine, causing a buildup which leads to infection." She jots something down on a piece of paper and hands it to me. "I am prescribing you a seven-day antibiotic treatment."

"Will these be safe to take with the baby?"

"Don't worry, they are fine. You should feel the symptoms easing up within a few days. Just remember to drink plenty of water throughout the day and try to drink at least one glass of un-sweetened cranberry juice a day."

I look at the piece of Rx paper, fold it up, and hold it in my hand. Watch the doctor as she cuts the lights down and wheels a cart over to the table I am sitting on.

"Lie back," she directs. "This jelly is going to be a little cold."

A little cold is an understatement. Makes me jerk at its abrupt-
ness.

The more she moves the little wand around, the more the jelly
begins to lose its effectiveness. Watch her face as she studies the
picture on the monitor.

"Hmm."

"Is something wrong?" I want to know.

"Well," she pauses, moves the instrument around some more.
The longer she stares at the monitor without answering my
question, the more I begin to worry. "Is everything okay?" I ask
again.

"When was your last menstrual cycle?"

"I can't remember offhand. Sometime in April, May. I'm not
really sure."

"See this right here?" She points her short finger to the black-
and-white screen. "This is your baby."

My baby. I finally see my baby. A tear rolls across my face at the
sight of the life I have created.

"You said you are ten weeks, right?"

I wipe my tear away, wipe my emotions away. "Please, Dr.
Nguyen. Is there something wrong with my baby?"

She removes the wand from my belly, grabs a cloth from underneath the cart and wipes the now warm jelly from my stomach.
She pushes the cart away, cuts on the lights, rolls her chair over
to the table with my chart on it. Turns and makes eye contact
with me. "My concern at this moment is your baby's size. How
did you come up with being in your tenth week?"

I lean back up on the table, pull my shirt down over my stomach.
Kick my legs to the side, let them dangle off the edge of the
table. "Let me be honest with you. About a week ago, I went to
an abortion clinic. I had an ultrasound performed by the doctor

then. He told me I was about nine weeks' pregnant and would have to pay more in order for him to perform the procedure." Dr. Nguyen's sorrowful expression makes me regret my previous decision to terminate. "Him telling me that was my sign to get my stuff and get out of there."

She crosses one of her legs over the other. "Some of these abortion clinics are nothing more than extortionists. They tell women anything to get more money out of them. In your case, he was somewhat right, but still off by a couple of weeks."

"I actually thought I was less than he told me. I didn't think I was more than six or seven weeks."

In my hand, Dr. Nguyen places my baby's first photo. She says, "Fatima, I am not here to judge you, I'll leave that up to God. But I will say that everything happens for a reason. I know the saying is older than old, but it's the truth. Maybe this is your second chance."

"Can you tell me something?"

"Sure."

My eyes dart across the room to the shut-down machine. "If I'm not ten weeks, how far along am I?"

"About twelve weeks."

"Twelve weeks?" I repeat for no other apparent reason other than to register it to my brain.

"That's right. A fetus in its tenth week would be just over one inch in length and a little over one-tenth of an ounce. Yours is over two inches in length and about half an ounce in weight. Which puts you at *at least* twelve weeks."

She keeps talking, but my ears no longer hear. If it weren't for the abortion clinic attempting to wipe my pockets clean, I would not be sitting on this table now discussing the weight and length of my unborn child.

Twelve weeks' pregnant.

That changes everything.

❂ ❂ ❂

"Table for one?"

"No, I am waiting on someone," I tell the hostess. My watch reads five minutes 'til eight. "He should be here any minute."

"Okay. Would you like your table now or would you like to wait at the bar?"

The Thai restaurant is packed tonight. If I don't get us a table now, we might have to wait later. "We can go to the table."

I follow the hostess through the crowd of people in the front to the secluded area in the back. I smell him before I can see him. That familiar, weakening scent of vetiver and tender violets. I tap the hostess on her shoulder and point at a table in the corner. "He's already here."

She takes me over to the table, places my menu down on the table. "Thank you," she says before walking off.

He gets up, gives me a hug. "Glad you made it."

I can't deny how good I feel being in his arms again. "I am glad you came, Cory."

He pulls my seat out, waits for me to get comfortable before pushing me under the table.

"I'm glad you called me," he comments once seated himself, his eyes twinkling with honesty. "You look good."

I smile.

He smiles back.

Both of us sitting in silence, unable to move forward from this moment. If I talk, it'll be about the baby. If he talks, it'll be about the same.

Our waiter brings conversation to the table. "You ready?" he asks while filling our empty glasses with ice water.

Cory grabs his menu, tells the man, "I'll have Pad Thai."

"Mild or Spicy?"

"Spicy."

The waiter looks in my direction, "And for you?" he asks.

"Pad Se Ew with tofu, please, and a bowl of jasmine rice."

He takes up our menus and tells us in broken English that our food will be out shortly.

"Have you been here before?" Cory questions.

"Yeah, Lauren brought me here not too long ago. The food was so good I wanted to go in the kitchen and slap the cook."

He laughs. "I agree. My first time here I had to ask for forgiveness for eating too much."

"Last time, I got the same thing you got, but I wanted to try something different, see if they're consistent."

"Oh, they are."

The situation is different for Cory and me. Last time we were in each other's presence, he put things in perspective for me. We are simply not meant to be.

I peep across the table at him, find him peeping at me.

"I know what you're thinking," he says.

"Oh, really? What am I thinking?"

His eyes forget to blink when he stares at me. "You're thinking about us."

"Ha." I have to cover my mouth to keep my outburst down. "And what makes you think that?"

"Because I've been thinking about you since the last time we were together." He reaches his hand across the table, attempts to place it on top of mine. "Fatima, I want to apologize for how I acted that day—"

I put my hand up to stop him. "Cory, you don't have to apologize."

"Yes, I do. My silence was just as tactless as me saying, 'What that got to do with me?'"

I don't know what to say, so I say nothing.

My silence just gives him more reason to continue talking. "I've been doing some thinking, soul searching as some would say, and I came to the realization that I want to be in your life. Will you allow me to be?"

"I'm pregnant, Cory."

"I think we've already determined that."

"So, what are you saying?"

"Exactly what I said. I want to be with you, be a part of your life and be a part of our baby's life. Will you let me?" he asks again.

I shake my head. My heart and my mind battle each other. "I don't know, Cory."

He clears his throat. "Like the song says, 'All you gotta do is say yes,'" he tries to sing.

Even though he is being totally serious, I laugh. "Um, leave the singing to Floetry, please."

"I'm serious, Fatima. I do want us to be together. I've never begged a woman to be in her life, never had to."

"So don't start now."

The waiter heads in our direction with two hot plates in his hands. He places them down respectively. "Okay?"

Cory and I look over our plates and nod.

Before he can walk away, I remind him about the rice.

"Okay," he tells me.

Cory inhales the aroma steeping from his plate. "My mouth waters just smelling this food."

While I wait for my rice to mix with my noodles, Cory pulls out his ringing cell phone.

"Hey, Cora. Been trying to reach you for three days now. Actually you did. Having dinner with Fatima. Don't say that. Yes, we're still seeing each other. Stop it. Well, she's going to be the mother of my child. Come on, that was uncalled for."

He looks up at me to see if I am listening. I divert my eyes to a couple seated a few tables away from us.

All of a sudden, my appetite is ruined. Just the mention of his sister's name brings back the feelings from our first encounter, how she made me feel. Made me lose my desire to be with her brother.

Cory drops his fork against his plate. "I know what I'm doing. Fatima is nothing like them. Why are you doing this? Yes, the baby is mine. She's right here." He hands the phone to me.

I shake my head adamantly. "No," I mouth, pushing the phone out of reach.

He's determined for his sister and me to reach an understanding. "Please, just talk to her. She's my sister." His dark eyes plead and beg me to take the phone.

Literally, I want to throw up. Matter-of-factly, I think I just threw up in my mouth a little bit. I swallow the bile as I snatch the phone from his hand. "Hello."

"Why are you doing this to him? Don't you know the hell he has been through from women like you?"

"First of all, you don't know me. Second of all, you have no right to compare me to those women, you have no right to judge me at all. And furthermore, I am not forcing your brother to do anything that he does not want to. He is a grown—"

She cuts me off, "Don't give me that BS. And don't sit up there lying to my brother. I refuse to let another one of you selfish-call-yourselves-loving-my-brother women take advantage of him anymore."

I hear her fighting back tears on the other end of the phone.

Hear the struggle every time she opens her mouth to slander me.

"Look, Cora. Your brother means a great deal to me." My hand shakes as I try to keep the phone to my ear. "My pregnancy has been a big shock to the both of us, but we both care about each other and are going to try and make this work. I am sorry if you can't handle that, but that's how it is."

Her voice trembles. "What's done in the dark will come to light. Put my brother back on the phone."

I hand the phone back to Cory, excuse myself from the table. Walk past a Buddha waterfall on my way to the ladies room. As soon as I can close the stall door, shut and lock it, all of my anger passes up through my throat and out of my mouth. Nothing but remnants of pure hatred reside on my tongue. Hatred toward myself for putting up with this nonsense.

✪ ✪ ✪

Back at the table, I can't get seated good enough before Cory is tossing his apologies at me like dollar bills.

"You shouldn't have done that," I say.

"Do you want to leave? We could have them wrap up our food and eat it back at my place."

"We're here, the food's here. Let's just eat."

It's obvious that he has lost his appetite as well; his food is untouched. He flags down the waiter.

"Yes?"

"Will you bring a glass of Black Label to the table?"

The man from Thailand nods his head.

Cory's eyes are so soft, sincere. So much vulnerability in them. "Did you mean what you said?"

"When?"

"When you were talking to my sister. You said that we are going to try and make this work."

If I ever felt confused about anything, it is no comparison to how I feel right now. My feelings are too strong for Cory to let his sister run me away again. However, on the other hand, this simply isn't our time. "I got caught up, Cory. I wanted to hurt her like she hurt me."

He leans back in his seat. "I see."

When our waiter brings him his favorite bronze drink, he slides it as far away from him as the table will allow.

"I have something to tell you."

"Save it," he says. "You know, I should have listened to you a long time ago when you told me to leave you alone. I wanted to be with you so bad that I have made a complete fool of myself. I'm just glad I'm seeing this now."

I want to know, "So what are you saying?"

He leans forward. "When you called me to meet you here tonight, I just knew that you and I were finally on the same page. I had accepted the fact that you were carrying my child, and I just knew that you would let me in your life. But I see I had it all wrong."

"It's not what you think."

Cory pulls a couple of twenties out of his wallet and lays them on the table. "Until I see differently, I take it for what it is," he tells me before excusing himself from the table for good.

I refrain from calling after him. It's best this way. Either we hurt now, or hurt later. No matter what, we'll end up hurting each other.

With my purse and Styrofoam container of food for later in hand, I head toward the exit just as I entered—alone.

On my way out, I am almost knocked over when this woman with bleach-blonde and bronze curls on the top of her head scoots her chair out without looking.

"Lauren?" I lean over and give her a hug. I laugh. "You almost killed me."

Unlike her very warm hugs that I'm used to, Lauren weakly greets me and her face is as pale as a black woman's with the wrong color foundation. "Fatima?"

"Oh, that's right. You haven't seen me since I cut my locs off."

I realize she isn't paying me any attention. I follow her eyes to the man sitting in front of her.

Everything becomes black.

❂ ❂ ❂

My eyes open. People are standing over me. "What happened?" I want to know.

"You fainted," Lauren tells me.

Slowly, it all starts coming back. I was showing Lauren my hair and...I look to my right, to my left, look for the face that caused me to be lying on a restaurant floor with strangers looking down on me.

A hand touches my shoulder. "Fatima?"

"Get your hand off of me. You have no right to touch me."

"We need to get you to the hospital, Fatima," Lauren says.

With clenched teeth I order, "I am not going anywhere until you tell me what the hell is going on."

The tall man on my left puts his hand up to Lauren and nudges his way in front of her. "Let me tell her," he says.

"I don't care who talks as long as somebody tells me something." Feel my temperature rise with each agonizing millisecond.

"Fatima, I don't know how to—" Lauren starts.

There's no time for hesitation. "Just say it."

She looks up at the man, then back at me. "We're sisters."

Fatima comes running out of Thai Cuisine, and people are running after her. I see Lauren's blonde curls bouncing somewhere in the middle.

I hear their voices. Everyone is yelling for Fatima to stop. She ignores them though, keeps running toward her car. She manages to get in before anyone can get any closer. The engine fires up.

Standing in front of her SUV, blocking her exit, is a tall, dark-skinned man. His hair is gray, looks to be twenty or so years Fatima's senior. Lauren buries her head in the man's chest. He wraps his arms around her, but his attention is in the direction of Fatima behind the wheel.

The strange man is adamant about his position, even though Fatima is inching forward. Her ride is just inches away from this man's legs.

Fatima blows her horn so loud it causes Lauren to jump out of the man's arms and over to the side next to the guy who waited on us inside the restaurant.

"I'll kill you, I swear I will," Fatima screams over the blare of her horn.

"Daddy, just move," Lauren begs on the sideline.

The truck continues to creep closer.

Again the horn warns "last chance."

People are ditching their plates and filing out of the restaurant to see what all the commotion is about.

"Watch out," someone shouts.

A man in all black rushes toward the figure standing in front of his death sentence and hurls him off to the side. Fatima's truck accelerates, screeches to a halt before charging out of the parking lot. Lauren runs after her.

My tires scream as I avoid sideswiping Lauren.

She hits the side of my car with open hands, a look of horror on her face.

I tap my horn and shift my focus back to Fatima.

❂ ❂ ❂

Fatima whips in and out of traffic like Tarzan through trees. Makes it hard for me to keep up. It's hard for me to tell if she knows that I'm following or if she even cares. Nonetheless, I keep my eyes on her as a few cars get in between us.

My mind is playing all sorts of scenarios as to what the hell is going on. Minutes ago, Fatima was glowing with words of her unborn child. Now, she's driving as if she no longer wants the baby to be a part of her and as if she no longer wants to be a part of this world.

She slams on her brakes, causing the car behind her to super-glue his hand to his horn as he swerves over to the right lane and throws that middle finger out his window at the silver beast.

That doesn't faze Fatima. She keeps on trucking.

I'm not far behind her.

She cuts to the right, no blinker. Turns a left at the next light.

I'm right on her trail.

The green light up ahead flashes to yellow. Fatima's brake

lights refuse to come on, yet she is too far back to try to make the light.

She ignores the red light in front of her and flies through the intersection. Her tires beg for mercy.

I don't chance my life with the light. I sit back and wait for the go signal. I've been down this route before.

Less than a minute later, my foot presses down on the gas. Pass the Hess gas station on my left, the Publix shopping plaza on my right. One light up, I make a right into Huntington Gates and then a sharp right onto Fatima's street.

Her garage door is still up. Take that as my answer that she knew I was following her and pull in next to her truck. Open my car door before it can come to a complete stop. Put the car in park, snatch my keys out. Press the down button on the panel by the door. The garage door hums shut.

I remove my shoes at the door and put them in the shoe rack just as I've done many times before.

It's dark inside. I try to navigate my way through the best way possible until my knee comes in direct contact with the edge of a sharp surface. "Damn." I grab my knee, try to smother the pain.

In the dark, the rest of my senses come to my assistance. My ears hone in on a wooden stick striking a phosphorus surface.

Light illuminates the room as Fatima leads the burning stick to a candle wick.

The pain in my knee decreases while my concern for her increases.

I move away from the pulled out drawer that attacked me and walk around to the side of the counter where Fatima is sitting.

"Why'd you follow me?"

I sit down on the other barstool next to her. "I was concerned." I pull her hand away from playing in the flame. "Still am."

"Thought I'd be a forgotten memory to you the way you left."

She doesn't look at me when she talks. Just stares blankly at the flickering light.

"What happened back there?" I want to know.

"What didn't is the question."

I tell her, "I was waiting for you. Didn't like the feeling I had when I left. Felt like I had done something wrong, so I waited for you in the parking lot. But when you came out, you were running and people were chasing you. I saw Lauren in the background, saw some strange man standing in front of your truck. Saw you contemplating a Clara Harris. I didn't know what to think. So I followed you here."

"What would you say if I told you that that strange man was my father?"

The calmness in her voice scares me. Makes me think that she'll flip the script on me at any give minute.

"I'd say he had some explaining to do."

She runs her hands over dry eyes. Maybe she's crying inside, but on the outside it's a different story.

Anger flickers over Fatima's eyes, hatred spills from her lips. "I was over him, over everything that he had done to jack up my life. Seeing him brought all of that back. I hated him for what he had done. For leaving me, for leaving my mother and making her leave me. I wanted to run over him, wanted to run him over a hundred times. Wanted to kill him a hundred times a hundred."

"Why didn't you?"

She gets up from the barstool, walks over to the door where her purse is hanging. She grabs it, brings it back to her seat. From it she pulls out glossy black-and-white photos and puts them down on the counter top where I can see them.

I see the pictures of the life growing inside her and my mind flashes back to the night Trish threw similar snapshots in my face. The only difference is the vile taste of my life being over isn't soiling my tongue. My throat isn't clogged with discontent.

"I want a better life for my child. I refuse to throw away all that I have been through by birthing my child in jail. My parents left me. I am not going to leave my child."

I hold the pictures in my hand and understand exactly why Fatima decided against mirroring her life. Same reason why I never wanted to repeat what I had experienced growing up. It's just not worth it.

She takes our existence from my hands, traces her fingers across the images. "As much as I wanted to take his life, the idea of leaving Lauren fatherless just didn't sit right with me. Even though the pretense of our friendship was false, I couldn't let her go through what I went through."

I overheard that bit of news back in the parking lot. Heard Lauren yelling over and over not to kill their dad; he didn't deserve it. In a way I know how she feels. At the same time, none of Zach's other kids tried to befriend me like that. "How do you feel about that? About how she manipulated her way into your life?"

"How do you think I feel?" She bites down on her chapped lips. "I feel betrayed. The only reason we became friends is because she was trying to get to know me as her sister. All this time, she knew who I was and I knew nothing. She saw me break down, was there when I made the biggest decision of my life. She saw me at my most vulnerable state. She was there for me as a sister would be and the whole time she knew she was just that, my sister."

"Damn. That's messed up."

Fatima's cell phone vibrates on the countertop for like the tenth time since I've been here. She picks it up, looks at the number.

"Speak of the devil." She hurls the phone against the wall. It crashes to the floor in different directions.

I pull her close to me. Hold her tight.

"I don't want to be in this place again." Her words muffled against my chest.

She tries to push away from me. The harder she pushes, the tighter I hold her.

"Oh my God, oh my God. I can't live like this."

She convulses in my arms. Feels like she's having a seizure. I rub her back, rub my hand over her hair. Give her silent comfort as she lets out her angst.

Fatima pounds her fists into my chest over and over again, treats me like a human punching bag. "I can't live like this."

All I can do is hold her. Feel like if I try to do anything else, she might make me her next target.

I let her continue hitting me until she wears herself out, until her inhales and exhales slow to a sedentary pace.

Fatima finagles her way out of my grasp and looks me dead in the eyes. "I'm leaving, Cory."

"Where are you going?"

"I don't know, but I am getting as far away from this place as possible."

I shake my head. "What about this house? What about your spa? Don't be irrational."

"You haven't seen irrational."

"Then what are you talking about?"

She puts some distance between us. Walks over to the sink, back turned. "This place holds too many bad memories for me. I can't trust anyone. Can't even trust myself. Moving to a place where no one even knows my name is the best thing for me and my child. Maybe then we'll have a better chance."

I walk up behind her, wrap my arms around her waist. Hands resting on top of the little knot in her belly. "You can trust me."

"No, I can't."

"Have I ever lied to you?"

"That's not the point," she refutes.

"Then what is?"

Again, she removes herself from my touch. "Why can't you just accept the fact that I need to move on with my life. Living here, being in the same town where yesterday refuses to stay in its place, is not conducive to my moving forward. Being in the same town with you is not conducive to my moving forward."

"Why are you running from me?"

She stands with her back toward the sink, her face toward me. "Things were complicated enough when we began."

"Life is complicated."

"Look, damn it. I am trying to push you away. Why can't you respect that?"

Fatima staggers back over to the barstool. Sits down and plays with the burning flame again like a stubborn child.

"I'm just trying to understand."

"Some things can't be understood."

The glow from the candle reveals tears in her eyes. None fall, instead they ripple from shore to sea.

I sit down next to her, pull her rebellious hand down from the fire and hold it in mine. Rub the softness of her flesh back and forth with the ball of my thumb. "I remember my mother coming into my room one night after a heated fight with my father. She came in and found me buried in the back of the closet. Her hand shook as she reached out for me. She told me, 'This is life, son. If I run now, I'll keep running. And if you hide, you gon' keep hiding.' After that, she pulled me out of the closet. I guess part of me stayed hidden. I refuse to keep hiding and so should you."

Fatima begins humming as if she is the only one in the room. The tune is unfamiliar. Sounds dismal, yet resurrecting at the same time.

"What song is that?"

My question goes unanswered as she hits a high note deep within her bosom and holds on to it in a way that if she stops, she'll stop breathing.

Her hand is still in mine. I continue stroking her velvety skin, hoping to bring some sense of solace to her debilitating world.

I open my eyes when her melodic words are no longer heard. Her eyes are on me. "Penny for your thoughts," she says.

"Just thinking about all that you have been through lately, especially in the last couple of hours and the fact that you still manage to make beautiful music."

She smiles. "It was a poem I wrote about six years ago that I turned into a song."

"Maybe I can hear you sing it on stage one of these days."

Her eyes dim, gives me a skeptical look. "What is it about me that keeps you around?"

I rub my palm against my pants. "I'm gonna be honest with you, I have no idea. I think you put something in my drink at the club."

She chuckles.

I laugh.

Fatima says, "I was so pissed off earlier that I could've seriously hurt somebody."

"You had reason to."

She shakes away my validation. "There's no reason good enough for that. I'm not here to punish."

"I hear you."

"If it weren't for you, there's no telling what I'd be doing or where I'd be right now. So, for that, I thank you." She reaches her arms out and pulls me into her.

I hug her back, but I tell her she doesn't need to thank me. "I'm here because I want to be."

She slightly releases me, digs her face into the groove of my neck. Her lips grazing my skin just enough to awaken my loins. My hands begin to caress her back, my fingers tracing the back of her neck. She inhales my scent, long and hard. Feel the heat as she exhales.

❂ ❂ ❂

Fatima escorts me into a room that I have never been in. A mattress is on the floor covered in black satin sheets. Everything in the room is black, including the walls.

"Take off your clothes. I'll be right back."

She leaves the room and I do as told. Wonder what this woman has in store.

A minute later, she flips the light off, tells me to lay on my stomach. Seconds later, I feel her bare legs straddle mine.

Her warm hands glide across my back in the most sensuous way. Makes me wonder if she touches her clients in the same way.

She massages me slow, deep, reaches down to the core of me. Penetrates through layers of hardness to the soft part of me that cries out to be loved. She hits that spot over and over until I feel tears engulf my eyes.

Even though my face is buried, I am thankful that this room is beyond darkness so she can't see my tears.

Fatima stretches her arms the length of mine, her breasts molding into my back. She raises herself back up as she traces her fingertips back to the center. The warmness between her thighs brushes against my backside as she moves her torso to rest on the back of my thighs. Her fingers kneading my lower back as if I am made of dough. A true professional at work.

I am totally relaxed as she squeezes the firmness out of my glutes, turns them soft like cotton. She slides further down my legs, leaving no inch of skin untouched.

"Turn over."

She helps me roll over and resumes doing what she does best.

Her fingers make love to my toes. Intertwined, she wiggles her fingers up and down in short movements. Excites me in a way I didn't think possible. She gives me a foot massage out of this world.

The only sound in this room is the deep moans that keep escaping from my parted lips.

She works her way up my thighs, stopping briefly at the piece of me that merged with a piece of her to make a part of us. I hear a subtle moan leak from her lips at his presence.

I wish I could see her, stare at the expression on her face, but the decor obstructs my view. It's so dark in here that with my eyes wide open it seems as though my eyes are closed.

My attention focuses in the direction of her face, her fingers still massaging their way up my body. I envision her butter-toffee complexion, her mesmerizing brown eyes, the tanned freckles on the tip of her nose. I envision her pouty lips and that deep dimple in her left cheek as she smiles her way toward me.

Heat spreads across my face as she lowers her body to mine. Skin to skin, flesh to flesh. Her fingers dance around my face. Fingertips smooth the thickness of my brows, outline my chiseled cheekbones—compliments of my third-generation Ethiopian heritage. She brushes my lips with hers, teases me beyond pleasure.

"I want you, Fatima," I hear myself say.

She puts her finger to my lips, shushes me from saying anything else.

Her body inches back down mine, placing passionate kisses on my toasted-almond skin.

I hear the sound of liquid being squeezed from a bottle. The sound of her rubbing her hands together.

Her hand oils the last untouched part of my body, the hardest part of me in her hands. I lay my head back, close my eyes, and let the feeling of bliss take over me.

❂ ❂ ❂

I am lying on my stomach in Fatima's bed. We came in here sometime last night after she rubbed me down from head to toe, after she massaged me to seventh heaven and wiped me down with a warm towel.

I'm restless, can't sleep. Keep having nightmares. I turn over on my side, reach for her to bring her warmth next to me. I reach for her and realize she's not here. Her side of the bed is cold, she hasn't been here for some time.

"Fatima?" I call out.

No answer.

I look around the room, find her propped up on a bench in the bay window. Her skin still bare. The moon's glow accenting the small roundness in her belly. If I were a photographer, this would be the perfect picture, a poem without words. I find myself wanting her more. Wanting her in my life no matter what.

She stares out the window, so many emotions etched in her innocent face. Her voice distant. "Can't sleep?"

"Doesn't look like you can either." I climb out of the bed, my feet heavy against the hardwood floor as I move toward her. Stand behind her, kiss the tip of her shoulder. "You okay?"

"I'm at peace," she says.

I stroke her supple skin with my hands, continue placing delicate kisses on her. She leans into me, submits to me. I kiss the back of her neck, follow the trail down to the curve of her spine. I sit down on the cushioned bench, she turns around on her knees, faces me. Our eyes on each other with immeasurable desire.

She hoists herself on top of me, wraps her warmness around my firmness. The only vision I have of her is in my mind as I close my eyes.

Her movements are slow, almost calculated. Not sure if she is being careful with the baby or being careful with me.

"Cory," she softly calls.

"Hmm?"

When I open my eyes, I see tears falling out of hers. My penetrations come to a cease, I reach up and usher her closer to me. "What's wrong?"

She bites down on her bottom lip, her tears glistening under the moonlight. "Oh, my God." She breaks down above me.

I hold her closer than close. "Talk to me, baby."

I am still inside her, feel her walls tighten around me with every effort she exerts to stop crying. Nothing works.

All I can do is hold her and hope that this too shall pass.

She mumbles a few inaudible words, clears her throat, and talks more clearly. "I am so tired of riding this roller coaster. My whole life has been filled with ups and downs, sharp corners, near-death plummets. Someone is always getting hurt and I am tired. I am truly tired."

"I'm not going to hurt you, Fatima. I just wanna learn how to love you."

She releases me from her, wobbles over to the bed, turns her back to me.

I don't run after her, I stay seated in the window. Empathize with all that she has been through. Give her some much needed space.

"Cory, please leave," I hear her say.

She's lying in the bed with the covers tossed to the side, lying there with her head and knees pinned to her chest in the fetal position.

"Why do you do this to me...do this to yourself? This torture is not fair to either one of us," I tell her, frustration stressed in every word.

"It's better this way. Now, please, just leave."

I can lead a horse to water, but I can't make it drink.

Hours after Cory walked out, I am still in the bed, crying. Tears flowing from oceans I thought had dried up and formed into deserts a long time ago.

I cry not only because I hurt him, my pillow is soaked because no matter how much I try to forget, life has a funny way of reminding me that things truly are out of my control.

I want to get out of this bed, at least gather some sense of control, no matter how little that might be. I want to do something for me. I want to, but I can't. I am too weak. These tears have stripped the last bit of energy from me.

The source of my pain threatens to cripple me. "Damn you, Lawrence. Damn you, Ruby. I won't let you destroy me."

I remember when I first started running, my legs would hurt like hell for days. "Pain is just weakness leaving the body," my trainer would tell me. The pain I'm feeling right now just proves that hating my parents has crippled me.

"Lawrence and Ruby, I won't let you destroy me." The more I repeat my affirmation, the more I find my tears drying up.

With a newfound burst of energy, I thrust myself from the bed, head straight into the bathroom and cut on the shower. I refuse to look at my reflection in the mirror because I know what I see might scare me.

Under the warm temperature I stand completely bare, let it rinse me from my head to my feet. Let it wash away the soiled tears from my skin, remnants from the oil I rubbed on Cory. Let it cleanse me from every memory of yesterday. Today *is* a new day.

All of a sudden, I feel a tiny flutter in my stomach. Feels like a baby butterfly.

My baby reminds me that I am no longer in this fight alone. I rub my belly, sing the words to a Destiny's Child song to my little boy or my little girl. "For you I live and love again. Open the path to happiness. For you I learn to smile again. I. Thank. God. For. You… I love you, I love you."

The shower door flies open. I'm soaked, but I jump out and move toward the mirror with a sense of urgency. I stare at my reflection. See a little girl with curly, sandy brown ponytails in her hair. Eyes too big for her four-year-old body stare back at me. She's so hurt and broken, so unloved. I stare back at her and, with as much affection that was in my voice as I sang to the baby growing in my belly, I tell the little girl in the mirror, "I love you."

She looks back at me with even bigger eyes as if to ask, "You do?"

I smile and see that deep dimple in her left cheek spring to life.

I tell her over and over again until all of her hurt and pain from being unloved through the years dissipates from her innocent face. I tell her over and over again until she becomes me. I wrap my arms around myself and continue saying the words that I've been so afraid of all of these years. "I love you."

And I weep tears of joy.

✪ ✪ ✪

"Girl, you look like I feel," Adrian says once I walk through the back door.

"The story of my life."

"This is not the time to be stressing about things you can't change, Fatima. Plus, you might scare our clients away with that four-piece luggage set under your eyes."

"Ha, ha. You're always trying to be funny during my time of misery." I put a couple of bags of snacks down on the countertop.

"Care to indulge me?" She takes a peek through the bags, pulls out a container of mixed fruit.

We both sit down at the table, forks in hand.

"Not really. It is what it is and I am so over it," I tell her. "How was your weekend?"

"Marcus has been sick as a dog. He caught strep throat from drinking off one of his classmates which, might I add, I've warned him about not doing since the last time he got sick."

"Poor thing."

"Poor thing, my behind."

"Quit being so hard on him."

She waves me off. "You'll see soon enough."

"How's he doing now?" I pop a piece of juicy cantaloupe in my mouth.

"Let me tell you, that little boy had me so scared, Fatima. His tonsils were so swollen he could barely breathe. Had a high temp and everything. We were in the ER for five hours before they called us back only for the doctor to swab his throat and give us a prescription for some bubble gum-tasting medication."

"Ooooh, the pink stuff. I used to love getting sick just to get some of that stuff."

She gives me a skeptical look. "He's better now," she says. "You on the other hand, I'm not so sure about."

"Yeah, whatever," I defend myself and swallow a too-bitter-for-my-liking strawberry.

Adrian gets up from the table. I watch her as she takes the rest of the goodies out of the bags and puts them in their respective places. Her locs sway back and forth across her shoulders, making me miss mine. But I cut them off for a good cause, so it's not much of a love loss.

She puts her thick hands on her high hips, mumbles some stuff about all the healthy food choices I got for the team. "What's up with this? You trying to send subliminal messages around here?"

"You know I've never been one to hide behind words. I say what needs to be said when it needs to be said, so no subliminal messages here."

"Well, come out and say it then. You think I'm fat, don't you?" There's no denying the self-criticism in her voice.

I choose my words carefully, try my best not to offend her. "You are a little on the healthy side, but it's not about that. I'm just trying to make better choices for this life growing inside of me."

The cut-the-malarkey glare on her face lets me know that she's not buying my story. "You don't have to lie to me, Fatima. I thought we were better than that."

I get up from my chair, walk over to her. Put a reassuring hand on her shoulder. "Girl, we are. You know that. Yes, I think you could stand to lose a pound or two, but like I said, my main concern right now is delivering and raising a healthy child. So please, don't take offense to my food selections."

She puts her weight against the counter. "I know. Guess I'm all on the edge 'cause Mr. Man has been complaining about the weight I've been putting on lately. Guess I feel like since he thinks I'm fat, then everybody else must feel the same way."

"You are not fat," I tell her. "And even if you were, that's the last thing he needs to be complaining about."

"I know."

"I'm not trying to knock your husband and all, but he's not even working. He sits his behind around the house all day and expects you to pay all the bills. I bet he didn't even go to the ER with you when his son was sick, did he?"

She shakes her head.

"Need I say any more?"

Her face is still hanging to the ground.

"Let me ask you…how do *you* feel about your body?"

Adrian shrugs. "I don't know. I guess I look fine."

Doubt is still in her voice.

"You guess or you know?"

She runs her hands down her hips. A smile creeps across her face. "I *know* I'm fine."

I pull her into me. Give her a tight hug. "That's right, girl. Now carry that attitude home with you. Don't let that man run your house and your mind. You've got the control over you, don't give someone else that position."

My friend of five years holds my hands in hers. "I'm always the one there for you, but you're on point today. I feel like the daughter in this friendship now."

"Every therapist needs therapy."

"Guess you're right." She still holds my hands in hers, gives me a kiss on the cheek. "You still look like a Gremlin."

"Leave my eyes alone." I playfully slap her across her arm. "You're always trying to crack on somebody."

She laughs.

"Do my eyes really look that bad?" I want to know.

She tells me she was just playing. "They're a little puffy, but nothing some Preparation-H can't get rid of."

"Damn, it's that serious?"

Adrian walks over to the table, ruffles through her purse. "Just rub a little dab of this under both eyes." She hands me the infamous yellow tube.

My face reads like a made-for-dummies book. "I don't know about this."

"Here." She grabs the tube from my hand, squirts a little of the white stuff on her finger. She gently applies it to the puffs under my eyes. Rubs it in enough to take the whiteness away. "See, better already."

I look away from my reflection in the toaster up to the clock above the door. "Thanks, girl. I need to get the room set up for my eight-thirty client."

"Oh, snap. Where'd the time go?" She tosses the cream back in her purse. "I might need this later."

We both laugh lightly.

She pulls me into her. Hugs me tight. "I really appreciate what you said earlier. It meant a lot. And whatever it is that you're going through, I know you're going to make it out all right. Just look at you, you've already come a long way."

I hug her back even tighter.

❂ ❂ ❂

Ten minutes later, I walk up front to meet my morning client. Erykah Badu's "Orange Moon" vibrates through the speakers.

The only person in view in the reception area is Danielle.

"Morning, Fatima. I was just about to ring you in the back." She rises from her too-comfortable chair and hands me a piece of paper. "Alex called and said he's running a few minutes late. He should be here within five minutes or so. He said to call him if that's a problem."

I walk around to the back of the desk, grab the appointment

book. Even though all of the appointments are input into the computer, I still keep a hard copy book in case any changes are made to the schedule. That way, appointments won't get mixed up or deleted from the computer by accident. All appointments are entered into the computer at the end of the day. Keeping two journals makes things much easier.

I look in the book to see who is scheduled after Alex. My next appointment isn't until after lunch.

"Just page me when he gets here," I tell Danielle.

Before I can get to the back, I hear the chime to the entrance door ring. I turn around and prepare myself to greet my client after all.

My stomach grows weak when I see Lauren standing in the doorway instead.

"Can we talk?" she requests.

"Do you have an appointment?"

"No."

"Well, there's your answer." I say that and resume walking toward the back.

I hear her footsteps coming after me. "Fatima. Please. Just talk to me."

I face her with eyes she's never seen before. "Do not bring this here. Do not." I put my hand up and walk away.

Once again, I hear her footsteps. "This isn't about me, Fatima."

"It's not? Then what was our so-called friendship about? Was that not about you?"

"I'm not going to lie, in the beginning I did want to know what it was like to have a sister. I grew up with two brothers and I always wanted to know what it was like to have a sister. I wanted someone I could play dolls with, share all my secrets with. Talk about boys with."

"Aww, poor Lauren." I cut the sarcasm and replace it with bitterness. "At least you didn't have to grow up alone."

She sighs. "I know how you feel."

"You don't know a damn thing about how I feel." I hear my voice raise and, temporarily, I don't give a damn about this being my place of business. "He left my family for you. Don't you ever say you know how I feel."

She backs away, but her desire for me to understand still persists. "Will you hear me out for a minute?"

"Why should I?"

"I just found out. All these years, I didn't know."

"And?"

"I had a high regard for my father. Thought he was the best dad in the world. I never thought he could do something like that."

I start walking toward the back because the chime out front keeps going off. It's starting to get crowded in here. No matter how upset I am, I will not have my place's high reputation go down the drain. Worked too hard for that.

Lauren quits talking as she follows me to the break area. At least she shows some respect for me in that capacity.

My bladder screams for relief. "Wait here. I'll be back."

In the bathroom, I line the toilet with tissue, then put a seat cover on top before sitting down. My head is heavy, heart is heavy. So much to think about. So much has gone on these last few months, so much has gone on in these last few days.

I wash my hands, then rinse my face with cold water twice. "You can handle this, Fatima," I say in the mirror.

Before going back into battle with Lauren, I step up front to apologize to Alex for the hold up. He does the same for his tardiness, but tells me that he has another appointment and can come back after that if I need him to.

"That would be great," I say. "I'll give you a ten percent discount for the inconvenience."

"It's not inconvenience, but I'll take the discount anyway."

We both smile and he walks out the door.

Now that that is out of the way, back to the issue at hand.

Lauren doesn't hesitate with picking back up where we left off. "Listen, I am not going to sit up here and give you a slew of excuses for what was done."

"As well you shouldn't."

I see the frustration burrowing behind her green eyes. "Point is, don't blame him for what I did. He had no idea that I had befriended you."

I shake my head, roll my eyes. "I can't help but feel that everyone has plotted to tear me down. I just want to know what did I do to deserve any of this. I thought you were a true friend, Lauren."

She reaches across the table for my hand. I slide it away.

"Even though you don't believe me, I am your friend, Fatima. I've been your friend since the very beginning."

"Only because you knew I was your sister. Am I right?"

She sits back in her seat, arms folded across her chest like a kid caught in a lie. "Initially. As soon as I actually met you, though, I forgot all about the sister factor. I wanted to get to know you as a person."

"I don't buy that."

"It's true. I honestly considered you my friend. You were my best friend." She moves forward in the chair again. "Don't take that away from me."

"You took that away when you neglected to tell me that you and I share the same blood." With that, I stand from my seat, hold my hand out to show her the direction of the exit.

"I will accept that. As hard as it is for me to say, I was wrong for that. I just didn't know any other way."

My hand is still pointing toward the door.

She stands, grabs her purse, pushes her chair underneath the table, and starts walking for the door leading to the hallway. "I understand that you are mad at me, probably will never forgive me. That's something I'll just have to live with, but I can't live without you at least talking to him. He really does love you, Fatima. He never stopped."

"Be sure to write that on his tombstone."

The library closed over an hour ago. I am the last to leave, but my car isn't the only one in the parking lot.

She sits on the trunk of her car, dark shades cover her eyes even though it isn't bright out. It's almost the dead of summer, yet she's dressed in sweats, hair smoothed back into a ponytail that is not all hers.

"Never expected to see you again."

"Always expect the unexpected."

I want to say, "Especially when it comes to you," but I hold my tongue back on that one.

I unlock my car doors, put my attaché in the back seat. Open up the driver's door to get in to drive away from the drama.

She hops off her car, taps on my window. "You just gonna leave me out here like this?"

Momentarily, I stare at her through tinted glass. Rev up the ignition so I can roll the window down. "We've said all we need to say. No point in wasting any more time."

"You're one callous mother fu—"

"I was this way when you met me, Trish."

I roll my window up, but her hand blocks it from making it to the top.

"Why? What did I ever do to you?"

"It's not a matter of what you did or did not do. We just weren't meant to be more than what we were."

"Did you ever even like me?"

I have never been dishonest with Trish in the past, so now is not the time. I shut the engine off and join her on the outside.

"Yes."

She stands a few feet away from me with her arms folded. Her face doesn't register anger, just hurt.

"But?"

"But what?"

"There has to be more because apparently like wasn't enough or we wouldn't be here like this."

I nod to her truth. "In the beginning, you seemed very independent and had an aggressive nature to you, a trait that I like in the women I date. But, as time went on, you became the opposite. I saw you as dependent and clingy, traits that turn me off. Every time the phone rang, it was your number that popped up. I felt like the life you had before me was replaced with me."

"That's not true."

"Say it isn't. Then tell me why you quit the job you loved so much?"

She doesn't respond.

I keep going. "What happened to all of your friends? Why were you skipping classes?"

Still she doesn't say anything.

"That's what I'm talking about. You stopped doing all of the things you loved, stopped hanging with your friends. Everything changed when you met me."

"Is that so wrong?"

"If you have to ask, then you know the answer."

"I loved you, Cory. Did you know that?"

"I was under the impression."

"Well, I did. My sister thought I was crazy for loving someone like you. Yeah, you were complicated as all get-out, but that made me want to be with you more." Trish sucks in air, almost gasps like a fish out of water. "I'll admit that I lost my focus, I lost me in you and, obviously, that was the fastest way to lose you. Would I take it back? No. There's nothing that I would do differently."

"Then it's safe to say that if I gave you a second chance, we would not work out then either."

She belts out a laugh that makes me think my comment was asinine. "First of all, what makes you think I would even give you a second chance?"

"Would you?" I'm interested to know.

"In a heartbeat."

I ask, "So is that why you're here now?"

"Don't get your hopes up."

She leans next to me up against the car and slowly removes her shades. Staring out into the darkening sky, she says, "After I lost the baby, I literally shut down. I wasn't eating, sleeping, talking. All I did was sit in the same rocking chair my mom nursed me in as a baby. I would rock by the window in the baby's room and watch time change from night to day. I felt like the baby was the final piece of the puzzle to us. You would've come around and we would've been a happy family. But that never happened. I didn't understand why you didn't love me. Didn't understand why my baby had to die because of it."

I watch Trish in my peripheral. She looks so broken, so unsure about the choices she made. For a minute, my heart mourns for her.

"One day, as I sat in that rocking chair, rocking my life away, a butterfly appeared on the outside of my window. It just kept flying and flying and flying, never leaving my view. It was beautiful, a rainbow of colors on its wings. The sun was shining bright that day. I don't know what it was, but it was as if God was trying to send me a message. He was trying to wake me up. I got out of the chair, walked over and put my hand up on the window. Seconds later, the butterfly flew toward my hand. At that moment, as I studied its wings, I had an epiphany: Life showers us many storms, but if we endure there is always a rainbow at the end. The sun *will* shine again."

Her chest rises high and falls. "My storm was losing you and losing my child, but my rainbow was finding me again."

I think about my past representing the storm in my life and how I thought Fatima was *my* rainbow. Boy, was I wrong.

After hearing Trish's revelation, I find myself asking an obvious question. "So why *are* you here now?"

"Closure."

After all that she has been through since dealing with me, I honor her wish. "Come here, Patricia." Her eyes twinkle at my newfound respect for her. I extend my arms out to her and let her in in a way I never had before.

Her embrace says a lot more than her lips ever will.

❂ ❂ ❂

As soon as I get in the car, I cut my cell phone on. It alerts me that I have a new voicemail. It's from Cole. Him, Carl, and Cora are on their way out to my place. I delete the message and call him back on his homing device.

He doesn't answer.

I hang up and call Cora on hers. She refuses to answer as well.

Instead of calling my younger brother, I send him a text message. Ask him to tell me what the hell is going on.

He replies back, *Don't know. Just as clueless as you.*

I shift into drive so fast it feels like I broke the knob.

❀ ❀ ❀

Cole reads the pissed-off tone in my eyes. He throws his hands up in defeat and points toward our oldest sibling, Cora.

"What's this all about?" I ask her. "When did you get back in town?"

"You going to let us in first?"

"After you answer my question."

Her arms are folded, lips pulled in. No sign of her conceding any time soon.

I open the door because the scene doesn't look right. Four Blacks huddled in front of a door with it's-about-to-jump-off-any-minute glares in their eyes.

I direct my frustration to anyone who's listening. "I don't appreciate this."

She gets in my face. "And I don't appreciate some whore taking advantage of my brother."

"You flew down here for that?"

Cole and Carl relocate to my spare bedroom, leaving me alone with Hell in Heels.

"What's wrong with you, Cory? I mean, really, what is wrong with you?"

The itch for a bottle of Johnnie Walker slowly creeps through my veins. I recognize the all-too-familiar beckoning from my subconscious. "I am a thirty-year-old, African-American male, who owns up to his mistakes and something is wrong with me?"

"Maybe you need to stop making all of them mistakes."

"I'm never going to win with you, am I? If women were going

around talking about me being a no-good baby's daddy and were seeking legal advice from you for some form of retribution, I'd be a loser then too, huh?"

"That's not the case."

This time it's me in her face. "It is the damn case. That's the problem. We men get dogged out either way. If we don't take care of the child, we get our privileges taken away from us and find ourselves behind bars. But if we do own up to our responsibilities, years down the line we find out the kids aren't even ours. So, what is a brother to do? Since you seem to have all the answers, can you answer that one for a brother?"

Cole marches out for the back room. "Cory, your voice," he warns and goes back to being out of sight.

For once in her life, Cora is at a loss for words.

I turn the volume in my voice down just a notch, but keep it high enough for my sister to know not to cross that line between what's right and what's wrong. "Don't ever question my choices again. If I decide to do the right thing in my life, it would be nice to know my family has my back."

"I do, *we* do have your back, Cory. We just don't want our brother to be dogged out. Trust me, your best interest is at hand."

"Do you hear yourself?" Steam flows out of my nostrils. "How can you have *my* best interest at hand without even consulting me about it? Seriously, you need to go on back to Chicago and keep my best interest from being any concern of yours."

I leave her in the living room and head for the kitchen in search of the Black Label I had stashed away for times like these.

It doesn't take her long to barge her way into the kitchen behind me. "I don't care what you say, that is not your baby."

"I slept with Fatima unprotected. Not only am I doing what's right, I'm finally doing something that makes me feel good about myself." I refuse to let my sister nor Fatima make me feel bad about my decision.

Cora slumps up against the wall. Her voice barely above a whisper. "That's not your baby," she repeats.

Both of my brothers appear in the doorway like they're security or something. "It's too quiet in here," Cole speaks up. "Is everything alright?"

"Why are y'all here in the first place?" I want to know.

"Cora asked us to come," Cole fills me in.

Cora puts her hand up, stops him from sharing anything else. Tells them, "We're okay."

As if on cue, my brothers step back out of sight.

"I asked them to be here," Cora says. "I needed the support of my family."

"What about my damn support," my voice raises. "And what do you need support for anyway?"

I open the cabinet under the sink, reach my hand all the way to the back. Lay my hand on the infamous bottle. Feel my nerves calming already just from the touch.

My sister walks over to the breakfast nook and sits down in one of the two wooden chairs. "How well do you even know this woman?"

"Doesn't matter."

"Like hell it does," she refutes.

"Is that the kind of language they're using in the courtrooms these days?" I smirk inside at my sarcasm. "Like I said, it doesn't matter. I can have a one-night stand and if the woman happens to get pregnant, how well I know her or not won't matter."

My patience runs thin as I pour me a hefty glass of scotch. I don't hide it from Cora either.

"See, she's even got you drinking again."

With my eyes closed, I savor the flavor as I take a huge gulp. Put the cup down on the countertop and stare eye to eye with my stress. "Actually, she's the reason why I stopped. I'm drinking because of you."

She gets up from the chair. She is in my face again. "I refuse to let you blame your alcoholism on me. You make your *own* choices. I have nothing to do with that."

"Then why are you here now?"

That shuts her down.

"Exactly what I thought." I get another taste of the drink that has been alien to me for months now. As it goes down my throat, I realize that I haven't missed the drink one bit, but I keep drinking it to spite Cora.

"I'm glad Patricia lost the baby."

I almost choke on the fire in my throat. "How can you say something like that?"

"Deep down, you know you feel the same way. Don't act like it was a loss to you."

The more Cora opens her mouth, the more I realize that I barely even know my own sister. Yet, at the same time, we finally agree on something. I'll never tell her that though.

"Cory, you are my brother. I used to help change your diapers, for goodness sakes. It kills me to see these women take advantage of you. And I refuse to see you take care of another man's child again."

I've heard enough. "Do you hear yourself? I mean, seriously. Do you hear what you're saying? Where do you get this stuff from?"

"I only speak on facts. That is not your baby in *that* woman's stomach."

"If you got something to tell me, I wish you'd just come out with it. If you have some proof that Fatima isn't carrying my baby, show it to me. Otherwise, shut the hell up and let me take care of my business."

I'm so mad my hands start to shake.

"Sit down, Cory. Please. I don't like it when you're like this."

I exhale. "You're talking crazy, for real."

She sits down instead. Face in her hands.

I put some space between us. Grab the bottle of Johnnie Walker and pour the rest of its contents down the sink. That part of my life is history.

"I know for a fact that she's not carrying your baby," Cora says.

"Damn, do you ever stop?"

"Cory, you can't have kids," she blurts out.

I shake my head, try to shake some sense into what I just heard. "What the hell are you talking about now?"

"Cory, there's no way possible that you can have kids. You're infertile."

I turn around and look her dead in the eyes. "You really don't want me to be happy, do you? I can't believe you'd stoop this low."

"It's true, Cory. I wouldn't lie to you."

I turn away from her, can't face her at this point.

"It's true," she says. "You were around seven. Daddy was really laying it on Mama. We were all scared. Thought he was gonna kill her. You didn't like what was going on and ran to her defense. He left Mama alone and turned his anger on you. His beating landed you in the hospital for three days. When we came to pick you up, I overheard the doctor telling Mama that you'd never be able to have kids."

"Quit lying. This is not true."

"I wish it wasn't, but it is. I promised Mama I would take this secret to my grave, but I can't keep letting you get hurt by these women and their lies."

I feel my anger mounting in a way that it never has before. "You have some nerve to be calling someone a liar. You've been lying to me my whole life."

Wood scrapes against tile as she scoots out of her chair. I hear her heels clicking closer in my direction.

One.

Two.

Three.

Cora screams as my hands clamp around her tiny neck. "C... Cor...Cory... puh...puh...lease...let me...go."

I feel two sets of strong arms pull me off of the woman below me gasping for air. Now I realize why my sister needed them for *support*. To keep me from killing her.

"Wasn't expecting to be hearing from you."

This is not the time to beat around the bush. "David, I'm pregnant."

"Are you serious?"

"Wouldn't be calling if I wasn't."

"How far along are you?"

"Fourteen weeks."

Silence.

"I'm a week shy of four months, almost in my second trimester."

"I know how to calculate." His tone is stressed, but it neglects to do a good job of covering up his excitement. "Why are you just now telling me?"

"It doesn't matter. I thought you should know."

"I'm on my way over there."

"For what?"

"I need to see you."

This is exactly why I didn't want to tell him. "Look, David. We slept together, we produced a child. Don't make it more than that."

"We produced a child together, there doesn't need to be more than that." His voice firm. "I'm on my way over."

"No, you're not. Meet me at the MoCafé on Slauson in about an hour," I say and hang up.

❂ ❂ ❂

David admires me as I walk toward him. He's sitting on a brown sofa, his eyes glistening as if I am walking down the aisle to meet him and stand together in holy matrimony.

"Fatima, you're beautiful."

He hugs me with more affection than I have ever felt from him, almost like he finally has something to seal this relationship in stone. I can't lie, it feels good, but to let him know that would be like giving away a one hundred-twenty-five-million-dollar lottery ticket.

"You wanted to see me, here I am."

He holds his hand inches away from my stomach. "Can I?"

I nod.

Even though I'm barely showing, you can see enough to know that there's a baby growing inside me.

David touches my belly with complete joy written on his face. "You're really pregnant."

I nod again. A faint smile etched on my face.

"So, are we going to have a son or a daughter?"

"Too soon to tell." The sofa calls out to me. Heels and pregnancy do not go together for me. Thought I could be cute for a minute, but even sixty seconds is too long these days.

I sit down. David sits next to me. Puts his arm around me and gives me an I-missed-you kiss on my cheek.

"Want me to get you something? A slice of cheesecake or a brownie and coffee?" he offers.

"I'll have an Iced Mocha Crème with Splenda."

This time, it's me watching David as he heads to the bar to get our treats. It becomes harder and harder for me to conceal the fact that I actually feel good right now, feel special. Finally, someone not only shows me affection, but gives my unborn child the same love. And it's obvious the baby feels it too.

He comes back to our sofa and picks back up where he left off. He puts my drink and his brownie à la mode down on the table in front of us. Reaches behind the sofa and pulls out a yellow bag with pink and blue ribbons hanging from it. "After you told me you were pregnant, I jumped in my car and made a mad dash to Target. I've been waiting for this moment my whole life, especially since we met. I'd like to have been married first, but at my age, a brother will take what he can get." He hands the bag to me. "Hope you like."

"Excuse me." I leave him there holding the bag.

The bathroom is my solace. The place where I can shed my tears and feel no shame. I rush into the first stall, my tears keeping me from breathing properly.

This is how I wanted it to be when I told Cory. I wanted him to look at me like I was heaven, wanted him to touch my stomach and coo to our seed. If only, for one moment, he'd told me that I made him the happiest man alive. If only—but he didn't.

❖ ❖ ❖

When I make it back out to the lounge, I see that David's ice cream has melted into his brownie, looks like a puddle of mud. My drink, a watered-down froth.

"You okay?" he asks without looking at me. His voice sounds wounded, like a man being stood up at the altar.

"Yeah, still battling the waves of nausea."

Finally, he looks at me. "I make you that sick, huh?"

A soft sigh exhales from my lips. "It's not that. Your excitement… the gift. It's all overwhelming."

"I've never hidden the way I feel about you. Ever since the first day you walked into my office, I knew you were special."

"I was just another world for you to conquer. You just got caught up."

"Who wouldn't, Fatima? You're beautiful. And with that little bundle of joy inside of you, you're more magnificent than the moon at midnight."

His words make me smile.

"It's true. You're glowing." He slides his hand over to my lap and touches mine. I don't pull away. "Man can't live by bread alone, but having you alone by my side, I feel like I can live without food for three eternities. You alone satisfy me."

"I'm not a hot air balloon, David. You can't inflate me and expect me to fly you over the world." My fingers intertwine with his. "But I'm not gonna lie, it feels good."

He pulls our hands up to his lips, kisses the back of my hand. He winks at me. Tells me, "I am so happy right now."

"Me too," I admit.

My confession surprises the both of us.

His eyes spread so wide I swear he's vying for a Guinness World Record. "Are you saying what I think you're saying?"

I release my hand from his and rub it through my fresh curls. "No, I'm simply saying that *this* feels good. Let's just leave it at that."

He nods. "When did you cut your hair?"

"When I accepted the pregnancy."

"Wasn't easy knowing that you had to deal with me for life, huh?"

"Didn't know it was yours until recently."

He pulls air in through his nose as if he's trying to suck the life out of everyone in this room. Exhales back out of his nostrils hard enough to do the damage of a Category 5 up in here. He does that three or four times. Enough times for me to know that I dropped a serious bomb on him.

"Let me explain," I start.

"What's there to explain. You've been sleeping with me and somebody else at the same time. You thought it was his baby, probably wanted it to be his baby. You found out that you miscalculated and here we are. Guess that's why you waited four months to tell me."

"It's not—"

He turns to me with so much pain in his eyes. It's written all in his voice. "I'm not going to let you continue to make a fool out of me." He lowers his tone when he notices a couple of stares in our direction. "This isn't the place for this."

"It's not what you think," I whisper. "Let's just go to my place and talk about this."

Here I am, begging David to give me his time, something that has always been his role. It's funny how tables turn.

"Right now, I don't think I can stand to be in the same room with you."

"Just let me explain."

❁ ❁ ❁

Twenty minutes later, I turn into my subdivision. In my rear-view mirror, David is not far behind me.

Oh, how I wish I could redo the last four months of my life. Things would be so different.

As soon as I make that left onto my street, I see it. See the teal green Chrysler that immediately floods me with memories of what could've been.

Cory.

I let the garage up, but I don't pull my car in. I get out of my car and rush over to David next to me. I tell him, "Go inside and wait for me." Against my better judgment, I give him the code to my alarm.

I don't wait for David to get out before I kick off my shoes and run across the street to where Cory is parked.

"What are you doing here?"

"We need to talk."

He gets out of the car. Stands over me like the Jolly Green Giant. His eyes roam from me to David's car to my stomach. In that moment, I realize he knows.

"Cory, please, just go. I'll tell you everything, I promise. But this is not the time."

He ignores my pleas, leaves me, and starts walking toward David as he gets out of the car.

"David. Go. In. The. House," I yell.

Neither of them taking their eyes off of each other.

David speaks first. "Cory?"

"Doctor Bryant?"

My mouth drops open. "You two know each other?"

Neither answers the obvious.

David asks, "Is Fatima the woman you were telling me about?"

"You're a smart man. I'm sure you've figured that out by now," Cory says.

I'm speechless.

"When were you going to tell me, Fatima? I deserved that much," Cory requests, still not taking his eyes off of David.

"I tried. Believe me, I did."

"Don't give me that bull—"

"Let's be adult about this, Cory," David intervenes.

Cory steps closer to David. Tells him, "I stopped writing you checks weeks ago, but since you want to give some unsolicited advice, check this out. Do you want to know how I found out that that's not my baby in her stomach?"

Cory looks at me, but directs his question at David.

"Cory, you don't have to do this," David says.

"No, wait, this is a good one for you to put in my file." He chuckles, but no laughter is in his eyes. "I found out I'm infertile. And you want to know how I found out? My own sister told me right before I tried to kill her. Yep, that's right. So you see, right now I'm having just a little bit of trouble trusting anyone. My daddy, my mama, my sister, my brothers, Brenda, Trish, my therapist, and even you." His eyes burn through me like summer in Texas. "Fatima, I thought you'd be the last one to betray me. I became a fool because of you."

"Cory," David and I say at the same time.

"Get away from me," Cory threatens.

Cory takes a few steps back, reaches behind him and pulls out a gun, death staining his dark eyes.

"Cory, wait," David says as calmly as a dove flaps its wings. "I know you're hurt, trust me. I'm just as hurt as you, but this is not the answer."

Cory points that hard piece of iron at David. "What do you know about hurt? You sit there behind your big desk all day and get paid to listen to other people's problems. You don't know a damn thing about pain."

"I don't know about pain, huh?" As David talks he inches closer to Cory, slow and deliberate, tactful like a negotiator. "When I was nine years old, I lost my grandmother, my father, my mother, and my twin brother when our house burned down."

Cory is taken aback by the pain he now hears in his therapist's voice.

"That morning, there was a strong smell floating through the house. My father went to the basement and found one of the pipes was leaking gas. He said we didn't have enough money to call the city out, so he put tape around it. We didn't have money for a lot of stuff." His voice becomes shaky, his poise growing weaker with every word.

"That night, after my father got home from work, the lights went out. There wasn't enough money to pay for that either. I was in the room with Grandma and Donald, and we were in her bed working on a crossword puzzle, which was our nightly ritual, when the lights went out. She told me, 'Baby, go get Grandma a candle so we can finish this puzzle.' I was the oldest by one minute, so I had to take charge. I looked everywhere and came up short. I snuck out the back door 'cause Mama didn't like having to ask folks for handouts, but I snuck out anyway to go ask the neighbors for some candles. Next thing I knew, my house and my family was going up in smoke. So tell me I don't know about pain."

Even though death is riding the night like the Black Plague, hearing David tell the story that connected the two of us together in the first place, both of us parentless by different means, brings tears to my eyes.

"We've all got pain, Cory," David continues. "Killing me, killing Fatima...none of that will change the tables of time. None of that will make you fertile again. This is just another pothole in your path, another bad movie on the TV."

Cory's hand shakes, tears forming in his eyes. "This is how my pain's supposed to end," he says and presses the gun against his temple.

Words run from my lips like a free slave. "Don't do it, Cory. I need you. I love you." I want to run to him and pull the gun from his hand, but I can't move. Fear keeps my feet planted in the soil.

His eyes pierce in my direction. Those black irises tell me the same thing.

"Cory, give me the gun," David says. "This is not how your story ends. Give me the gun."

Every fist my father laid on me, every time my mother let him. Every day my mother refused to tell me the truth, every day she refused to tell me that my father took away *my* ability to be a father, every day my sister refused too. Every seed I was told I planted, every woman that lied to me. Every pain I've experienced in my life begs me to pull the trigger. Begs me to end my never-should've-been, to end my thirty-year misery.

My finger pulls the trigger closer to the grip, closer and closer to my death. Hear the bullet rounding the chamber.

Click.

Nothing happens.

Fatima sobs in the background.

Dr. Bryant and I stare eye to eye. I look in his eyes and see myself sitting in front of his desk again, emotionally unclothed, no part of me hidden. He looks in mine and sees at this moment I want to die.

He raises his hand in a plea for me to give him the gun. "You don't have to do this, Cory."

Too much has gone on for me to go on from here. The gun in my hand steadies. I push it further into my temple. "There's no other way."

"Tell me why *don't* you think there's any other way."

I know what he's doing. "It's not going to work this time, Doc. The cards are different."

He lowers his hand, sticks them both in his pocket. He's throwing in the towel. It's in his eyes. "Well, if your hand is that bad, throw your cards in. Quit playing. Can't make you see something you don't have. Losers give up, winners keep playing. When you're ready to win, you'll see that you *can* no matter what cards lie in your hand. You got to learn to play with what you got and make it work."

If I do this, everyone who did me wrong wins. Everyone. And I still end up losing.

With the gun still pointed at my head, Dr. Bryant searches my eyes for my final decision.

Just like the burdens in my life have become too much for me to bear, so does the gun. It falls from my hand like a fallen angel from the heavens.

I didn't want to kill him, didn't want to kill Fatima. Didn't even want to kill myself. Just wanted to make sense of the situation. Wanted to make sense of the pain. But, to make sense of my life would mean that I have all of the answers. I had no choice in how my story began, and I definitely have no control over how my story ends. Like Dr. Bryant said, *this* is not how my story ends.

Dr. Bryant walks closer to me, kicks the gun further away from me. He stands there with arms open wide and, just like a child being forgiven, I fall into his embrace.

Fatima runs her hand across my face. "You okay?"

My faint smile answers her question.

"I'll be right back," she says.

She leaves me alone with my cup of hot black tea. Goes outside to have some words alone with David.

I admire the man. His ability to make his pain transparent in order for me to see that I'm not the only one who has suffered in this life is admirable. Not to say that I thought that, but I was able to see that there are two sides to every story. The side people allow us to see and the other for their eyes only.

What Dr. Bryant did for me went far beyond therapy. He used his ability to put his own pain aside in order to not just save his life, but mine as well. In some twisted way, it's a good thing that Fatima is carrying his child because had it been someone else's, I doubt I'd be sitting here right now. It's funny how things happen.

"What are you laughing at?" Fatima startles me.

"How long have you been standing there?"

"Long enough."

I can tell that she's scared of me. Probably thinks I'm some psychotic fool ready to blow again at any given minute.

Fatima grabs her cup of tea off of the island and sits on the sofa next to me.

I ask, "Did you mean what you said out there or were you just trying to save my life?"

"I meant it."

Feels like my heart starts beating again. "How long have you felt that way?"

"Since the night you followed me home. It showed me that you cared. Even though you didn't want this baby, you still cared about me."

"Why didn't you tell me?"

She looks at me, so much fire in her eyes. "I tried."

"No you didn't. If you had tried, I would not have had to find out from my own sister."

"Let me be honest for a minute." She puts her cup down on the ottoman. "I never told you it was your baby to begin with."

"Oh, so it's my fault you led me on."

"That's not what I'm saying. I really thought this *was* your baby. I believed that more than anything. I also knew having a child was the last thing you wanted, especially after just finding out about Brenda and losing the baby with—" She stops herself in mid sentence.

"Well, now we know *that* wasn't my baby either." I laugh.

"That's not funny."

I lower my head in shame.

We let the silence continue our conversation for a few seconds.

"I thought you were different, Fatima. Wish you would've told me that I was just a possibility." Feel my discontent creeping back in.

"Do you remember the night I came to Patchouli's, the night we had to pick your sister up at the airport?"

I nod.

"I came to tell you that I was pregnant. I knew your issues with kids, but I wanted to tell you anyway. Felt like you had a right to know."

"Just like I had a right to know that I was just a possibility," I repeat.

"We can sit here and debate about that all night and that won't change a thing." She leans back on the sofa. "That night, I was so happy. I felt beautiful and I wanted to share that with you. I wanted you in the worst way and I believed you wanted me just the same. But you got that phone call and it changed everything. Changed how I felt about you. Changed how I thought you felt about me. I felt so disrespected to where I wanted to erase any trace of you. Cory, I felt so hurt that I went to get an abortion. Carrying your baby proved to be the last thing I needed in my life."

"An abortion?" I lick my lips, they feel drier than dry.

"Cory, you don't understand. I had gone from feeling like I was capable of handling anything to not even feeling like I was able to handle myself. The only power I had was to cut the ties that bind. I had to rid myself of you, of you and all that you came with."

For another minute, there's silence. Both of us tangled up in our own thoughts. Had I just walked out her door and stayed out when she told me to a long time ago, I would not be in this situation right now. I would be somewhere else being lied to by the next woman.

"My sister tried to protect me, yet in her protection she left me unprotected. To be lied to by my own family hurt me more than life itself. Instead of owning up to it, she took it out on you. Yeah you lied, but she did the same thing she was accusing you of."

"You really tried to kill her?"

My heart is heavy, causes me to close my eyes. No matter how wrong Cora was, I had no right putting my hands on her. I change the subject. "How long have you been dealing with David?"

"Too long to remember."

"How'd you meet him?"

She sighs. "Used to be one of his clients."

"Never pegged you as one to seek therapy."

"Hey, like they say, sometimes you got to do what you got to do."

We both nod in agreement.

"I was going through a lot at the time. Was trying to channel out all of my negative energy. I was in massage therapy school, still living with my grandma, dealing with my need to have a father figure in my life. I was toting it all around and realized that I couldn't do it by myself anymore." She puts her back up against the arm of the sofa, swings her legs up. Her feet graze against my thigh.

My curiosity grows. "How did you go from being his client to his bedmate?"

"To be honest, he had this authoritative disposition that commanded my attention. He asked me questions and pulled so many things out of me that I never knew existed. He gave me advice, gave me antidotes to the plagues of life. He represented something in my life that I never had. I mistook the unfamiliarity for an attraction. One thing led to another. I'm sure you can figure out the rest."

She pulls her legs in closer to her, wraps her arms around her knees.

"I see."

"David and I only recently turned things sexual. Like I said, I mistook one thing for another and let my guard down. It was a mistake. Knew it the moment it happened, but I let it happen again and again. Right before I met you, I called things off for good. I just felt like I was simply another victim for him to save."

"So how'd we end up in this triangle?"

"I went back." Fatima blows out air through tight lips. "I was confused. You came along and introduced me to a new set of feelings. Maybe David had already lit the match inside of me, but you came with the gasoline and set me on fire. I didn't want to feel like that, so I went back to David to bring me down from my high. He was like a Newport and you were Ecstasy."

"Great comparison." I turn my head from her. Tap my foot against the ottoman.

"You know what I'm trying to say."

"You're carrying his baby. Where does that leave the two of you now?"

A loud, long yawn falls from her lips. Moves me to look at the time. It's almost three in the morning. We both have jobs to go to in a few hours.

My question doesn't need an answer. It just went with the flow of the conversation. I get up from the sofa, prepare to leave.

She stands up with me. "Don't go. Stay here tonight."

"It's not right."

Fatima's eyes tell me that it's too late at night to have a debate between right and wrong. "You can sleep in my guest bedroom, even sleep down here if you that makes you feel more comfortable. I just don't want you to be alone tonight. I don't want to be alone either. If you stay here, my mind will be at ease."

I don't want to be alone tonight either, even if it is only for a few hours.

She walks over to me, stands one exhale away. "I meant what I said earlier. I do love you, Cory. I love you, but I love my baby, too."

As the sun plays peek-a-boo with the clouds, I watch Cory walk to his car. His stride is somewhat staggered, shoulders holding a lifetime of insecurities. Nothing like his attention-grabbing walk that first caught my eyes.

He knows I'm watching him. His pause before getting into his car lets me know that. If he turns around, I swear I'll run out there after him. He doesn't. His eyes stay focused forward, toward the future. And now I know things between us will never be the same.

Cory drives off and I feel an emptiness inside. Feel like I am losing a part of me, like I'm losing my right to breathe. I want to pick up the phone and call him, tell him to come back so we can run away from this world together. Make our mark on another planet where soul mates are the only souls that mate. A land where we write our beginning, present, and future. I want to call him and tell him we can erase what's been and rewrite what's to be. I want to, but I don't.

Perspiration on the concrete across the street is the only evidence that Cory was here. I could stand here for an eternity, but that wouldn't change a thing. He is gone and there is nothing I can do about it. I tear myself away from the despondent reflection. Submerging myself in the one-degree-below-boiling water in the tub is my only consolation.

❃ ❃ ❃

It's a quarter to nine when I walk my last client of the night to the front to pay for his services. "See you next month," I tell him.

Once he leaves, I lock the door behind him.

Danielle hands me a printout of our profits for the day. "We were hustling around here today."

I look over the paper, realize I had eight clients alone. Two Brazilian and underarm waxes, one sixty-minute deep tissue massage, two Swedish massages, a seaweed body wrap, and two Parafango body wraps. I don't even remember doing all of that. Adrian and my five other staff members did just as much as I did.

I hand the paper back to Danielle for her to put in the book. "Advertising is worth every dollar spent. We keep spreading the word, business will be like this every day."

She finishes closing up shop while I head to the back. Adrian is nearby, stripping sheets off her massage table. I step inside her room. "I'm going to get out of here. Danielle is done up front. All's left to do is cut off the lights and cut on the alarm."

"You going to be okay?" she asks.

I nod in the affirmative.

"Call me if you need me."

I tell her I will.

She stops doing what she's doing to give me that you-better-do-what-I-say motherly look she does so well. "I'm serious."

I give her a wink and leave her to get my things out of my locker.

As soon as I get in my car, my body decides it wants to crash. Now is not the time.

I cut the car on, pop in my new Corinne Bailey Rae CD, put the car in reverse and make that twenty-minute drive to the north side of town. Her song "Trouble Sleeping" takes my thoughts back to last night when I had trouble sleeping, but for different reasons. So much has gone on in the last seventy-two hours. As tired as I've been, I have not been able to get a decent night's sleep in ages. But somehow, through the rollercoaster sequence of events from last night, I managed to close my eyes long enough to dream.

Last night, or this morning rather, I dreamt of my father.

It was one of those crazy what-the-hell-was-that-all-about type of dreams that left me feeling like I had way too much sleep.

I was on the porch, lying on an old, wooden swing. The early September breeze was calmly sending me into an afternoon sleep. The house was located in the deep woods, surrounded by dirt roads and trees. A place I did not recognize, yet I was comfortable enough to close my eyes.

It was mid-afternoon, but with my eyes closed, it looked as though the sun was trying to close its eyes. It couldn't be. I opened mine and almost fell out of the swing.

The sun had turned pitch black. I freaked out, ran inside the house screaming at the top of my lungs, but no one came to my aid. I ran upstairs and heard my parents arguing. For a second, I was confused, but I went into their room anyway. I said, "The sun...something is wrong with the sun."

My dad looked at me. Mom kept yelling.

I turned to her and started yelling at her. "It's not about you right now. The fucking sun just turned black and you're still concerned about you."

She moved toward me like she was about to slap the mess out of me. "Who do you think you're talking to?"

The look of death in her eyes didn't scare me one bit. I raised my arm in her direction, bent my two forefingers and gave her the curse Celie gave Mister in *The Color Purple*. Told her, "You've ruled my life for too long. No more."

Daddy grabbed my arm and rushed me out of the room. He shook me. "Fatima, what's wrong with you?"

I didn't answer. Just ran down the stairs and back out the front door. Pointed to the sun. "Look."

He briefly glanced, then pulled me into his chest and covered my eyes with his hand. "I've been trying to find you so I could tell you about that."

"Daddy, I'm scared."

He kept holding me tight. "Don't be. I'm here with you now and that's all that matters."

I moved my head away from his hands, wanted to look at the sun again. It was moving closer to Earth like the asteroid in the movie *Deep Impact*. And just like Téa Leoni in the movie, I was standing in my father's arms in our final minutes.

But we didn't die.

He picked me up and carried me inside, sat down in a chair, and sat me in his lap.

Mama came down the stairs. "What the hell is going on?"

There I was, a grown woman, sitting in my father's lap again. It was like old times before he left. For a moment, I felt peace.

He ignored her, looked me in my eyes and said, "I've wished for this moment since the day—"

Beep beep. Beep beep. Beep beep...

My alarm clock was trying to tell me that it was six-thirty and I needed to get ready for work. I tried to ignore it and finish my dream, but it was no use. For a second, I just lay in bed wondering how in the hell did I have that senseless dream. Black sun, cursing my mom out, sitting in my father's lap. It didn't make a lick of sense.

Maybe it was from my lack of sleep.

Or maybe, deep down I want to connect with my father again.

❂ ❂ ❂

I pull up in front of Leonardo's, a pizza joint that keeps late hours every night of the week. The baby is making me crave a nice, juicy portabella mushroom and green olive thin-crust pizza. Mmmm, my mouth waters just thinking about it.

Before I grab a table or place my order, I have to relieve my bladder. The bathroom isn't as clean as I'd like, but at a time like this, it doesn't even matter.

When I walk back out to claim a table, that's when I see him. He's sitting in a booth not far from the front door. Dark blue Polo shirt, gray slacks. Looks just like I remember him, as if time stood still for him. He sees me, hesitates. Lets the anxiousness in his face dissipate.

"I thought you were going to stand me up," are his first words.

"Unlike you, I don't turn my back on my commitments."

"Ouch."

He takes my brashness hard. Sits back down gently like he's in need of some Preparation-H.

I slide into my side of the booth feeling like the cards are in my favor.

"Fatima, I didn't come here—"

I cut him off. "You walked out of my life twenty-five years ago. Did you expect me to come here with a dozen roses? Let's not act like you just went out of town on business."

"Wow." He looks around the empty restaurant. Other than the staff, we are the only two in the place. "I was just hoping that we could talk about this like civil adults."

Give-me-a-break is written all over my face. "Don't you tell me about being civil. Did you forget you walked out on your wife and daughter because you got another woman pregnant?"

"It's not how you think. You were only four."

I lean back in my seat, arms folded. "Explain it to me, then. I think I'm old enough now."

He sits quietly, contemplates his next choice of words carefully. "Why'd you drop your last name?"

"Didn't want any part of you."

That hurts him.

Does exactly what I want it to.

He bites down on his bottom lip, a nervous habit he passed on to his children. "Do you hate me?"

"At one point in time, I did."

My father shakes his head. "*Do* you hate me?" he questions again.

I think about what he's really asking me. Think about how I felt over the years when I gave him too much power over me and my emotions. Gave him control over how I wanted to feel. As much as it would appease my ego to puncture his, I am not in that place anymore. "No," I tell him the truth.

He relaxes some in his seat. The tension in the air thinning like a woman's cervix before giving birth.

"I never wanted to hate you, but you broke my heart. You were my father, for goodness' sake."

"Still am."

Finally, I am presented with the opportunity of a lifetime, the chance to ask my father the million-dollar question. "Why did you leave?"

His nostrils flare as he takes a deep breath. I can hear the air being pulled in through his nose like he's about to bench press a thousand pounds.

I fiddle around with the ice in my cup, not sure if I'm ready for the answer I've been waiting to hear for twenty-something-odd years.

"No reason is good enough, Fatima."

I push my cup back, stare at my need-to-be-trimmed fingernails. Flashes of the worst heartbreak of my life travel through my mind. "When Mama left, I thought my life was over. The world as I knew it ceased to exist. I experienced more emotions in one night than most people do in their entire lifetime. Probably cried enough tears to fill the Atlantic Ocean three times. There I was, four years old, feeling like I couldn't trust anybody. If my own mother and father couldn't be trusted, who could?"

"I didn't know Ruby had left."

"You didn't?" My voice reeks of sarcasm. "Something tells me deep down you knew she wouldn't stay."

His eyebrows curve down toward his nose. "Why would you say that?"

I reach into my purse, pull out the brown suede journal that was sent to me. "It's all in there. She didn't want me, you knew that. So why would you *think* leaving would make her stay?"

He looks at the journal then back at me. Looks at the journal. I slide it toward him.

He doesn't pick it up immediately. Instead he reads my face for any sign of emotion. Any sign of hurt or anger. Anything to let him know if he should run out of my life again or come over to my side and give me a hug.

He runs his fingertips across the velvety texture. "Ruby had a lot of layers. A lot of dimensions. Every inch I got into her was like falling in love with her all over again. She had such an innocence about her, a delicacy that made me weak in my knees. We would lay under the moonlight and write poetry together. I was a photographer and she was my muse. She made me happy to be alive, made me happy to be in love."

He sighs through his trip back in time of happier times.

"Shortly after we got married, I told her that I was ready to start a family. I wanted to share all of what life had shown me with another part of me, another part of her. I wanted us to create something beautiful, something magnificent. That's when I found out that your mother and I didn't share the same vision. It was like my wants to expand our horizons brought out a different side of Ruby that I had never seen before. She became lukewarm. I never knew which way she was coming, if she was coming or going. She would often fall into a deep funk. She basically stopped communicating with me. It was through a telephone conversation that I found out she was pregnant. When I confronted her about it, unable to hide my happiness, she slipped into a deeper funk. Days later is when I found her at the clinic."

All of this is too much for me to hear. I pick up the phone on the wall next to me. Order a medium thin crust pizza with my two toppings on it. Hand the phone to my father for him to place his order. Do that to get our thoughts on something else for a minute. As hungry as I am, I couldn't eat even if I wanted to.

"Fatima, she went behind my back and tried to end a life that I helped create. I've never forgiven her for that."

I look at him with soft eyes. "When I read about that in her journal, I wished you had never found out. I wished she had succeeded in ridding her life of me, in ridding me of this life."

He looks at me with the most compassionate set of hazel eyes I've ever seen. "How could you say something like that?"

"It's how I felt. Imagine reading how your own mother didn't want you and how she'd rather die than give birth to you. Wouldn't you wish the same thing?"

His silence says it all.

"That was the hardest reality I ever had to face," I say. "Carrying me made her so depressed that she wanted to end her life and mine in the process. Was I that much of a burden? Did carrying me make her that unhappy?"

He doesn't say anything, just grunts at my never ending questions. A hard sigh helps me fight back the tears.

"I hate that you feel that way," my father finally says.

"Sometimes, in the back of my mind, I look at you as a hero for saving my life that day. But, at the same time, I see you as a man who gave up, retired his cape, and left me out to die. For something you wanted so bad, how could you do that to me, Daddy?"

His eyes come to life at my reference to his relation. "My dearest Fatima. For the rest of my days, I'll regret that one moment in time when I made the worst decision in my life. I never meant to leave you. I never meant to hurt you. I never meant to do to you what your mother did to me. You've got to believe me."

My heart wants to believe him so bad. I want to reach across the table and fall into his arms like a sinner at the cross.

He reaches in his back pocket, pulls out his wallet. From it, he slides an old photograph across the table. "You were three when this picture was taken."

I stare at it. I stare at it real hard.

My mother and I are sitting outside. I'm sitting between her legs with a wooden bowl in my lap and a small, pink Baskin Robbins spoon in my hand. My hair in half an afro on one side, the other side has my mother's hands in it. I look so small and innocent, my big eyes staring straight into the eyes of the person behind the camera as if I'm begging to be taken away from this unhappiness. Like I'm begging to be rescued from the woman who I've made unhappy.

I ask, "Did you take this picture?"

"Yes," my father answers.

I don't take my eyes off of the photo when I ask him that. My eyes focused on the distant gaze in my mother's eyes. She's staring at a place far away from where we are as she does my hair. Looks like she's staring at another life, a life before me. A life before things got complicated for her.

I hand the picture back over to him. "I never felt loved by her," I tell him.

"Me either," he says and puts it back in his wallet. "I loved her more than anything, but sometimes love just isn't enough."

"Why do you keep that with you?" I want to know.

"To remind me of why I left."

I let out a deep sigh that lets him know his rationalization is ridiculous. "If anything, looking at my face in that picture should've made you stay."

"I know this isn't a good reason to leave your family, but to answer your question, I no longer felt loved or needed. Ruby shut down and shut me out. I tried everything to bring the Ruby I fell in love with back. She was too far gone, though. Living in a home where you don't even know who you're living with wasn't a safe environment for me, or you for that matter, so I prepared to leave and I was taking you with me. That didn't go over well with her. She made all kind of threats. For your safety, I stayed. Emotionally, I was gone. I couldn't feel for her anymore." He pauses while our pizzas are placed on the table.

I ask the server, "Can we get some to-go boxes?"

My father waits for the boxes before he continues. "I am a lover, Fatima. Being in a relationship where I could not be me, where who I was, was jeopardized, left me searching for an outlet where I could be free. And unfortunately, that lead me into the arms of another woman. It was wrong, but I couldn't help but feel liberated. I felt free as a bird with her. Before I knew it, I was caught up. My ideal fantasy of what love really felt like became my reality. She ended up pregnant and I had to make a decision… the one decision which cost me you."

I lick moisture back into my lips. "I don't understand. You said you were going to take me at one time. Why didn't you take me then?"

"Ruby was trying to call my bluff. She never would've let me take you with me. Even if she didn't want you, she didn't want me to have you. You and Ruby were a package deal."

I box my pizza up. My appetite stolen by my emotions. "You know what, Lawrence? You were right. No reason will *ever* be good enough."

"Even though I was not there, I never stopped thinking about you. Wrote you letters, sent you cards for your birthday every year," he tells me.

"Cards? Letters? I couldn't care less about that. I wanted *you*. I needed *you*."

"I'm sorry, Fatima. That was the only way I could reach out at the time."

"Well, I never got 'em."

"They were returned to me. Everything but the money got 'returned to sender.'"

I look up at my father, the pain in his voice too sincere for me to ignore. "Wish things were different."

"Me too, Fatima." He smiles at me. "You know, I named you that the moment I held you in my arms for the first time. You were a blessing, a *great* blessing."

For the first time in my adult life, I smile at my father.

For a second, his eyes twinkle. Maybe it was the reflection from the lights. Or maybe it was a hint of a tear that faded with the memory.

"Do you think you could ever forgive me?"

I shrug, shake my head. "That's a lot to ask."

"Your agreeing to meet me was a lot."

He's right. When I got his call earlier today, I could've turned him down, but I didn't. Maybe it was the crazy dream I had. Or maybe deep down, if I'm willing to travel that far into my vault of feelings, I will see that I want my father in my life again. Maybe I want to be daddy's little girl again. Or maybe it's these crazy hormones. Either way, we're both here. Father and daughter.

He says, "I was in town on business, I leave in the morning. I'm in town often, visiting Lauren. Next time I'm in town, I'd like to see you again." He pauses and looks in the air for a second, almost like he's searching his brain for something else to say. "I can actually come back next weekend. I would really like to spend some time with you."

My response is dry. "We'll see what happens."

For now, my answer satisfies him.

I watch my father as he walks up to the register to pay for our uneaten food. I watch him and on the inside I smile. I'll never know why the currents of life shifted us in this direction, but we are here for a reason and we are a part of each other. He is blood of my blood and I am flesh of his flesh.

When he gets back to the table, I grab my pizza and purse, tell him thanks for the food, and head toward the door.

Neither of us say anything as he walks me to my car. We both stand at my door, hesitating, as if we're not quite sure how to end things.

He speaks first. "I saw the frown on your face when I mentioned your sister's name. Don't blame Lauren. She—"

I put my hand up to stop him. "Please, let's not go there. She knew exactly what she was doing."

"Hear me out, please." He fights her case anyway. "She just

found out, okay? Her and her family came to visit one weekend. Lauren went crazy trying to find a photograph of herself when she was sixteen. She kept rambling about 'closure.' She looked through album after album with no such luck. Her and my wife ventured off into the attic. Isaiah and I were on the lawn bar-bequing when Lauren came running outside with a picture in her hand. Her eyes were red as Georgia clay, she was screaming. My wife wasn't far behind, tears in her own eyes. Lauren found a picture of me and you when you were just a baby. Lauren knew it wasn't her because she had curly hair since the day she was born. I knew then I couldn't keep my past a secret anymore. I never wanted her to find out about her father's faults. I had already hurt one daughter, the last thing I wanted to do was hurt another one."

He pounds his fist into his chest. Makes me grip the keys in my hand a little tighter. "I have failed as a father, Fatima. My short-comings have caused enough pain. Your sister is hurting. Please, don't let me be the cause of you two not being able to at least be friends."

I open my car door and look at his pathetic behind one good time before I get in. "You're right, Lawrence. You *have* caused enough pain."

39 / CORY HINES

It's funny how time has a way of repeating itself.

Here I am, sitting in front of Dr. Bryant again. We're not in his office though, we're in his home.

"Can I get you something to drink?" he offers.

I decline.

"Bet you're wondering why I called you over."

I nod.

He relaxes in an antique-style deep brown leather sofa. Hands crossed in his lap. "First of all, how are you?"

"I'm not going to lie, David. This is awkward." No need in calling him doctor anymore.

He bobs his head in agreement. "Then let's move past the small talk. I called you here because, as we were both recently made aware, we have something in common. We both share Fatima."

"I don't share women," I quickly let him know.

"Neither do I. Can't change what is, though."

"She's carrying *your* baby. Can't change that either." I get up to leave.

"But she loves you."

His admission stops me in my tracks.

"I'm not sure how to begin to understand what I'm feeling, Cory. What I'm about to say is hard as hell for me to admit, even to myself, but it's a reality I've been facing since the other night."

I sit back down.

This time, the good doctor puts his feelings on the line. "As long as I've known Fatima, I have loved her. Everything about her. I accepted the good and the bad, her rocky past and everything in between. She wasn't easy to love, but that was okay with me. I accepted what little she did give me. No matter how hard I showed her that I loved her, no matter how many times I showed her that I wasn't going anywhere, she never looked at me the way she looked at you. I was insanely in love with Fatima. Was willing to lose myself in order for her to know that what I felt was real. I did all of that, but she never loved me back."

Hearing him open up like that in front of me, a former patient, lets me know that everyone is vulnerable for something or someone at some point in time. Having a PhD couldn't save him from heartache. He hurts the same as me.

"Cory, what I'm trying to say is," he clears his throat, "I want you to be with Fatima. I want you to make her happy."

The pain from loving, from not having his love reciprocated stifles the air like the smog in L.A. The disappointment in his voice, hearing him tell another man to love his woman makes me uncomfortable.

"She's carrying *your* child," I say again.

"We've already established that. I can't make her happy, haven't done so in all these years. You did what I had been trying to do in a matter of months. Can't stop what's to be 'cause it's going to be regardless."

"Damn," is all I can say. Insane was an understatement.

"I bet you think I'm crazy."

Now he's reading my thoughts. "That goes without saying."

He chuckles. "I'd probably think the same thing if the situation were reversed."

"I'm sitting here listening to you, trying to make sense, but any logical reasoning fails me right now. This just does not make sense."

"Remember in your last session, when you told me that you were going to make things work?"

I nod in the affirmative.

"If I had known you were talking about Fatima, I would've given you some different advice."

This time a chuckle vibrates through my lips.

"Seriously though, let's look at the cards on the table. You were willing to go against everything you taught yourself to accept about yourself by being a father to your child with Fatima. That took a lot of courage. A lot of heart. Unfortunately, you now know the baby is not yours. The DNA has changed, but the story is still the same. Don't stop writing the book just because the plot changed. Change it again. You've come too far not to."

"I don't know, Doc."

"I'm not here as your therapist, but as someone who cares about your well-being. I know there are some skeptics out there who think all we do is sit and listen to strangers tell their problems day-in-day-out, hand out advice like it's popcorn, and cash checks, but we really do care how your lives turn out. It's more than a job for some of us, for me. Your situation is no different. It just hits a little closer to home."

Once again, he's right. His words have always made sense to me. They've opened my eyes and helped me to see things a lot differently. Shoot, his words have saved my life. Why shouldn't I listen now?

My curiosity peaks though. "Okay, so if I still *try* to be a part of Fatima's life, where does that leave you?"

"I'm going to be right here." He looks me straight in the face to make sure there's no misunderstanding. "My lack of a romantic involvement with the mother does not mean I can't or won't be a father."

"I knew there was a catch." I still have my reservations about the whole situation.

"It is what it is."

I say, "Fatima might not even agree to this. She's got a lot going on right now. I doubt she'd be able to handle this."

"Say she does, then what?"

The thought crosses my mind. "I don't know."

"Cory, you're a strong man. You've treaded through some rough waters and you made it through all right. Hard times come to make us strong. Think about it, you're still standing. Be that strength for Fatima. I wouldn't trust you with her if I thought otherwise."

I nod my appreciation. Means a lot to hear a grown man tell me that.

He says, "After losing my family, I wanted to lose myself. Had it not been for a certain fireman–who stuck by my side from that day until a fire claimed his life fifteen years later–I more than likely would have lost myself. He always told me, 'Sometimes people are in trouble and can't save themselves, so God has to put people in their lives to help them find their way out. Can't save everybody, but at least we can try. Because of him, I tried to save everybody I saw in trouble. I couldn't save my family, but I could save myself and anybody who came in my path."

He moves forward in his seat, gets closer to me. "Point is, I threw myself into my cause, into my mission. I focused so much on saving folk that I was almost in my forties and realized I had given up all hope for having a family. Imagine that, I tell everyone else they can do and have, but didn't believe it for myself. Then Fatima showed up and changed my faith. She became my cause, became my mission. Unfortunately, we didn't work out, but she is giving me my family. Do you understand where I'm going with this?"

I bob my head up and down. "I believe I do."

"I can't have Fatima. You can't have children. In spite of that reality, if we all work together, we can all have what we want."

Again, I get up to leave.

On my way out, he stops me. "Can I give you one piece of advice on the house?"

"Sure."

He doesn't skip a beat. "Your sister was wrong, but two wrongs don't make a right."

No need for him to say anything else.

❂ ❂ ❂

It takes three days before my sister accepts my phone call. "I know I'm probably the last person you want to hear from," I say as soon as she picks up the phone.

"You tried to kill me." Her voice scarred.

I sympathize with her angst. "If I tell you I'm sorry every day for a thousand years, it still wouldn't be enough. Cora, you've got to believe me. It was never my intention to hurt you."

Silence.

"You still there?" I want to know.

More silence.

"I'm sorry, Cora."

"You tried to kill me," she finally says again.

"I know, Cora, and I am sorry. I wish there was a way for me to take time and rewind it back, but I can't."

"My own brother tried to kill me."

My breathing grows tight. I contemplate hanging the phone up.

There's movement on her end of the phone. Sounds like *she's* the one about to hang up.

Her voice resonates with remorse. "I should have told you."

She's right, but I don't tell her so. "That still didn't give me the right to put my hands on you."

I can hear her fighting through the tears on the other line.

"I was trying to protect you."

My anger grows. "Protect me from what?"

"From people who don't give a damn about you. None of these women out here care about you."

"Some would argue that neither do you."

She sucks her teeth. "How could you say that?"

My voice climbs up a notch. "You did the same thing you accused all of those women for doing. You lied to me. Lied to me my whole life."

"I was going to tell you, Cory."

"When? After I took my last breath?"

"That wasn't fair."

"Let's not talk about fair. That is not something you should have kept from me. Instead, you tried to make everyone else look like the bad guy."

She coughs, blows her nose. "Mama made me promise to take it to my grave."

"I wouldn't have kept something like that from you."

"She made me promise."

"Come on, Cora. Mama knew you couldn't hold secrets. She didn't want to have to tell me. She only told you not to so that you would."

"Fuck you."

"Whoa. Is that why you're the best divorce lawyer in Chicago?"

Silence.

Silence is on both ends.

Seems like the more we say, the deeper we dig the cut.

"No matter how we look at it, we were all wrong, Cory. You, me, and Mama."

I ask, "So what do we do about it? Where do we go from here?"

"Maybe it's time we had family counseling. All of us. We need to get rid of the curse on this family before it tears up all we have left. Daddy did his best to destroy us. I won't let him succeed."

"Won't that be a little hard with you being up there?"

She blows her nose again. "I'm moving back, Cory. I'm coming home."

Her news surprises me. "Why?"

"Because I left for all the wrong reasons. I was trying to run, trying to forget, but I could've run to Kalamazoo and my past would've still followed me. It's a part of me. There's no getting around that. But I left at a time my family needed me the most. I should've been there for you, for all of you, Mama included. It's just time for me to come home. It's time to take off the bandages and let this family heal."

I disagree. "This is us, Cora. We are who we are. This is our story. We're okay."

"No, we're not okay, but we will be."

And with every fiber in me, I believe that we will.

"You've been silent for way too long. I need some answers and I need them now."

"Here we go again. I done told you all I'm gon' tell you."

"Which hasn't been much of nothing."

My grandmother stands behind the screened door, refuses to open it and let me in. "So why you keep asking?"

I pull at the door. It's locked.

"Fatima, you're a grown woman now. You don't need nothing else from me."

"I saw my father."

She puts her hand on the door, then steps away. "I told him not to bother you."

"You've talked to him?" I pull at the door again. It's still locked.

"He came by here looking for you."

"When?"

"A few days ago."

The last time I was here was a few days ago. I remember Grandma being all discombobulated in Ruby's room. Remember her begging me not to leave that night. Also remember a car zooming by me on my way over here. Must've been him rushing off to find me. "Will you open this door so I don't look like a fool out here?"

"You knew you'd come back. Shouldn't have left your key."

"Did what I had to do at the time."

"And I'm doing what I have to do right now."

I stand outside with my arms folded across my chest, my patience running thinner than the hairs on the head of someone suffering from alopecia. My grandmother stands the same way on the opposite side of the locked screen door.

"Why did you send his letters and cards back? Why did you keep my father from me?"

"He kept himself from you when he walked out that door. I didn't do nothing he hadn't done already."

"That was so unfair." I feel tears on the horizon, but I won't let them fall.

"Just leave," she says. "There's nothing else left here for you."

What's the point in trying to argue with this woman? She will never understand my angst, nor will she concede to my understanding of her own. This is the life we live and some things should be left in the land of the unknown.

In the last couple of months, in the process of searching for the secrets of my life, for the answers to the whys of my life, I have lost my dignity. I have put myself in compromising positions, put my life on the line, even caused someone I cared about to make an attempt on his own life, all because I couldn't leave yesterday alone. Searching for my past has done nothing but cause heartache. It has caused me to lose the little bit of who I was, yet at the same time, it allowed me to really learn who I am. To learn what makes me...me.

Grandma Pearl is inside, sitting at the breakfast table. Her back is toward me. Maybe she thinks I'm gone, but I'm still right here. Right here watching her and dropping my past off on her back door. For yesterday is gone, today is all I have.

I tap lightly on the screen door.

She doesn't turn around. Maybe she knew I was still here all along.

I tell her, "This is it. I'm not coming back."

She gets up slowly, takes slow steps toward me. "I think that's best. For you and me." She closes her eyes tight. "And Ruby."

I want to ask her why does her child cause her so much pain, just the mention of her name, but I don't. I can't keep living like that. And looking at Grandma, she can't either.

Walking back toward my car, I realize walking away is the best decision I could have made. Today is a new chapter in my life. From now on, I will dismiss the things and the people whose only purpose is to exist as a constant reminder. My life is not a rearview mirror. Neither is my future.

Fatima sees me as soon as she walks out the back door. My presence catches her off guard, can tell when she drops her keys on the ground.

I get out of the car. "I'll get 'em."

"What are you doing here?" She doesn't look at me when she asks me that.

I hand her the keys. "Wanted to see you."

A hint of a smile etches across her face. "How long have you been here?"

"Maybe an hour or so."

"That long?" She locks the door. "Why didn't you just come on in?"

"Figured you would be busy. Plus, it's your job. Didn't want to make you feel uncomfortable."

"I think we're past that stage and then some."

We share a light laugh.

I ask, "So what're your plans for the night?"

"Haven't made any."

Fatima struggles to bend over. I stop her. "Let me help you."

"Thanks."

We walk in the direction of our cars. She leads the way. "Feels good out, doesn't it?"

"My favorite time of the year," I say.

It's not quite dark out yet, but dark enough for the street lights to be on. The temperature feels like summer is in the backseat sharing a sneaky kiss with fall.

She pops open the trunk to her SUV for me to put the bags in. "So, why did you want to see me?"

I debate if I should tell her what the good doctor, well, David, and I talked about. I decide against it, at least for now. "Because I knew it was something you wouldn't expect."

She sits on the edge of her open trunk. "When you left the other morning, I thought I'd never see you again."

"Is that what you wanted?"

She cuts her eyes up at me. "You already know the answer."

I sit down beside her. "Do you think we have a chance?"

"That's the big question, eh?" Fatima gets further in the trunk, sits Indian-style with her back up against the inside. "Considering everything, when I really think about it, I think we have possibilities."

"Guess *anything* is possible."

We make eye contact. Not just looking into each other's eyes, but we make there's-a-meeting-in-my-bedroom type of eye contact.

She licks her lips, makes her signature deep dimple in her left cheek pop out when she gives me a seductive smile.

I rub the outside of her thigh, but my mind isn't on sex. I tell her, "The past few weeks have been hell."

"That's an understatement," she adds.

"True. I mean I lost my mother, tried to kill my sister. Found out not one, not two, but three kids who were claimed to be mine don't have my genetic code running through their veins." I didn't bother letting Patricia in on my recent discovery. No need in reopening that wound.

Fatima shifts from my touch, shifts in her shame.

I didn't say that to make her uncomfortable. Just stating where my life has taken me.

"I never told you this baby was yours, Cory."

"And you never told me it wasn't. Didn't even tell me there was a fifty-fifty possibility."

"You were too busy throwing your own pity party, you wouldn't have even heard me if I tried." She blows out a hard puff of air. "I'm not going to let you blame me for your assumption."

"An assumption? Is that what y'all call it these days when a brother steps up to his responsibility? Come on now. You told me you were pregnant. What else was I supposed to do?"

She unfolds her legs, swings them around to the ground. She moves with a quickness. Moves so fast she twists her ankle. "Shit." She almost hits the ground.

I jump from the truck. "You okay?" I ask helping her regain her balance.

She pushes me off of her, stands away from me, hands in the air. "I don't need this right now, Cory."

I agree. This isn't what either of us need right now. I keep enough space between us to where both parties are comfortable. "Look, Fatima, I'm trying to get some sense of control over my emotions. I'm trying to understand A, B, and C. Some things aren't making sense, but I am trying to understand."

"You don't think I know you're hurting? Who isn't? We're all trying to put the pieces together in our lives, but in the process we can't tear down another's logic, what makes sense to them. For me, right now, I'm making sense of my life and I do not need you or anyone else for that matter bringing your own sense into it."

For the first time, I honestly listen with my ears and not my emotions. I hear exactly what Fatima is saying. I hear her so well that I feel for her. She's been through a lot, more than I'll ever know or understand. But what I do know is I don't want this to be the end for us. I tell her just that.

I close in on the distance between us, wrap my arms around her waist. She doesn't flinch, doesn't fight me. Makes my heart smile. I look her in those beautiful, brown eyes of hers. "I want you in my life, Fatima. More than anything. For the good of us, collectively and individually, we can't be right now. I have work to do on me and I won't allow you to be with me until my transformation is complete. Can you understand that?"

She wraps her arms around my shoulders and pulls me into her. Holds me so tight I feel like I'm the one carrying a baby.

"I can understand that and I respect you for doing the right thing, not just for you, but for us. All three of us."

She pulls back, iris to iris. She kisses me. No tongue, just her lips pressed against mine. Kisses me hard enough to let me know that once we get our lives together, we will be together.

Weeks pass when I finally pick up the phone to talk to David again. What we had was never easy, but what we have now will bind us for the rest of our lives. To deny him his paternal right by not allowing him to take part in the rest of my pregnancy would be selfish and plain old unfair. I could not do that to him, not even if I wanted to. He is a good man, just not the man for me. But he will be a good man for our child.

David has been spoiling me like crazy too. As my belly grows, he takes pleasure in massaging me down with Shea butter, giving my swollen feet weekly foot soaks in peppermint and eucalyptus, and running around town like a madman to appease my ridiculous cravings. One night, I wanted a Hawaiian-inspired serving of ice cream. He went up the street to Walmart, bought a pint of Blue Bell Homemade Vanilla ice cream, a fresh pineapple, and a jar of macadamia nuts. Mixed them all together in the blender, poured the creamy delight in a bowl with drizzled chocolate on top. With a spoonful of goodness on my lips, I swore I was in Heaven.

Several nights, we stayed up talking as he rubbed my feet. We would mostly talk about how we were going to raise our child. But on certain nights, Cory's name would creep into our conversations like the winter cold through an unlit fireplace. I would try not to think about him, try not to remember his touch. Try not to miss him so much. My efforts denied me. After not hearing back from him after my umpteenth call, I promised myself I would try to forget him a little harder.

Months roll by like the credits at the end of a movie. I find myself wanting to rewind time and catch a piece of life I missed the first time. It wouldn't matter though. I am happy right now. Happy living, laughing, and loving me and my unborn baby.

❂ ❂ ❂

Business is booming. The spa is gaining more and more clientele every day. I haven't been on my feet much lately though, so I've spread all of my clients evenly with the rest of the team. I will gladly welcome them back once I come back.

I watch Adrian walk toward me at the front desk, sadness in both of our eyes.

"Are you sure you want to leave?" I ask her.

"Don't have a choice. I told my husband if he got a job in Minot, North Dakota, I would move with him. Told him I had his back no matter what as long as he got a job." She pouts. "You know I don't want to leave, but I got to support my family."

"I know. Just gonna miss you."

"At least I'm not leaving until after the baby is born."

A smile crosses my face. "Thank God. Doubt I'd make it without you."

She looks at me with all seriousness in her eyes. "You heard back from her yet?"

I shake my head. "No phone call, no thank-you card. Nothing."

"Guess it's for the best." Adrian shrugs. "At least you got me."

"Yeah, but not for much longer." I feel lonely even though she hasn't gone anywhere yet.

"See, why you had to go there?"

"I know, I know." I stick my bottom lip out something serious. Feel tears forming on the rims of my eyelids.

Adrian comes around to my side of the desk, wraps her arms around me. "Girl, you better stop before you have all of us crying around here. You act like you're never going to see me again."

The bell to the front door chimes. Forces us to put on our professional faces with a quickness.

It's a solicitor trying to get us to purchase a fancy three-temperature water dispenser. Adrian politely refers the man to the "no soliciting" sign on the front door. He hesitates, then hands her a pamphlet before heading off to another business to harass.

She walks back over to me and tosses the brochure in the trash. Tells me, "Don't forget, dinner tonight, my house, eight o'clock sharp."

I lightly slap my hand against my forehead. "I totally forgot. David is taking me to The Cheesecake Factory tonight."

Disappointment is in her eyes. "How could you forget?"

"I'm sorry. This pregnancy has my memory acting up every now and then."

"Whatever, Fatima."

"I'll make it up to you. We'll do dinner next week. How about that?"

"And you say you're going to miss me," she says and walks off with no confirmation for next week.

❂ ❂ ❂

David and I make it to the restaurant famous for its cheesecakes almost a quarter after eight. The hostess leads us to an area in the back.

I tap her on the shoulder. "Are there no tables closer toward the front?"

She looks at David then back at me. "It could be at least a thirty-minute wait." She lets her eyes dance around the full restaurant as if to prove what she's saying is true.

"We'll wait."

David interjects, "Come on, Fatima. It's Friday night. It might take longer than thirty minutes. Let's just go to the table. If you still don't like it, we'll come back up and wait."

After a couple of would-you-get-from-in-front-of-my-table glares from other patrons, the hostess swings her shoulder-length brunette hair and resumes her lead toward the back.

I don't know why they always want to take the black folks to the back. I swear. Even in a town full of us, there's still blunt forms of racism. Nothing hidden about it.

I'm too busy fuming inside that I neglect to pay attention to what's going on around me when I hear in unison, "Surprise."

In the room is the whole team from Conscious Kneads. Adrian is at the front of the table, holding enough balloons in her hand to float her to another side of the world.

"Oh, my goodness." I'm in such shock I can't say anything else.

David whispers in my ear, "Surprise, baby."

I look up at him, his face beaming with joy. "I can't believe this."

The hostess in black tells me, "Enjoy your evening."

Immediately, I feel ashamed for my negative thoughts. This had nothing to do with race. I blink her a million apologies with my long eyelashes.

Adrian walks over and gives me a huge hug. "You didn't think you were going to get off that easy, did you?"

Uncontrollable tears run from my eyes. "You did all of this for me?"

She looks at David who throws his hands up. "I had nothing to do with this."

"Me either," Adrian says. She moves behind me, covers my eyes with her hands. "Keep your eyes closed."

I do as told and feel myself being spun around the room three times.

"Open your eyes," Adrian's voice instructs.

Standing in front of me is Lauren. My sister.

Adrian says, "This was all her idea."

No words form on my lips. Lauren looks at me, I look back at her. We stand that way for what feels like hours.

"Surprise," she finally says.

"I guess that's the word of the night?" I say.

That gets a chuckle out of everyone. Loosens the thick tension in the air.

I take two steps forward and open my arms for Lauren. She accepts. And whatever reason she didn't respond to my attempt to make amends with the complimentary spa package I sent to her a couple of months ago no longer matters. The here and now is all that counts. This is our chance to put what's happened behind us and build a relationship based on truth for a better future. For both of us. We *are* sisters after all.

Two-and-a-half weeks later, at six thirty-three in the morning, Bennet Amir Bryant takes his first breath. Blessed and full of life. Dr. Nguyen places my son on my stomach, lets me look into the face of my child for the first time.

He struggles, but finally, with a couple of pats on his back, he lets out his first cry. The sound of his tiny little voice makes my heart melt double times over.

"I love you," I tell him over and over again.

Nothing can wipe this smile away from my face. Nothing.

My son validates me. Makes my living worth everything I have been through. I would go through it again a million more times just to feel what I feel right now. I feel loved and I love more than love could love. Sounds crazy, but it is truly how I feel right now.

Adrian and Lauren stand to my left, tears of pure joy in their eyes. David kisses me on the forehead before rushing over to the corner where the nurse has taken Bennet to wipe him down and check his vitals.

It wasn't easy letting Lauren back into my life, especially after the way our relationship began in the first place. But as she told me before, "Yesterday is gone and there's nothing that can be done about it." Now, we both know where each other is coming from

and I can look at her and say that I am glad she is here to welcome the life of her nephew.

I hear a camera flash twice, then hear it flash again in my direction.

"Will you get that camera out of my face?" I try to sound mad,
but like I said, nothing can wipe this smile off of my face.

"I'm just capturing the essence of this moment."

I look at my father and my lips spread even further.

It wasn't easy welcoming my father back into my life either. He
left for reasons I may never understand. All I know is he is back
and now we have a second chance to have that relationship fathers
and daughters should have. I have the chance to be his daughter
again and he has the chance to be my father again. It is because
of his blood I am able to welcome the life of my blood.

He winks at me.

I wink back.

David walks slowly back toward the bed, our bundle of joy in
his arms. So much adoration is in his eyes. He places our son in
my arms and plants another kiss on my forehead. "Thank you,"
he whispers.

I place a hand on top of his. "No, thank you."

My father snaps another picture. Captures another moment in
time.

❂ ❂ ❂

The room is finally quiet. Everyone left shortly before visiting
hours ended. With all of the excitement and entertaining, we all
failed to realize that I needed some rest. David wanted to stay the
night, but I insisted I needed to be alone. "I want to spend the
first night with Bennet… alone," I told him.

I look down at my son snoozing away in my arms. He looks so
peaceful, looks so at home in my arms.

There's a light knock at the door. Probably the nurse coming in to check on us.

"Come in," I whisper.

He doesn't say anything at first. Flowers in one hand, a welcome-to-the-world balloon in his other. "Congratulations."

"Wanna see him?"

Cory moves closer, puts the flowers on the table. The balloon floats as high as the ceiling lets it. "He's so little," he says.

Bennet makes soft movements in my arms. "Cory, meet Bennet Amir."

"Can't believe I've run from such an amazing blessing."

"Wanna hold him?"

Cory passes. "He's so little," he says again.

"He looks just like my dad when he was a baby."

"Really?" Cory takes his focus off of my son and asks me, "How's that working out?"

"We're making the best of things, you know. Him and Lauren are a part of my life. They are a part of my son's life. Can't change that, no matter how screwed over I feel."

Cory nods in agreement. "I'm glad to know things worked out."

"Me too. They've been a big help. Now, Bennet has a grandfather and an auntie, not to mention a couple of uncles that I have yet to meet. He truly is blessed."

"So are we. We've made it through some serious stuff."

This time, I nod in agreement.

"Thanks for the flowers," I say. "They're beautiful. And the balloon...I think Bennet likes it."

Cory looks up at me in the dimly lit room. "You're beautiful. Not a day has gone by that I haven't thought about you. That deep dimple in your left cheek, the freckles on the tip of your nose."

My eyes close momentarily. When I reopen them, I stare into

the darkest eyes I have ever seen. "Why didn't you return any of my calls?"

He sits down at the foot of the bed. "I wanted to. Every time I saw your name pop up on the screen, I wanted to pick up and hear your voice. I wanted to hear you say, 'I love you,' and I wanted to say it back. As hard as it was, I couldn't. I didn't want to break my promise. The next time I talked to you, I wanted to be the right man for you."

We keep our voices low.

"So, why now?"

"My sister moved back down and we've been going to counseling as a family. I still have a lot of luggage to drop off at Goodwill, but my load is nowhere as heavy as it was before. I'm still not all the man I can be…I just don't want to do this without you."

I reach out my hand toward his. He meets me halfway. "I don't want to do this without you either."

Cory kisses my hand, gets up from the bed. He looks into my eyes for approval before he plants his lips ever-so-gently against mine.

"That was nice," I tell him.

He kisses his fingertip and rubs it across Bennet's face. Cory winks at me, pulls a chair right next to the bed. Places my hand back in his, leans his head against my shoulder.

Just like that we fall asleep.

Just like that, everything we've come to be.

ABOUT THE AUTHOR

Julia Blues is a storyteller on a mission, and that mission is to help people live better lives with every story she tells. *Parallel Pasts* is her first novel of many. She resides between here and there in search of a place she'd like to call home. To read more of her story, visit her website at www.JuliaBlues.com.

REFLECTIONS FROM THE AUTHOR

From conception to delivery, the process of *Parallel Pasts* has definitely been a journey to keep close to my heart.

My life as a writer began in the midst of working a boring job for a temp agency. I had to field calls and direct clients to the company's new location. I felt like I had exhausted all resources to keep me entertained until—as if my boredom could be felt in another world—someone came up behind me, tapped me on my shoulder and whispered in my ear, *"Monica Brown, that's my name, ask me again and I'll tell you the same."* Though I knew I was the only one in the office, I turned around to see who this Monica was. All I saw was my reflection in the window. I tried to get back to the Spades game on the computer screen, but the raspy voice of this strange woman kept replaying in my head like the memory of an old lover you try to forget. I shrugged my shoulders, cut off the game, opened a blank document and told Monica, *"Tell me more."* She sat down in a chair in front of me and told her story.

As the days passed, a collection of papers grew into a thick stack that I carried with me home and back to work again. I had grown accustomed to and comfortable with these strange voices in my head. I became intrigued with their stories. I wanted more. I needed more. Within a few months, I was staring at a finished novel.

What I thought to be a complete book turned out to be everything but. It took a lot of months and that many more years to say THE END and mean it. Every time I sat down to revise, I learned something different about my characters. Monica had given me an alias because she was hiding from her true identity in case the parents who abandoned her came looking for her one day. After digging, I uncovered her real name to be Fatima No-Last-Name. And Cory tried hard to forget the woman who gave birth to him, the woman who was no smarter than a fifth-grader, giving him and his siblings four-letter "C" names. They evolved, they revealed more of themselves as they began to understand *who* they were and *why* they were the way they were. They were naked in front of me which allowed me to be naked in front of them.

I had just as much fear and frustration in my life as they did. We shared our pain together. I cried when they cried; they hurt when I hurt. As they exposed their truths, I too, got honest with myself. Through it all, we grew together.

And I grew as a woman and grew into an author.

Parallel Pasts liberated me.

For that I am grateful.

I longed to write these reflections before I even learned of having a book deal. My plan was to talk about how this book came to be, then thank all of those who played a part. When I got the call from my agent, my life was in a different place and it has taken me until now to write these words.

Today is Thursday, November 22, 2012. Thanksgiving Day. As I sit here with a belly full of macaroni and cheese, kale greens, carrot soufflé, fried turkey, cranberry sauce, potato salad, and bread rolls, I find myself digesting a myriad of emotions.

"Be Grateful" by Walter Hawkins & The Love Center Choir

plays softly in the background on vinyl. *God has not promised me sunshine, that's not the way it's going to be, but a little rain mixed with God's sunshine; a little pain, makes me appreciate the good times.*

2012 has had its share of pain mixed with joy to the point I've been stuck in the middle of both.

Since January, my soul-sister had been in the hospital due to a rare blood disorder. Once I learned of its severity, I traveled to Atlanta to sit with her in ICU through the night. I traveled month after month, most times with her being in a medically-induced coma and unaware of my presence. She began to make improvements, enough to be released to a rehabilitation facility. Just a few short days later, she was back in a coma. A week later, I got a call from my agent with the good news that my first novel had been picked up. This was the call I had been waiting for since I began writing. After thanking God, calling my family to share the good news, I called my soul-sister's mom. I told her when she went to the hospital that day to make sure she told "Butterfly" because I knew that would make her smile...wherever she was. Two days later, I was off to Jamaica for a pre-planned vacation that just so happened to be at the perfect time to celebrate my new book deal.

The weekend I got back from my vacation, our 20-year-old kitty was walking around the house looking disillusioned. We took her to the vet on Monday. She did not come back home with us. She was in severe kidney failure and we had to make the decision to let her go. She had a long life filled with love. To keep her here would be for selfish reasons. We'd had her since I was thirteen, so it hit real hard. She was my fur-sister, and for some reason I had the feeling she'd be around forever. As I was trying to get grips on that reality, news of my soul-sister's health took another blow out of me. The doctors didn't see her returning from her coma. Again, I was back on the road. When I returned home, as if I wasn't distraught enough, my brand-new car decided to break down on me. I had only had the car for a week. In the days it took the dealership to figure out what was wrong with the vehicle, the call came that my dear friend had transitioned.

Two losses within three weeks of each other was a tough pill to swallow. I tried to keep my mind on the positives in my life while dealing with the car situation and more heartache and pain. My father had to go to Florida to see about his ailing mother. During that time, my twelve-year-old kitty started showing signs of illness. I was at the vet just about every day, trying prescription after prescription with no luck. Trying to keep my head above water as the levels continued to rise proved difficult as the call came that my grandmother had passed away. As fireworks were being fired into the sky left and right on the Fourth of July, my grandmother had taken her last breath. Seven days later, I made the decision to be with my kitty as she took her last breath. To date, that has been my hardest decision to make.

Verse two of *Be Grateful* says: *God desires to feel your longing; every pain that you feel He feels them just like you, but He cares too much to let you feel only good…then you can appreciate the good times.*

I was living that song. Seemed like the moment I began to experience joy, I was hit back to back to back with pain. May. June. July. In three months, I had to say goodbye four times. I began to feel like the characters in this book. Just like Fatima and Cory, as soon as I took one step forward, I was pushed three steps back.

My dream of becoming a published author was happening right before my eyes, but it was overshadowed by circumstances beyond my control. Part of me began to believe I had not received the call of the good news to begin with. Circumstances left me blah.

Luckily, my sanity came in the form of another pre-planned vacation to The Netherlands. God knew I needed to do like Southwest Airlines' *Need-to-get-away?* commercials suggest. The day after my grandmother's funeral, I was on a ten-hour flight to another continent. God's sunshine like no other.

Holland felt like home. It was something about being there that brought me so much peace, a peace I had not experienced in a long time. The thirty days I was there, God allowed me to see so much of His grace and mercy, and how much He strategically plans out every detail of our lives. Days after arriving there, my father sent an email saying I had mail from my agent. He held it up for me during our Skype conversation later that day. It was the contract for my book deal. It *had* happened. It wasn't a figment of my imagination. That was the moment it became real for me, the moment my dream came true.

I AM a published author.

For that I am grateful.

I am grateful for God. None of this would be possible if not for Your grace and mercy, Your love, Your patience. It was You who breathed this gift into and birthed this through me before I was even born. You knew every road I was to turn down to reach Your appointed destination for me. You sustained me through all of life's disappointments, every closed door, the depression, the heartache. You said YES while everyone else told me no. You. Kept. Me. You ordered my steps and now I am walking, living, and breathing my purpose and am fulfilled unlike ever before. For that I say, "Thank You, Jesus!"

I am grateful for my parents, Barbara and Gary Williams Sr. You have been here for me every step of the way. You've supported me through every career path—and there have been many—until I found my true calling. You've laughed with me, got mad at me, but most importantly, you've been there for me. You've held and comforted me through many tears; you've felt my pain. You've helped rebuild my faith and my hope in my darkest hours. Maybe one of these days I'll remember that when playing Boggle so one of you can finally beat me! Love you, Mom and Dad, and I thank you for allowing me to be who I am.

I am grateful for my brother, Gary Williams Jr. You're the best brother I've ever had. Come to think of it, you're the only brother I've ever had. Ha! Thank you for supporting my dreams and visions with your encouragement along the way. For listening to me ramble about what I'm going to do, the story ideas I have when you'd rather figure out all the specifics of your new electronic gadgets. Thank you. Love you, Brudder.

I am grateful for my best friend, Devisteen Conley. You were there to hear all about Monica from day one, and was okay when she became Fatima. You were there when I became me and haven't changed your views of me one bit since. Thank you for shuffling through my scattered dreams, supporting and encouraging me to keep writing and bettering me no matter what. You're a fantastic friend, though, I wish you'd pick up the phone more. You can't let that raggedy mail truck get in the way of our friendship, 'cause guess what, Shame? I'm on the bookshelves! Love you, Devo.

I am grateful for my writing buddy and friend, Del Sandeen. Who knew a natural hair care forum would bring us together and help form a great friendship due to our love of writing?! Many times you've helped me keep my sanity through this profession we've chosen to be a part of. Thanks for listening to my rants and for giving me a good laugh when I needed it most, and thanks for letting me be that for you. You're next! Love ya, girl.

I am grateful for my agency, The Sara Camilli Agency. Sara,

you and Stephen have been an asset to my dream coming to life. You are a testament that delay is far from denial. Thank you for seeing something in my work that you were willing to stand behind. Your taking a chance on me truly means a lot. I thank you and may God continue to bless you both.

I am grateful for Strebor Books. Zane and Charmaine, it is because of you giving me this opportunity that I am able to say I am a published author. Thank you for standing behind my words enough to put your banner of representation on. I thank you beyond words.

I am grateful for KC Turner of Brand Diversity PR. The work you've done before this book even went into print leaves me nearly speechless. *smile* You've definitely been a driving force in this journey. I thank you, and celebrate with you all that is to come in this part of your journey.

I am grateful for those I can call my friends: Miriam Pollock, Shirley Joyner, Monica Tolbert, Jazmine Howard, Monica Rogers, Karla Barefield, Kinta Turner, Kenyatta Malone, Donald Smith, Mary McCarter, Toshii Cooper, Shauna Clarke, Latika Ross, Craig Wilson, Bobby Rhoades, Tekea Hines, Jackie Edwards, and Mrs. Wylene Adwater. Thank you for being a part of this journey with me. Your support has meant a lot through the years, each in your own way. Thank you for being a friend and for allowing me to be yours. Love you.

I am grateful for Shonia Brown. You were the very first person to publish one of my short stories in your anthology a few years ago. I appreciate you for seeing something in my writing that you were willing to stand behind. Much success to you as you pick your pen back up.

I am grateful for L Kimberly Smith and Mo. Thank you for reaching out and giving me the experience of my first interview.

Being able to talk about the art of writing to your listeners without actually having a book out made my night. Thanks for that. Many blessings to you.

I am grateful for Adrienne Adams and Bridgette Outten of It's Not Enough To Dream Women's Circle & Magazine. Thank you for my second blog radio interview and for the opportunities to write for your magazine and website. It was an honor to be a part of your dreams coming to fruition. Continued blessings to you.

I am grateful for social networking. There are a host of people I have met along the way who have helped me in this journey thanks to MySpace, Facebook, Blogger, and Twitter. You've inspired, motivated, encouraged me in so many ways. You've asked about my work, and some of you have harassed me about when my work would be in print. Trust me, I was just as anxious as you. I hope I've made you proud. I thank each and every one of you for all that you've done. Lolita Files and Robin Caldwell, thank you for our chats. *smile*

I am grateful for music and these artists: Bilal, Me'Shell Ndegeocello, Kem, Raheem DeVaughn, Corinne Bailey Rae, Mary J. Blige, Jaguar Wright, Vivian Green, Mint Condition, and Floetry. Your music kept me going in those moments I felt drained and not able to push forward. This book wouldn't be what it is if not for your gifts. Eric Roberson and Lalah Hathaway, "Dealing" stayed on repeat to help me churn out the dreaded synopsis. Thank you.

I am grateful for every lesson and every person who has made me who I am and my journey what it has been. To old friends and to new, thank you.

I am grateful for you for picking up this copy *Parallel Pasts*. I wrote this book for you. It is my hope that something in this story of Fatima and Cory helps you live better in some way. I'd love to hear how at JuliaBlues@outlook.com. But, be warned, I can get long-winded (as if this isn't enough proof), LOL!

I am grateful for Fatima and Cory. Thank you for choosing me.

Just like them, and in my own journey, I've come to find that there'll always be circumstances in life that seem to put our dreams and visions, and even our very life itself, on hold, but the thing to keep in mind is "this too shall pass." Life teaches us many lessons through our circumstances, our trials and tribulations, our past, our heartbreaks, our challenges, our illnesses. If we pay attention and listen to what life is telling us, we could heal a lot faster and our wounds wouldn't leave such ugly scars. It's okay to hurt and mourn our losses, but if we're not careful, those very things can end up ruling our lives. It's a step-by-step and day-by-day process. Keep putting in the work and you will begin to see a difference in your life for the better.

We're all in this struggle together. Let's keep each other encouraged. And know, no matter what you may experience in life or are going through at this very moment, if you find the littlest thing to be grateful for, your circumstances won't seem so big. Your change of perception will change your life. As the last words of *Be Grateful* says, "*For it (everything) will be all right.*"

Until the next book...

Abundant blessings and peace to you!

Julia Blues

"And this same God who takes care of me will supply all your needs from His glorious riches, which have been given to us in Christ Jesus."
—PHILIPPIANS 4:19 (NLT)

1 / SYDNEY HOLMES

My hand shakes as I unfold the letter.

I know the words by heart because I wrote them. Wrote them six years ago on the eve of my wedding day. Wrote them to my husband to tell him I wasn't going to meet him at the altar the next morning.

I made a mistake.

That night I should have gone to his hotel and slid the letter under his room door like I had planned. Should've done that and taken the taxi to the airport, hopped on the flight I purchased a ticket for the night before and flown to another life where nobody knew my name. Should've done all of that, but I didn't.

"Mommy, are you crying?"

I stuff the letter back in the shoebox, toss a worn pair of shoes on top of it. Shove it under the bed just like I did my heart when

I stood in front of family and friends and God, and promised to love a man for the rest of my life who I couldn't even love at that moment.

Before my son can see my face, I grab a tissue off the nightstand. "No, honey. Mommy's not crying. It's my allergies." I blow my nose to emphasize my lie.

I knew it the moment the doors opened and I placed my feet on freshly sprinkled rose petals that I was making a mistake. My heart begged me to turn around, save myself before committing to a lifetime of insecurity. But my right foot betrayed me, then my left. Moments later there was only a breath standing between us. I closed my eyes as his lips touched mine. Deep down I prayed that when I opened them, it would have all been a dream. A really bad dream.

It wasn't.

Almost seven years later, I'm still hoping to wake up and realize I'd been placed in the *Guinness Book of World Records* for the longest, uninterrupted nightmare.

My son stands in front of me, stares me in the face to see if I'm really telling the truth. "Your eyes are red."

I pick him up and sit him on my lap. "Well, that's what they do this time of year, EJ. Let's just pray you don't grow up to be allergic to everything like your mother."

He shakes his head so hard it makes me feel like I have a bad case of vertigo, then runs his tiny finger down my nose. "I don't want to be allergic 'cause it makes you look bad."

Wow. I don't know if I should be insulted or laugh at his truth-telling innocence. I catch a glimpse of myself in the full-length mirror in the corner of the room. Bags under my eyes large enough to incur an overweight baggage fee. There's nothing laughable about my image. I put Eric Jr. down and pat him on the butt.

"Go tell Kennedy it's time for bed. I'll be in to check on you two in a minute."

"But I'm not sleepy, Mommy."

I give him the look of looks, one that lets him know I mean business tonight.

He shuffles out the room yelling for his sister to go to sleep before she gets in trouble. Just like him to threaten his sister with his punishment.

Kids.

I go in the bathroom, grab a rag and saturate it with cold water. Sit it over my eyes until it loses its cool. Rewet it with more cold water. Then I add a few drops of the liquid that promises to take the red out, let it marinate behind my eyelids. I do my best to get rid of any evidence of breakdown. Not that my husband would notice anything were wrong, I'm just not in the mood to tell any more lies. This might be the one night I set the truth free.

"Mom." This time my daughter comes barging in the room yelling at the top of her lungs. "EJ just squeezed all my toothpaste in the trash."

"Kennedy, calm down. I've told you, no one can hear you when you yell. Now, what's the problem?"

Why do these kids insist on working my nerves tonight? Don't they know I'm near my breaking point? Don't they know that if either of them so much as sneezes, I will walk out that door and not look back?

My daughter repeats her distress and marches down the hall to their bathroom to show me the evidence. "See." She points to the trash. Pink gel with a ton of sparkles splattered all in the trash and on the floor.

"Eric Holmes Jr.," I call out. No response. I look under the cabinet and hand Kennedy a new box of her favorite toothpaste.

"Brush your teeth and get in bed." That seems to settle all her problems for now.

Heavy footsteps climb up the stairs. "What's all this noise up here?" the man of the house questions.

I tell him, "Your kids doing what they do best."

He pulls a smaller version of himself from behind his back. "This one was hiding under the dining table."

I point to EJ's room door. "Bed. Now."

He scurries to his room like a dog with his tail tucked between its legs in its moment of chastisement.

"I'll have them asleep by the time you get downstairs." My husband kisses me on the forehead, tells me, "The dishes are done and I left the DVR up so you can catch up on your shows."

I stare at him momentarily. Do my best to convince my conscience that I did the right thing six years ago by not giving him that letter. And for a moment, it works.

I wink at him. "I'll be up shortly."